THE GLASS WOMAN

THE GLASS WOMAN

Kaaron Warren

PRIME BOOKS

THE GLASS WOMAN: A COLLECTION

———

Prime Books
www.prime-books.com

Donna Maree Hanson, editor.

For more information, contact Prime.

ISBN: 978-0-8095-7296-0

Dedicated to Mum, Dad, Sandra, James . . .
and Graham, because I said I would

TABLE OF CONTENTS

ACKNOWLEDGEMENTS
To Sean Wallace, Cat Sparks and Geoffrey Maloney,

for making this book happen.

FRESH YOUNG WIDOW

———

The fresh young widow washed her husband's body. She dipped her cloth into cloudy water and rub rubbed at him, cleaning the pores, washing away dried blood, picking at it with her long, strong fingernails. She closed her eyes as she touched his body but he was so cold she couldn't imagine him alive. She laid her head on his belly and let her tears wet him.

There was a gentle knock at the door.

"Marla, they are wondering if you will see someone. An old woman who walked here eight days from Baristone. She thought the penance would help."

The widow put down her sponge. "Connie, I am washing my husband."

"I'm so sorry, Marla. But they told me to ask. She had a son with her. He's very distressed."

At this the widow walked to the door and opened it. Connie stepped inside, her head bowed.

The widow said, "Did he find his beloved husband knifed to the bone? Did he hold him as he bled to death? Did he wait for last words and hear none?"

"No, Marla."

The widow patted at her wild and unbrushed hair, tried to straighten her filthy clothes.

"Oh, Marla," Connie said. "Oh, Marla."

The sympathy was too much to bear and the widow sank to the floor, weeping great painful sobs. When she quieted, exhausted, Connie said, "I'm so sorry about your husband. We all are. It should never have happened. Why do they even let the tourists in?" Connie began to cry. Marla felt so old around Connie, though the difference was just two years.

The widow knew most girls in the town had loved Brin. He had been funny, handsome and flirtatious. She knew he kissed them, sometimes. Nothing more.

He liked to kiss.

"I'm going to finish with my husband, now," the widow said. She felt no strength in her voice. "Tell the son I may be able to get to his mother. Tell him the stories are not true. There will be no clay walk. No great resurrection. Dead is dead. All there will be is a monument to her. Okay?"

The young girl said, "Okay."

Marla said, "This is new for me, too, Connie. I'm sure we'll get used to each other."

Connie nodded. She placed a box just inside the door. The widow knew it would contain offerings, bribes, and she felt a childish sense of anticipation.

She had three buckets of clay ready, collected as the sun rose. Soft and slippery. She took up a handful and squeezed, loving the squelch between her fingers. The fresh young widow worked the clay. Picked out stones and sticks, any small impurities. She dropped handfuls of clay into a large bucket of water, where small motes drifted to the top. These she skimmed off. She sifted the sludge through her fingers and when it was silky smooth she poured it onto a long flat sieve outside. Cloudy water dripped onto the ground and she left the clay to dry. When it was no longer sticky to the touch she could work it, kneading it until the smoothness of it satisfied her.

Then her real work began.

She added three of her fingernail clippings, a link from his mother's chain, and a pinch of coriander, his favourite spice. She rubbed her fingers together and sniffed them, the smell evoking such an intense memory she smiled. She and Brin had been married only a few days, just returned from their honeymoon in the city, where everything was delivered on the asking; food, drinks, books. She was tired, exhausted, and so was he. He had enjoyed lovers before. She had not. Her learning with the clay was so intense not much else filtered through. She had friends but not close ones. She was popular without people really knowing her.

It had made her blush, returning from her honeymoon to all the attention. All the assumed knowledge. Everybody had smiled at her, nodded.

"How did you go?" her mother said, arriving at their home dusty, clay-smeared, her hair clumpy.

Marla nodded, too embarrassed to speak. Her mother had laughed.

"You poor young thing. It's all a bit terrifying, isn't it? What's he cooking you tonight? What are you cooking her tonight?" Her new husband came out of the bathroom, rubbing at his hair.

"Amazing how you forget about the clay when you're away," he said.

Her mother said, "What's for dinner?"

"Oh," he said. "Yes. Aha, can't you smell it?"

The two women sniffed. A rich, rough smell.

"It's my specialty. Ground Nut Stew."

He led his wife into the kitchen and ground some spice for her to sniff. She coughed.

"It's strong. But the flavour is so good. Beef, potatoes, ground nuts, cinnamon. You'll love it. I hope you'll love it."

He kissed her, and she tasted onion.

"He's a good boy," her mother said later. "He understands. Just like your father. We have a little work to do before dinner."

"It's ready now," Brin said. "Can't we eat first?"

"I guess the dead don't travel so fast we can't catch them. I'll leave you to your meal."

"Stay, Mum, eat with us. We'll call Dad and eat together," Marla said, holding her mother's arm.

"What about your parents, Brin?" her mother said.

"They'll come tomorrow," Brin said. "Go call your husband!"

They had eaten together, a happy meal. The men talked, the women, too, but Marla and her mother had thoughts behind their words, thoughts of what lay ahead.

After dinner the women walked to the workshop. It was a large, bright room, angled to let in the morning sun, but not the afternoon sun, so it never got too hot. The floor was slate, easily wiped clean but still ingrained with the red clay they worked with.

They had worked in silence, each intent on the process of covering the body in a way which was beautiful yet would not crack. This was an elderly woman, a resident long gone away but come home to die. Many of them did that.

After a while Marla had realized she was doing most of the work. She rested back on her heels and looked at her mother rocking by the door.

"Are you all right? Tired?" Marla said. Her mother had smiled. "I am, a little." The clay slip filled the small lines in her face, exaggerating them, making her look older and tireder than she really was. "But, mostly, I like to watch you. You're very skilled for one so young."

"You were young and skilled once," Marla said. Her mother had nodded and looked away.

"Your marriage has got me thinking," she said. "Thinking about now, rather than when."

"I'm not good with riddles, Mum," Marla said. She worked a piece of clay and smoothed it over the belly of the woman.

"What I mean to say is, I'm feeling some resentment about this job. This … placement. I'm feeling I need to get away, see the world."

"And Dad?"

"I'll take him, too," she said. She rubbed at her face. "What do you think?"

"It's not a good job to do resentfully," Marla said. "I know we don't choose it, but I accept it. You go. Let me be the Clay-Maker. It will be okay."

Her mother had fallen to her knees beside her.

"Thank you. Thank you. You kind and beautiful girl."

Her parents had left the next day. They were gone three weeks when Brin was killed.

Marla wiped away the tears brought from remembering that time, dropped a pinch of spice into the clay, then began to cover her husband.

First his toes, feet. The ankles were tough; too bumpy. The shins, knees and thighs. The room was cold to stop the clay drying too quickly.

She covered his genitals, his belly, his back, slapping on the clay and smoothing it, shaping it.

She sat with him, not eating or drinking, until the first layer dried. This needed patience. Each layer needed to dry before more clay was placed on top, or the whole thing would sink, sag, slump. She felt like sagging herself, her weariness was so great.

Then her parents arrived to be with her. Marla never found out who contacted them, or how.

"Marla, my poor darling," her mother said, pushing her way into the workshop. "We came as soon as we heard." Her father hovered in the doorway, his face grey, shocked. Both of them had aged.

"Dad," she said, and he held her while she cried.

"I should never have left you," her mother said.

"This has nothing to do with you leaving. But I'm glad you're back."

"We came to comfort you, but also we need to talk. I have something so important to tell you. Let's go sit by the wall."

Marla and her mother walked together to the clay wall. "I know where I want us to sit. I remember where everybody is," her mother said. She trailed her fingers over the clay faces then stopped. "Here," she said.

They sat down.

"You will need to act. I wish this talk could have waited many years, but this chance can't be missed, as terrible as it is. It is better to make the child with someone you love."

"So who was I born of? Someone you loved more than Dad?"

Her mother said, "No. No. You were born of my mother. She stands behind this clay man." She waved her arm. Marla looked. The man frowned slightly at her, his features a little askew. "He wasn't a very nice man," her mother said. "He bit people." Marla saw his clay teeth, larger than life, like a rabbit's. She closed her eyes and listened to her mother's words.

Marla walked her mother to the house. It was not the biggest house in the town; that belonged to the Chief Mason. The Clay-maker lived in a modest but beautiful home, paved with baked clay tiles, walls of pale terracotta. Beautiful furnishings, gifts from the people of the town.

Marla felt a little dazed. She was not old enough for this information, this task. Yet the task was hers.

"Have some lunch first. Fill yourself," her mother said.

"No. He's waited long enough. I must get to him," Marla said. She walked slowly to the workshop, though, stopping to talk along the way to anyone she saw, accepting their condolences, asking after them. She wondered if her face looked different, now she knew.

Brin grew fuller, thicker. Marla wondered if she could get him through the door, he was so large. She built him into a giant. She built the image of a girl on the clay case; vagina, breasts. Then she smoothed it away.

Knocking came. It was the masons. "Is he ready, Marla? Ready for the Kiln?"

"Not yet. Wait," Marla called out. She fashioned Brin a penis and she made love to her clay man. She sent his seed back to him, kissed his clay lips. She felt the dryness of the clay in her throat, and she coughed and choked as the masons entered. They did not flinch at her appearance. They knew she did not wash, did not change clothes, for the time it took to do her clay work.

For all her hard work, an impurity in the clay gave his face a scowl she had not intended. A downturned mouth she tried to fix but couldn't.

The masons stared in silence at his face.

"I told you we needed to find his killer," the oldest mason said. "You said no violence for violence, but look at his face."

The masons muttered together. There was a clamour at the door. The other mourners.

Two masons lifted the clay man so it appeared he walked, aided, between them.

They carried him outside. The widow staggered into step behind them, tears waterfalling from her eyes. She didn't sob; she was beyond noise.

The wailing around her began. His mother collapsed at his feet. She kissed them, huge sloppy kisses that left small damp patches on his clay toes. She rose, her lips dusty.

"It's wrong, so wrong," she wailed. Her husband and friends supported her so she walked almost like her clay son did.

The widow felt intense pain in her shoulders, her fingers. She had worked feverishly on her husband, making the clay warm between her fast fingers, giving it blood warmth. They carried Brin to the Kiln, a tin shed outside the walls, set amongst the burning sand. Here he would stand in the searing heat until his clay case baked hard. Here her work would be tested; a single flaw and the case could crack open.

As the time came, people gathered by the Kiln. There was a sigh as Brin was brought forth. The case was perfect, uncracked. The procession marched through the streets of the town to the wall. The wall rose just a little higher than the tallest mason, so if he stood up on his toes he could peer over it. It was broad, though, thick with clay people. Solid with clay. There were no gaps. These were filled by the masons as they appeared. The clay changed little in its shading, testimony to the unchanging environment of the town.

Marla was very proud of the wall. There, two more masons waited with cement.

They placed her husband Brin next to the doctor's wife, in the wall two weeks now. Marla could not help noticing how perfect her work was; no cracks in the clay woman, and the expression captured perfectly her kindly nature.

"It should be that tourist here instead," Brin's mother shouted. "He should be the dead one, not my son."

"But then Brin would have been a murderer," Marla thought. She held her mother-in-law tight and closed her eyes, resting for a moment.

"Into the wall we cement thy physical being," the Chief Mason said. "May your soul be free to roam until the great clay walk. May your body stay safe within the wall, an empty vessel awaiting your return.

"May your physical being keep this town safe from outsiders and repel evil from within us all.

"May we serve you and you serve us until the time of the great clay walk."

Marla collapsed at Brin's feet, clutching her belly.

"May the seed you planted within me grow, my love. I love you so much. I had so much more time for you." The snot ran down her chin, tears down her cheeks. She felt she was masked with her own fluids.

There were murmurings around her, high-pitched murmurings of hope and excitement. "A baby! A baby! There has not been a baby born here for two years!" They were almost as barren as the clay.

Connie stood staring, a fixed smile on her face. "Congratulations," she said.

"It's all right, Connie. You can care for both of us. You will be with me for life." Although the widow had deliberately misunderstood, Connie still smiled. "Your place is safe," the widow said.

The Chief Mason and the youngest mason came to her. The Chief Mason said, "I can tell you, Marla, that we are outraged by your husband's murder. He was a great man. A good mason." His eyes shifted there and the widow knew he was lying. Her husband had not been a good mason.

He didn't have the seriousness for it, the rock-solid dedication needed to build. He was too funny, too rebellious. He liked being the husband of the Clay-Maker. It gave him many privileges and he could shock the others so easily. The Clay-Maker's husband merely had to laugh loudly to be noticed.

"Thank you," she said. She swallowed. "Can you tell me how? What? All people tell me is the tragedy of it, the waste. I want to know what he did."

"It wasn't his fault. He was a funny man. He liked a joke. And the tourist was being disrespectful. He was drunk, and he poked and squeezed at the girls, joked about them being full of clay until he made Connie cry. Brin told him to leave her or he would turn to clay. He called the tourist some names, some cruel names," the Chief Mason said.

"He had a sharp tongue," Marla said.

The youngest mason blushed, and Marla wondered if images had popped into his head of the widow and her husband's sharp tongue. He stammered, "None of us expected the tourist to do what he did. He was skinny, you know? And pathetic. A bully. Brin turned away, we thought it was over, but the tourist leapt on him. Brin was down before we could react. Then we took him to the doctor's and fetched you."

The tears ran down her cheeks and drooled saltily into her mouth.

"Thank you," she said. "And the tourist? Where is he?"

"We'll find him," said the Chief Mason. "We'll find the killer and bring him back. Then perhaps Brin will smile as he watches over us."

Marla nodded. "You know what you will be sacrificing in leaving this place?"

"We do. We are prepared to age a little to see our brother at peace."

"You are good men," Marla said. She allowed herself to be held by the Chief Mason.

They were gone for over a week.

The clay had changed little over the last hundred years. The statues circled the town, staring in, watching the people. Her husband was part of the third row. He stood in front of a child, dead twenty years. The widow's mother was the clay-maker then.

The fresh young widow went to him at night, when all others were asleep.

She fell to her knees, weeping. Then she took a small hammer from her backpack.

She tapped hard at his belly, and the clay cracked. A sighing sound emerged. She lifted out the pieces and reached inside.

A baby girl was in there, gasping for air. She cried with a dry throat. The widow lifted her out and wiped clay dust from her face. Cleared her nostrils. The widow tucked her into the folds of her skirt.

Then she reached into her backpack and pulled out things to fill the clay case with; a dead cat, a sack of flour, some stones. She sealed the case again with new, wet clay.

Then she bundled the baby up and took her home, walking over the rough ground. There was the smell of paint in the air. The ground was green, freshly painted for the newly arrived batch of tourists. The ground was too full of clay for grass to grow. Visitors were advised to bring their own drinking water. The stuff in the town was so full of clay you needed to be born to it or your insides would clog up and you'd be constipated for a week. Washing water was the same; showers were red tinged and gritty. A good rough facial scrub people paid good money for elsewhere.

Marla washed her baby in warm, soapy water and placed the baby into a cardboard box for a bed. Then the grieving son from Baristone arrived.

"Are you busy?" he said. He was an idiot, thick-faced and stupid.

"I'm always busy. Always someone to attend to." She was desperate to lie down and sleep beside her baby.

"I promised my mother I would do this," he said. "She died at the wall. Once she'd seen it. She died right there. I wish we had come sooner. You all look so youthful here. Glowing."

"You should never promise anything which relies on other people."

He hung his head.

"Come with me to collect the clay then. You're lucky; no locals are waiting. My husband is in the wall, now."

"I'm sorry for your loss," he said.

"Not sorry enough to leave me alone."

Marla strapped her baby onto her back. There was a growing hubbub as she walked, "She's had the baby, there's the baby, when did she have the baby?" Her mother had told her not to worry about deception and to forget about trying to fool the people into believing the child had been born naturally. It was part of the mystique of the Clay-Makers. Let the people guess at the process. Let it add to their respect of the Clay-Makers.

She took some of the children with her to search for the clay. It was an adventure for them, outside the walls, and she could send them out clay-hunting on their own, once they knew how.

"We look near river beds, even ones no longer running. Look for puddles; clay holds water so water is an indicator."

One of the children shouted, "Here?" Marla walked over. It was gritty there, and pale. Not perfect, but she saved the best stuff for the locals. This stuff would do for the woman. "Good," she said. She scrabbled with her fingers until she had a palm-sized lump.

"To test it, we roll it into a coil and tie a knot in it. This is good clay – no cracks or breaks when we tie it. Not too much sand or gravel. Well done!" The child blushed with pleasure and the others rushed to impress, too, digging hard and vying to carry the most clay.

They took it back to her workshop. "I will need to prepare the clay," Marla said to the son. "Come back tomorrow."

He was there at dawn.

Marla was awake. "What have you brought to add?" she asked.

The son had a small paper bag. "Some of my father's ashes. A clip of my baby hair. And this is a scrap of material from my sister's wedding dress."

She nodded. "That's good. That's nice. All right. You sit over there. This will take some time."

He sat in the comfy chair while the widow kneeled on the floor and stripped the mother naked. She washed the old woman carefully, treating her as she had her own husband.

The water left a fine sheen of clay on the woman's skin.

The widow mixed the clay with the things the son had given her, kneading, squeezing, squelching.

She layered the woman, took care with her face. She scraped the clay off her fingers into the little opaque pots lined up on her bench. When she had filled twenty and the son had gone out for air, she called out, "Connie! Connie! Some pots!" Connie was still nervous in the workshop. It was so new to her. The Chief Mason had ensured there was no time Marla was alone; he moved Connie in the moment Brin died. "It's all right. Come in. Wipe the pots clean then get them ready for boxing."

While Marla worked, Connie cleaned the pots, found their lids, put stickers on them.

"Is it really magical cream?" Connie said. She rubbed clay between her fingertips.

"They say so. Glowing reports from the women who use it. They pay a fortune for it."

"My dad says we should start a factory and make heaps more," Connie said, packing the pots into a small box. "He says we'll all be rich if we sell more."

"We're rich enough," Marla said. She scraped her fingers off into the next pot. "It's the rare nature of it that makes it worthwhile. You tell your Dad to not be so greedy, like a pig in the mud."

Connie giggled.

Marla worked the clay gently around the woman's face, smoothing the large pores, filling the nostrils. Then the smell of something cooking made her stomach rumble.

"Brin? What are you cooking?" Marla said, and she jumped up, wiped her hands and walked to the kitchen. She pushed open the door, smiling.

Connie stood at the bench, chopping vegetables. She said, "I found a recipe book, and I'm making something from it. It looks very nice." Marla stared at her. For a moment, just a moment, she had forgotten. Just for a moment, Brin was alive again. Marla sat down and cried.

"I can make something else, if you like," Connie said. Suddenly she seemed too wise to be so young. Her eyes filled with tears. "I miss him," she said. "I'm sorry Marla, but I miss him. He made us all laugh so."

"You more than most, I think, Connie. That's one reason you were chosen to be my cook. My helper. You were a good choice to take his place."

"Some of the younger men thought it might be them."

Marla smiled. The thought stopped her tears. "I'm not ready for a new husband yet. Not nearly ready."

"Oh, no, nothing like that," Connie said, blushing.

"But we know what proximity does, don't we, Connie?"

Connie shook her head. "No, Marla."

"No. It's alright, cook what you were cooking, Connie. Eating his food is a good idea." Brin's food was always grainy, gritty. Three weeks of dinners. Twenty-one meals he cooked for her.

The son slept, to her relief. His gaze was very intense. Her child slept, too, growing so quickly she wondered the son didn't run in fright.

Connie whispered at the door, "Are you okay? I'm sorry about the recipe book."

Marla smiled. "Come in, Connie. It's okay. It just made me think of him."

Connie hugged her. "We have an order for four dozen jars."

Marla nodded. "Good. I'll do the rest this afternoon."

"Payment in advance," Connie said. "We've got lots of goodies arriving soon. A feast is planned."

"Bring me a plate," Marla said. "I'm not quite up to celebrations yet."

"No. I'm sorry. It's not a celebration, really. A welcome back for the men returned."

Three masons came to her workshop. "We have the tourist who killed your husband," the youngest mason said. It was not until he spoke she realized who he was. The men had aged dramatically. Far more than she had envisioned.

Marla felt a chill. "You have made a great sacrifice in leaving the walls of our town," she said. "Thank you. I have a woman here ready for the Kiln. Can you keep him till she's done?"

"Yes. We'll keep him."

They took the woman from Baristone to the Kiln.

"There's so much waiting," the son said.

"This gives us time to say goodbye," Marla said. "We can't rush it. You can eat now. Join the celebration while you wait." She led him to where the others had gathered in the Chief Mason's house. Connie paid the delivery man, who brought the food, wine, clothing, all the things ordered for the celebration. He arrived with his smell of the city, his big, loud truck and his air of superiority. He took the money and said,

"I know you must like it here, and it brings in the tourists, but those statues give me the creeps."

"Is anywhere else better?" Connie asked.

When the old woman was done, Marla led the son to the wall, the procession following behind them. The son coughed, his throat dry from the clay dust. "How do you breathe with all this dust?" he said.

"We get used to it," Marla said, though she wondered as she spoke if it was normal to feel the air in your lungs, to be aware of the tight filling of the chest with every inhalation.

Maybe other people didn't feel that.

The son said, "Oh, my god, all those faces staring at us. It feels like they're watching everything. Who was the first one covered? How did it start?"

"Many hundreds of years ago, one of the great men of the town disappeared. It was thought he'd left for the city but there was no word. Three years later, when it hadn't rained for most of that time, someone noticed a clay face in the dry creek bed.

"They dug it up. It was our missing man. Set solid.

"No one wanted to crack him open and nobody wanted to bury him like that, so while they decided they placed him upright on the town's limits. Already strange statues stood there, placed before local memory began. A woman died before they decided what to do. Her husband said she was just as important, so he had her covered in clay and set beside the man. They clayed the cracks to keep the statues standing, then an old man died, then a child, and already the wall was emerging."

She left the son trailing his fingers across his mother's face in the wall and went home to her baby.

They brought her the killer. Every centimetre was bruised or cut. His hair was all pulled out; his cheekbones shattered; his genitals cut and scabby; his shoulderbone exposed and his ears sliced to the skull.

They stood there silently, all of them, presenting her with their great gift. The man could not stand. He whispered, "Help me." Marla bent to him and stroked his hair back from his forehead. She looked into his face and said, "Take him to the Kiln." The masons nodded.

It took five days for the man to die. After the third day all they could hear was a scrabbling noise, like a mouse trying to break through into a food cupboard.

The masons carried him to Marla.

"Thank you," she said. "Would anyone like to stay to honour this man into the clay?" They all backed away.

She stripped him naked. He was blackened. His fingers, the ones that held the knife that killed her husband, were all broken.

She didn't wash him clean. She walked outside the wall, through the gateway made of brick. It was her wall, her family's wall. They had made it. And she was so proud of it. It was raining a little and tears ran from the eyes of the clay people. Rain pooled like piss at their feet. But the clay stayed firm. The mix of cement, gravel and a little fatty soap kept it strong.

Her buckets were light as she walked past the wall. The flowers in their pots were blooming, sending their perfume to her like a generous gift from a stranger.

She swung the buckets. She couldn't help it. Her step bounced, lifted by the warm air like a balloon. She started to skip, the exuberance of the day filling her with lightness.

She passed the masons, resting on this day with nothing to do but repairs. The people believed the wall kept them safe from all evil. And there had never been a calamity. Evil still occurred but it was blamed on external things, or a crack in the wall.

They were always finding cracks in the wall.

"Good to see you looking happy," the Chief Mason said. "You're like a young girl, bouncing along like that."

"She is a young girl," the oldest mason said. He was a friend of her father's. "A young girl with heavy responsibilities." She looked at him to see if he was serving her notice to behave, but he was smiling. "It's good to see you happy," he said. "Here, have some cheese. It's a good one. Imported."

She sat and ate the cheese with them, laughing at their teasing. It felt good to be teased, to laugh.

There was good rich clay around the sewerage plant. She never used it because it stank. It reeked of waste, and she would never use it for good people. She collected three bucketsful for the murderer. The smell made her retch. She carried the buckets back with her nose pressed against her shoulder.

In all her career, she had never been disrespectful.

Marla added nothing to the clay. He didn't even deserve her piss. She didn't prepare the clay as she usually did. Let the small rocks dent his flesh. Let the sticks scratch at him. The baby had awoken and sat up, watching her. They grow so fast, she thought. She gave the baby a piece of good clay, not the foul stuff she was using on the murderer.

The baby ate it. The widow laughed, tears coming. "Funny baby," she said, but the sight of it brought the taste of clay to her mouth, and she thought of her clay husband's kiss.

Marla's mouth felt so dry she could barely close it. Water quenched her thirst, but she had a sudden, intense desire for strawberries. She washed her hands and carried the baby over to the farming district. Here, they carted in dirt from outside, fertile dirt, rich and loamy. They piled it into large flat boxes, like giant's bed bases, and they raised these off the ground, as if the clay would suck out all the nutrients like leeches do.

Beautiful things grew there, tended by talented farmers. Greens, reds, oranges, food which nourished you even by looking at it. Here they kept the clay wetted down, not wanting dust to land on the produce. Things seemed more in focus.

"Marla, Marla, my dear girl. My poor dear, darling, little girl." The farmer held her in a bear hug from which she struggled to be released. The baby squirmed between them.

"No woman should be a widow so young," he said. "It's wrong. It's against nature."

"It is," she said. His sympathy made her cry, and she was caught up again in the bear hug.

"What will make you feel better? Anything. It's yours."

"Just some strawberries," she said. "Do you have any?"

He winked. "Wait'll you see them." He plucked a dozen, deep, dark red, dripping with juice.

She sunk her teeth in, unable to wait. The sweetness brought a bitter thought. Brin. Brin loved strawberries. He would have loved these. The baby clutched at her and Marla fed her a strawberry. The baby cooed in delight.

Back in the workshop, she gave the baby another piece of clay. The baby squeezed it, gurgled, played with it happily. She was already sitting up, getting ready to crawl. Marla thought of her own easy tiredness, her deep weariness, and wondered if this rapid growth did not leave time to build endurance.

She covered the killer with one layer. Then another. She built feet where his head was, a leering idiot face at the feet. Let him spend forever on his head.

If it should be these clay people were resurrected, she liked the idea of him heading down into the dirt.

She called to the mason waiting outside, "He's done."

The mason came in, wrinkling his nose. Politely, he said nothing. Marla laughed. "It's not me, you idiot. I used the sewerage clay for him."

The mason smiled. Marla didn't tell him the killer was upside down in his casing. They took the case to the Kiln and when he was done, the Chief Mason called the mourners.

This was a very different procession. There were jeers and snarls, no tears. There was laughter and chatter.

He was placed in the wall beside the woman from Baristone. "Good he's not next to my son," Marla's mother-in-law said. "Curse you on your clay walk."

There was a celebration afterwards, wine and beer, food and laughter. It was always like this after a procession, even a devastating one. Marla's mother said, "There is a certain satisfaction in what we do. It's like we have settled the answer of death. We've got it sorted out. It's comforting." People stopped to listen and Marla wondered if people would ever listen to her in the same way.

"But will it really happen?" Connie said. "The Great Clay Walk? The Resurrection?"

"It will be many generations away. You will all be safely in the wall, and many more beyond," Marla's mother said.

Connie shivered. "I don't know that I want to be awoken. It sounds terrifying."

Marla's mother smiled. "Frightening, yes. But for the chance at eternal life?"

"Here's to the Great Clay Walk," shouted the Chief Mason. "And here's to the clay, and the great Clay-Makers."

Marla watched them all, the clay dust in their pores, broad smiles on their faces, and she wondered which of them would be able to break free from their clay case on the day of the Great Clay Walk.

THE GLASS WOMAN

Feeding time. The Glass Woman in her glass box swallowed tomato soup, home-made, bright red, and we watched as it travelled to her stomach where, when she moved gently, it swayed like liquid in a wave machine.

We watched as she ate a dinner roll, tiny mouthfuls and she lolled her head back and let the chewed food slip down her throat. We watched it bounce as she swallowed.

We saw her blood. If we watched closely, paid extra to stand with our palms against the warm glass box, we could see the blood river, flowing, flowing, the rhythm matching her heart which we could also see.

It was my fourth time to see the Glass Woman. I was still not comfortable coming to this neighbourhood. I didn't have the style, the shoes, the clothes, the walk. I didn't have the sex. This is a man's neighbourhood. The women here stay indoors, because everything is provided within each high house. There are worlds in there, movie theatres, swimming pools, beds which make movies as you lie on them.

The men are on the streets. They walk to their cars, to another home, they meet at this house where the Glass Woman lives, and they are comfortable; they know how to walk on marble floors.

I didn't disguise myself. They would pick me out, anyway, you're not one of us.

I'm nothing like them. And yet I cannot keep away from the Glass Woman.

She watched us sometimes. She watched us when she masturbated using private items the men gave her. Paid to give her. Although the items are poked through the contact hole in a clump, she always stared at the person who provided it. Looked them in the eye and blinked.

The Glass Woman has no past. Her owner says he blew her when that was his job, and now he wears thick glasses and can't see through his cataracts, vision damaged by the great heat in his workshop.

"What else did you make?" I asked on my fourth visit. The men were gentle around the glass case, tempting her to spread her legs, begging her to press herself against the glass so light would catch in the prism.

Her owner sat on his stool at the back of the room. His fingers were never still. They fluttered like a beetle's legs, scurried so quickly, my eyes crossed watching.

His fingers were thin and strong.

I had not the courage before now to touch those fingers. If I scratched them, hurt them, he would never be able to make another glass woman.

On my first visit, the Glass Woman asked for my scarf in payment. Extra payment. My man had paid in full, he said, big, full amount of money. I had been warned she would take something of mine. That she was glass come to life without any manners.

My man took me there, and all I wore was the scarf and a thin dress. The Glass Woman squinted at me. She hadn't seen many women.

"She likes the girls," her owner said.

She didn't talk. She pointed at my scarf, and I unwound it and passed it through the contact hole. She grabbed so quickly our fingers touched and I gasped.

"Her fingers were warm and soft," I told my man when we were home. I didn't expect him to answer. He was angry with me because I had asked him for a new scarf.

"You can't bear the slightest sacrifice, can you?" he said. His voice was not tender. But I had given up a place in the Women's Home to be with him. I would not receive that chance again.

"I have made sacrifices," I said.

He smiled at me. "Of course," he said.

He had not touched the Glass Woman. He could pay extra money, a lot of money, and stay behind with her, alone together with just glass walls to separate them but he had not done so. This was because of me.

"You are not merely adequate," he said. "You are a find."

That was true. I had been working as a shop girl, my legs always bruised in the race to find a customer, and I smiled at him when he chose me to take his money.

He told me later he had never seen such desperation in one so beautiful.

I was not desperate, though. I was doing my job.

He paid many visits to the Glass Woman before inviting me along. He liked to tell me all about her, and was so descriptive I had to see her for myself. He said she was horrifying to look at, and I did not often see ugliness. She had taken from him his wallet, though she handed him back his money.

The second time we went to see her we stayed a little longer. Her owner recognised me and gave me a honey-coloured drink. It was bitter and made my limbs feel light, plastic. I smiled at him.

"Nothing wrong with smiling," he said, and he shrugged at the Glass Woman. Why should she smile, or cry? She is a woman made of glass, nothing more, she has no past, no background, no memory. She folded a pair of socks and placed them carefully beneath her. I could see the material through her thin glass body; blue wool. A man walked barefoot like an elf.

When there were not many people left, she strapped herself in and somebody took the controls. We laughed as he ordered her limbs to move. He split her in two and her limbs looked like toffee, glass toffee. Men's hands left sweat marks on the walls.

We left.

I had not touched the Glass Woman again. Her gaze frightened me a little, and her certainty. She always knew precisely what she wanted.

I didn't. My man took me to his little forest, eight trees with his initials on them. One was dead, its giant trunk hollow, and I stood inside it and stretched my arms up.

It smelt of moss and old wood. A smell I could live with, if I had to live inside a tree trunk. People could feed me, feed me, and I wouldn't exercise, and soon I'd fill the whole trunk. The bark would mark my flesh.

My man tied two ropes to a low branch of his tallest tree.

"Come on out," he said. He tied me like a puppet. When he tugged a rope my arm lifted. When he tugged another, my leg bent up.

He laughed. It was dark now. I couldn't see him, but I could feel his heat around me. He tugged so both my arms were raised and he licked me with a feather tongue until I giggled. Then he kissed me and caressed me with the soft leaves of the trees. There was no one to hear and I cried out, and his fingers squeezed me, my legs, he bit me with his gums.

He untied me and took me home.

On my third visit to the Glass Woman a man spoke to her. His voice was obscene. I watched the glass case shake with its tenor.

"You look a little like my wife," he said, "when she was younger."

"The Glass Woman is an original," said her owner from the back.

"As if he copied," I whispered to my man. He pinched me between to shut me up.

"Do I?" the Glass Woman said. She had a woman's voice, not a child's or a doll's. Someone near the front had to sit down. He looked ill. Green.

She had a voice. "Do you have a photo of her?" said the Glass Woman. The man nodded.

She tilted her head at the contact hole. He pushed the photo through. Without looking she sat on it.

Her owner chuckled. "You won't see that again. Keeps all her things in a little box, never even looks at them."

"Is it a glass box?" I said to my man. He pinched me again.

I did not visit the Glass Woman for a while. My man said I spoke too much and made her restless. He said I was far too keen on the Glass Woman for my own good, and there had been complaints about women. He continued with the visits.

She asked for things and you had to bring them. An old bowl. Some ugly paint. Odd things which cost nothing and she didn't seem to use.

I stayed at home and practised floating in the bath. I smelt sweet for my man.

He didn't come home one night after visiting her. I thought, he has spent our money to stay longer, and I was angry but I didn't go to the house. I waited, but he did not come home.

A week later I visited the Glass Woman for the fourth time. I was alone.

I had not been alone outdoors before. I walked proudly, like a man, but my backside could not help but stick out, and I was spat upon. I closed my eyes and imagined myself protected, worshipped, safe.

The Glass Woman's owner allowed me to enter unaccompanied. He knew me very well.

"I am shocked to tell you my man didn't come home," I told him.

"She does that to people," he said. "Stay a little later tonight. Share my food."

He gave me a stool by his, and I sat at the back with him, drinking the bitter honey. There was no way you could escape the magic of the Glass Woman. Even as an observer I could not keep my gaze from her.

She danced that night, when the man pressed the buttons. Her arms like the swizzle stick in my drink. Her legs still crossed, because there was no room to stand in the glass box. She bent over, and we could see through her anus and out her mouth. There were men on the other side of the glass box. Their features flattened by the glass. My man was not there.

"Where is my man?" I said when the dance was over. The men were leaving. Just one stayed behind.

"We'll go and eat," the Glass Woman's owner said.

"I'd like to watch," I said. I recognised something of myself within him.

Fear.

I had feared discovery when I began to read my man's books. He had so many lovely ones, and I could read because we learned at the Women's Home. I was careless; I said things I could only have known from the books. I remember my sudden silence, my fear that I had revealed myself, that I would now be blinded for my arrogance.

My man was kind. The women in the Home would not believe that but he was truly kind. He said, "No more books, girl," and he paddled me with them, smack smack smack. That was all.

The Glass Woman's owner now looked fearful.

"I want to stay," I said.

"All right, but be quiet. Don't let them know you're here." The Glass Woman and her man did not care.

"We're off now," the Glass Woman's owner said. They did not hear. I hid behind the door.

The man circled the glass box, and she turned on her haunches. She licked her lips. He began to take off his clothes, dropping them to the floor like he was being paid. They like to show us what we don't have, those inches of hard flesh bone.

She swayed by her contact hole, twisting her lips. He walked there, his erection a magnet. She placed her mouth over the hole.

And his cock went in there.

I could see it down her throat, in and out, the pink of it obscene in the glass vase of her neck.

He held onto the glass and dribbled. I could see saliva drip, a thick rain-drop, then stop at the contact hole.

She drew her lips back and bared her teeth.

"No," I thought. "Is this my man last week? Is this the price you demanded of him?"

No. She dropped backwards, without warning, and semen splattered the wall of her glass box.

The man sat down, head in hands.

"Tired?" she said. He nodded. "Poor love," she said.

She looked up, winked at me, then curled at the bottom of her glass box and went to sleep.

The man gathered his clothes and left. The Glass Woman's owner collected me and took me to eat.

"What else did you make?" I said. He fed me food so light I couldn't taste it. Doll's food. He took the Glass Woman's dinner to her and was gone an hour.

"I made a lot of things," he said. "I blew a perfect glass cat with a nasty nature, and I blew glass ants with all their legs."

"Always living things?" I said.

"I blew a cushion for a mouse king." He stretched across and stroked my brow.

"Do you miss your man?" he said. An odd question.

"He's gone," I said.

He nodded. He leaned over to kiss me but all he could do was puff his hot breath down into my lungs.

I slept by the fire in the room in which we dined and I visited the Glass Woman before breakfast.

It was the first time I had been alone with her. She sat, staring at the door, waiting for life to enter. She seemed to envy life, wish she was me.

That was what I thought, anyway.

"Hello," I said.

"I only talk if I have an audience," she said.

"You'll have an audience next week," I said. "The Captain is coming."

"The Captain," she said.

Then her owner walked in. "Now, now," he said. "Girls don't chat together. Girls never chat."

The Captain was the man every girl would like. He was the man, and if you were his, you would be the woman. If I were his I could have my own Glass Woman, and she would not need to have an audience to speak.

The Captain had white hair, like my man. White hair showed the dirt but looked so clean when it was clean. I washed my hair so it shone, although I would have to wash it again before the Captain arrived.

When the men were in the room with the Glass Woman, I walked amongst them, smoothly, my skin pale, my cheeks red.

"Hello, doll," they said. But they loved the Glass Woman.

Later on, I watched again.

The Glass Woman's owner could not keep his fingers still. He would be rich when the Captain came. He could keep the Glass Woman for himself, keep her safe, and I would be a friend as well.

The Captain was man as these men were men to their women.

He knew about the contact hole, the magical Glass Woman who was not real. He knew about the gifts you left behind.

The Captain arrived. He had eight men with him. I didn't stand by the Glass Woman's owner; I did not want to belong to him. The Captain sat at the front, hands on knees and waited. He was used to being entertained.

"You need to start her off," I said, bold, memorable. I had crushed rose petals into my underwear; I could feel their moistness.

He leaned forward and flicked the glass.

It shivered.

We saw her hand sneak up, turn on the light she was allowed to control.

But she was not there. A little girl was there, a young teenager, with white hair, a pale face. She had a scarf around her neck and "Eat it" written on the long sleeved t-shirt covering her flat chest. She wore a tartan rug as pants and blue woollen socks. Around her there was history; a wallet displayed, holding a photo of herself, a book, a page from a letter. She smiled open-mouthed and we could not see through her. She squatted, turned. I could see the crust of my man's blood on her wig.

"This is an ordinary girl," said the Captain. "Not a magical woman."

"Yes, but underneath she's glass, cold, transparent." The Glass Woman's owner was desperate. I walked around the box, thinking she must be hiding on the other side. She could not have escaped with those limbs.

"She's so beautiful your eyes will bleed. Take off the shirt. Take it off. Her cunt is made of cut glass. Fuck her and you'll bleed to death. Fuck her. You'll bleed to death."

I put my hands on the glass and stared through at the men. They seemed to wobble. They stared at me.

The Glass Woman's owner moved to the glass box and made a click. He lifted the lid, reached in, lifted her out. He dropped her to the floor where she shattered into a thousand diamonds. The men scrabbled for a prize. Only I saw, as the Glass Woman's owner lifted me into her glass box, only I saw the T-shirt, the pants, the scarf, stand up and walk to the door.

Only I, Doll Girl, made of porcelain and fed on sugar cakes, only I saw her turn and wink at the backs of the men bending over my cleverly jointed body.

THE BLUE STREAM

My brother will be home soon. Home from the cool Blue Stream where he has been floating for seven years now, since I was four, and where I will soon be floating; but you sink first, a cold, fresh shock, and as you rise you begin to float. It's just like being back in Mum's womb, apparently, only you're there for longer. I don't see how anyone can actually know that. My brother will be amongst the first Streamers to emerge, so how can they know? It's like saying if you dream you're dead then you're dead. How could anyone know that?

"Streamers Stream-Line the Future" we see everywhere. So my brother's going to be some sort of hero. They all are. Coming back to do all the jobs the adults don't want to do. Hopefully some of them will be teachers. The ones we've got now are so stupid. We have whole classes about How To Welcome a Streamer:

1. *Smile pleasantly at them.* If I used to smile at my brother he'd snarl. But I suppose that's the whole point, isn't it? The whole idea of the Blue Stream?

2. *Speak to them in a friendly fashion.* About what, though? What've you been up to, big brother? Learning how to swim?

3. *Invite them to join you and your friends for lunch.* But they're OLD. They're all twenty. Why would we want to eat with them?

Thanksgiving Day today. So much to be grateful for.

We are thankful for peace that exists in our homes, on our streets. We study riot behaviour at school—I had to memorise what a riot was because I kept forgetting. We watch old news, funny, jerky-looking pictures of big-eared teenagers. They smash and run, run over each other sometimes. We saw one, it was supposed to be a celebration of the New Year (how weird!

To be happy that another year had passed!) but it looked terrible to me. Thousands of teenagers crammed together, drunk on alcohol, smoking cigarettes and burning each other with the red end. Then we heard a clock ringing twelve times and they all went mad. They poured beer on each other, threw bottles. They started to fight! They ran in fear, pushing, squeezing and when some fell over, others just jumped on them like they were rubbish. We would never treat people like that. Then there was the next day: all the teenagers (except the dead ones) were gone, and there were the adults to clean up the mess as usual. They showed us the face of one of the dead kids, before an adult lifted a sheet over his head. His face was calm. We give thanks for there being no more riots.

Since the Streamers were set afloat, our world has been far more peaceful. Not on a global scale; we still have wars and terrorism, that sort of thing. But we are thankful that stuff will go, when the Streamers begin to emerge to grow older and take their place in the world. Soon everyone will have a position, and know their limitations, be accepting of their situation and be able to face the reality of it. We are thankful for that. We are thankful for no teenage pregnancies. And we are glad that those bad habits, like cigarettes, alcohol and drugs, are not formed at an early age, only later when a person can cope.

We give thanks for the safety of our belongings. Vandalism is gone, and our houses are safer. Not totally safe, but safer. The teenagers can't reach us from the Blue Stream, and we are thankful for that.

Before the Blue Stream there were more suicides than road deaths. Now there are far less of both. For this we are thankful.

Some of the adults are getting worried. There was a meeting at the hall, which everyone had to go to. Mum and Dad took me because I was too young to be trusted at home alone. Not everyone was a parent there. A lot of them had never had a child and didn't care if they never saw a young person again. There was a big group of them who shouted louder than the rest.

"Why take the risk? We've waited this long." That sort of thing. My parents wanted Jim back, so they were on the side of letting them out.

My Dad said, "We can't leave them in the Stream forever," and most people had to agree.

I was pleased with my father that day. All those other adults don't think the teenagers have grown enough. They think another year will do it, or two, maybe. They are just scared of their own plan. It's been easy to talk, the last seven years, of how the world will be, how wonderful. Now the proof will appear, or the evidence. I can't remember the difference. There was a survey in one paper, "Should we release the children?" They're just scared of what they've done. None of the questions matter, though. They have to stick with what they said. They have to. I do twenty sit-ups every day so that they won't leave my brother in there any longer.

And then there he was, climbing carefully out of the back seat and staring. He is a stranger to me. He has been gone from sight, floating through the country for seven years and now he is back. I don't recognise his face, I don't remember his smell.

How To Welcome a Screamer more like. He hasn't shut up—though his throat's getting sore so it's a bit quieter now. He'll stop eventually. He's started to look around and notice things, his gaze flicking about while his mouth still screams. They're all doing it, and everyone thought at the same time to call them Screamers. The PR company quickly sent out ads saying, "The Water-Babies are here," as if they'd never called them Streamers, never thought of it. But Water-Babies is almost as bad, because they're like new-born, full-grown babies, not wanting to leave the safety of the Stream for the big world where they are told what sort of person they will be.

"It's important to know who you are," my father said, the family sitting around him as he spoke of the perfect world we were helping to create. "Teenagers were troubled by their lack of identity, by the great nothingness which faced them in the mirror. We are simply supplying the identity to fill the nothingness."

"Nothingness," my brother said, "that's what it was."

"You see what society has saved you from?" my father said, nodding like it was his idea.

"The Blue Stream was the nothingness," Jim said, aping my father's nod because he is still learning and can't always connect action to meaning.

———

Jim has been home for nine days. He hasn't screamed since two days ago, only his wake up scream. He carries a little satchel, which he was given as a welcome present. In it, papers grow; he receives them in the mail, pinned to his pillow, under his plate. If he sees something written on the ground, he is to write it down.

"As a Mature Person, you will Look Your Best" (found on the bathroom mirror);

"As a Mature Person you will Perform Disagreeable Tasks Without Undue Delay" (Stapled to an invitation to a job interview) and

"As a Mature Person you will Be a Good Family Member" (In the bar under Dad's favourite glass).

Some of Jim's Friends came to visit and they all sat in the lounge room with the same frightened smile on their faces.

"What's wrong?" I asked him. I was helping him get drinks from the bar.

"I don't know who they are," he said. "Were they Friends of mine before?"

"I was only four. How would I know? Why don't you ask them?"

"I don't think they know either."

There was silence as we sat. I sat close to him. It was nice to be able to do so.

"Haven't been out today?" one of the girls asked him. She has these big boobs she barely knows are there; pinned to one was a badge. Everyone in the room had them except my brother.

"Minimise Daydreaming," she read, twisting the badge so she could see it. The others read theirs aloud, too;

"Overcome Anger and Fear."

"Avoid Complaining."

"You'll get one if you go up the street," the girl said kindly.

My brother was staring at her chest. I pinched his elbow.

"Don't be rude," I said.

They know as much as me, these Screamers. No more. After primary school they went straight into the Stream. Some, now, will go to high school, but not many. There are too many urgent jobs to be done. Some will go to Uni if they have to be doctors or something. My brother won't. He has to be a gardener.

"Happy Birthday," Mum said to me. She was the only one excited. She brought out a cake with twelve candles on it. Jim stared at the flame like he didn't know what it was, just stared and upset me so I couldn't blow out the candles.

"Blow out the candles," Mum said, "then we'll have some cake in the backyard."

We didn't go anywhere else. Jim still gets nervous when we go out anywhere, if it isn't part of some stupid Screamer instruction.

Sometimes I really hate him being a Screamer. He's supposed to involve his parents in his activities, but they're my parents too, and they hardly ever leave me alone. So I have to go. Today Jim had to go to the beach so we all had to go. People I knew were there and saw me with my parents. Jim would have gone purple with embarrassment if he wasn't a Screamer. The whole time we had the radio on, it played only one song, which happens to be Jim's favourite–same with all the Screamers. It's like a chant, slow and boring, and it just sings about what a great time you can have with your family.

Go to the beach
Read a sto-ry
Watch TV
or TELL a sto-ry
Take some lessons
Try a square dance
Do some sewing
Maybe some pants
Work on puzzles
Play a Game

Blah blah blah. I don't want to do any of that stuff. I think Jim is supposed to go all the way through the song, doing one of everything. I can't wait till he gets to square dancing.

I saw a terrible accident today, and it's all because of that boring Sara from school. She couldn't learn her rationale and the teacher said that I had to help, because I was smart and we both had a sibling home from the Stream. So I had to go to her house to help her. I made her try to remember on the way home.

"Teenagers have identity crises."

"Teenagers have identity crises."

"They develop negative personalities."

"They develop negative personalities."

"They join gangs."

"They join gangs."

"They rape."

"They rape."

"They riot."

"They riot."

"Once the physical changes have occurred, they will take their places as confident members of our society."

"I can't remember that."

She's a stupid girl.

We got to her house and her mum was crying.

"There's been a terrible accident," she said, "in the bathroom."

There was Sara's sister, empty pill bottles around her, vomit in her hair, a note clutched in her hand.

"It doesn't look like an accident," Sara said. Not so dumb.

But it was. The police said so. And in the newspapers, underneath the advertisements that said, *Be tolerant of other peoples' opinions,* was a headline:

"SCREAMER ACCIDENT RATE ALARMING." Sara brought the article to show me.

"Mum wouldn't let me read the note. She said I shouldn't have any new ideas before my birthday next week."

"You're lucky. I've got months to go."

"Yes, I can't wait. The peace, the rest, the water lapping my ears, cooling my forehead, washing me so I don't have to have a shower for seven years. I hate showers. And I won't commit suicide due to the confusion of my loyalties."

She has finally learnt the rationale.

Jim got a note today he didn't understand so I had to explain. He found it pinned to his towel in the bathroom.

"Be not dominated by others' opinions nor in constant revolt against social conventions."

"It's just that you're not supposed to listen to what your Friends tell you, only what the adults tell you."

"And what's revolt? Like that casserole Dad made?"

It's good being smarter than your older brother.

"You're not supposed to argue when they tell you what to do."

"But if they tell me everything, I might get sick of it."

"Well, if you do, don't tell anyone. You'll get into trouble."

He could understand trouble. It meant the withholding of the nothingness which comes at the end of the lives of people who have been good. I don't like the thought of nothingness, myself, but then I'm not a Screamer.

My brother keeps telling me stuff that I'm not meant to know till I'm a Screamer, and he lets me watch stuff that's meant to be private.

He feels sorry for me because most of my friends have gone into the Stream. I was smart and they put me up a grade, but now all my friends are early into the Stream. He feels sorry for me because I'm lonely, and he's been given so many Friends.

I hid behind the couch so I could only hear what was going on. It was called a *"Give deserved credit or praise to other people"* party, and it is the only party they are allowed to have. They are getting very good at them.

Jim sat on the couch, and kept dropping soft lollies for me to chew quiet as I could. His friend Barry was there; I could tell his deep voice and the way he felt so unused to it—he has only just emerged. And there was June; she has a lovely soft voice. Andrea, who kissed everyone (you're not meant to do that). Beryl, Big Beryl I call her, though my father says "*Nicknames Breed Contempt.*" And Mark, who is nearly as nice as my brother and wouldn't tell if he saw me behind the couch.

"Who wants to start?" June said.

"Me," Barry said. "Andrea, I admire your friendly nature and the way you make people feel comfortable."

"Thank you," Andrea said. "June, you are a gentle and kind person and you will make a marvellous instructor."

"Thank you," June said. She's got that lovely voice; I wish she was one of my teachers. "Jim, I think it's admirable the way you helped me prepare my college application even though you won't be going yourself."

"Thank you," my brother said. "Beryl, you are a most marvellous cook, and the lunch you prepared today was a great accomplishment. Thank you for bringing it to my parent's house."

"Thank you," Beryl said. "Mark, I think you are very handsome."

"You can't say that," June said. "That's a compliment for something he has no control over. Think of another thing."

"I'm not very good at this," Beryl said. There was a bit of a silence. If the others were anything like me, they would have been thinking, "Useless." But then they're not like me. They're Screamers.

Beryl finally said, "I think you're very good being nice to Jim's little sister."

My ears burned.

"Thank you. Barry, I appreciate the fact that you are very generous with your car and don't mind picking us all up to bring us here."

"Thank you," Barry said. They all stood up then, all saying thank you, thank you. The party was over. What a rage.

Jim and I went walking to get out of the house. It was hot, he had taken his shirt off and tied it around his waist. I thought he looked nice, such a big chest, hardly hairy at all, still smooth and soft from being in the Stream. Better than Dad's wrinkled and greying old thing, which luckily I only see if we go swimming.

A man with a whole pile of purple pieces came up. He shuffled through them and handed my brother one, smiling. Like a teacher does when he knows you're going to get the answer wrong.

"Behave acceptably in public," it said.

"But it's hot! This is acceptable!" Jim said. He knew what he was supposed to have done wrong.

"Put your shirt on, son. None of us want to witness your naked body," the man said. It was Mr Thompson from down the road. His two teenagers are in the Stream, and he has a Screamer back and his wife is quiet and ugly. I could imagine his chest; worse than Dad's, not even any muscles and probably covered with pimples. He has them on his face and neck; why would they stop there? I stared at this ugly man who was trying to cover up my beautiful brother.

"It's rude to stare," he said, and after my brother had put his shirt on, Mr Thompson left.

I found Jim lying in the back yard, amongst the grass he had just mown.

"I don't get it about daydreaming," he said. "I was just trying to see if I could daydream at all, and I can't. I've got nothing to think about."

"What about when you were a kid?" I said. I always daydream nice memories, from when I was five or six.

"I can't remember my childhood," he said. That sounded terrible.

"What about what you want to be? Or who you'll meet?"

"I'm supposed to be a gardener and I've already been introduced to June," he said. I moved closer and, the smell of cut grass filling my throat like sugar, I whispered, "But what do you WANT to be?"

He looked at me and there was a little smile on his mouth. "Nothing. I want to be nothing. I want to assume my duties as a citizen."

The sky-writer had smoked that into the blue sky earlier.

"Yes," he said. He went indoors and made good Friends with Dad. Dad gave him alcohol.

At least it isn't hard for him to assume his duties. He is told exactly what his duties are. At least he doesn't have to figure it out for himself.

Jim often went to the pictures with his Friends. In the morning I would ask him, "What was the movie like?"

"What movie?" he would say. He wouldn't remember. He smelt before he had his shower. He smelt like nothing I've ever smelt before.

———

"Is there a Stroking Party today, Jim?" I asked. I felt really cool, calling it what the Screamers did.

"What do you reckon?" he said, nasty voice. "Has there been a Thursday since I've been back when there hasn't been one?"

I hate it when he talks to me like that. I don't know what's wrong with him today. Something's up. Something's upset him. He won't even look at Mum and Dad, let alone get close enough for them to boss him around. Dad hasn't noticed, but Mum has. She keeps looking at me. Not as if I know what's going on, but in a thoughtful way, like she's trying to figure something out, something about me. It's confusing with the whole family gone weird.

I got into my spot behind the couch, but there were no lollies coming over. Five Screamers, my grouchy brother included, sat there saying nothing.

"Who'd like to start?" Beryl said. She must have thought it was her big chance.

"Mark's not here yet," June said. "Didn't you notice?"

"I thought he wasn't coming," Beryl said, "I thought he might be sick."

"He's not sick, he's in hospital," Jim said. There was this big noise, yelling and shouting and that. I couldn't tell who was who.

My dad slammed the door open and came into the room.

"Why was this door closed?" he shouted. "What's all this teenage rubbish?" That was a bad insult. He'd never called Jim a teenager before.

"We're just worried about Mark," Jim said. He is getting smarter and smarter.

"Mark will be released in the morning, Jim, you know that. He's learning his lesson early, he's lucky." There was quiet. My father left, without shutting the door.

"Arsehole," my brother said. I couldn't believe it. I didn't think he even knew a word like that. The others laughed, nervous but excited, it sounded.

"I can't think of anything nice to say," Beryl said, and that was the party finished with.

I never got to go to parties when I was growing. No one had them, no one had a big brother or sister to tell us what parties were like.

There was no one but our parents and teachers to tell us anything. Things like, when I wanted to go out late one night, to stay over at the twins' and sit up all night, my mum said NO, and I couldn't say but Jim is allowed. He wasn't there for me to say it about. I had to learn it all myself.

He won't come out of his room, only to do his chores and eat then back to his room. Dad gave him a bottle of whisky and I heard him in the night, crying in the voice I remember before he went away.

When it was party time again, I took my own lollies and ducked behind the couch.

But I had to peek my head around when Mark came in.

He didn't look very good. He was all yellow around his eyes and his arm was in a sling.

"I bit my nails," he said.

"But I thought we only had to *avoid the mannerisms*," June said. "I didn't think you could get hurt for them."

"Arseholes," my brother said. I think it's the only swear word he knows. I hid back behind the couch in case he told me to get. I heard a paper, then his voice, his nasty voice:

"Mannerisms to avoid.

1. Biting nails—you already discovered that one, Mark.
2. Sniffling
3. Playing with hair
4. Putting pencils in mouth
5. Drumming with fingers
6. Wiggling a leg back and forth
7. Twitching mouth
8. Twisting nose or ear
9. Moistening finger to turn page
10. Eating noisily
11. Playing with jewellery

And there I was, making little plaits in my hair!

"I think it's a bit much," June said, "but I think Mark is showing remarkable strength of character."

"Thank you," Mark said. "I think Barry was very brave for volunteering to take the food tins we collected to the city."

"Thank you," Barry said. I couldn't hear the rest. I blocked my ears and cried into my tucked up knees.

We had dinner with the Thompsons tonight. It was really boring. I was the only young one there, plus the parents, plus Jim and the Thompson's Screamer Laura. I was sitting there and I wanted to tell everyone about school, because I got best in maths, I got everything right and the teacher made me go to the other classes and read out my answers. It was really embarrassing.

I was telling everyone about it, thinking they'd be interested because they're all so boring, when I noticed how uncomfortable everyone looked so I shut up.

"*Don't talk about yourself all the time,*" Laura said, in that voice the Screamers use when they've learnt something off the purple pieces.

"*Don't talk about operations or dental experiences,*" Jim said.

"I haven't had any," I said. I was really annoyed.

"*Don't talk about controversial subjects, unpleasant happenings, or death,*" Laura said.

"I thought death WAS an unpleasant happening," I said. My mother, I'm sure, winked at me.

"What should we discuss?" Mr Thompson said. He already knew the answer.

"*News items and the interests of others,*" Jim said. It was the most boring night of my life, AND we had to eat chops.

Jim and Dad were drunk in the kitchen. Jim tried to tell Dad about some music he likes that Dad doesn't like. Jim said, "But it gets you, you're into it, it lifts you away."

"Sounds dangerous," Dad said, "Sounds like daydreaming. Where did you hear this stuff? Some backyard?"

"It was on the radio. They said music for all ages. You just don't understand," Jim said. He was lying. They don't play music like that on the radio.

"No, you're the one who's supposed to understand. You have to put yourself in **my** place and understand **my** point of view."

Dad pointed at the purple piece he had carefully stuck on the fridge.

"But it doesn't make sense," Jim said, and I got nervous. He was saying stuff like that now. "It's easier for you to understand me cos you've been my age. I've never been your age."

"Never mind, you will," Dad said. Jim said nothing, which made me even more nervous.

"I love you, Dad," Laura Thompson said. I was at their place, watching Mrs Thompson make a cake. I looked at Mr Thompson and wondered how anyone could love him, even if they were told to. Especially if they've been gone seven years and come back a Screamer.

I looked puberty up in the dictionary. No other rude words were there. It said, "From the Latin 'pubertas' meaning 'age of madness'." That seemed weird, but it was a brand new dictionary.

We went to a movie with June and her mother. I was depressed because the twins had gone into the Blue Stream, they were my last friends. Luckily, Jim didn't mind taking me. It wasn't really a movie, it was more like a lecture. It was about this really dumb woman who kept getting into trouble. There was one bit where she had a mental at her children, threw things at them.

Jim said, "My mother has such a good temper, you really have to try to make her angry."

June and her mother smiled at him. I was amazed. Didn't he hear her yelling at me this afternoon? Just because I was late home from saying goodbye to the twins? She won't leave me alone; she wants me there all the time.

Running along the bottom of the screen through the whole "bad mother" scene were the words, *"Show Pride in your Parents in Front of your Friends."*

At the end, a man stood up and said, "Isn't it nice to know exactly how to behave, even in the most embarrassing of situations? This hasn't always been the way. At one stage of the Human Struggle, people ignored the rules. It was a terrible time." All the adults and lots of the Screamers clapped, but the kids, old enough like me to be there, and the rest of the Screamers, just watched the titles. If they were thinking the same as me, none of them showed it.

I was thinking, "So you CAN break the rules. People have done it before." Funny to think of that.

There was trouble after the movie was over. The adults gathered in the foyer, leaving kids and Screamers in the cinema. Then they let the Screamers out one by one, and us kids had to wait for hours.

Jim said that the adults were angry at the Screamers who hadn't clapped after the man's speech. They said, "We know who you are. We know each and every face."

They pointed at the ones who had clapped and cheered. Those Screamers were allowed to go. They were given a prize—money, Jim said, but he couldn't quite see.

I was sent home then. We filed past the bad Screamers, who were standing facing the wall. Some of them were crying, and the adults said, "Don't cry like a baby. *A Mature Person does not Indulge in Childish Emotions.*"

The Screamers tried to stop, but that just makes crying worse. Jim told me they had to watch the movie five times. He got home at breakfast time, his eyes red and tired.

"Enjoy the movie?" Dad asked.

"It was educational," Jim said. Then he had a shower and went to work.

Jim received a purple piece of paper with his pay cheque. *"Take Disappointment Gracefully."* I was very disappointed myself; I thought if I met him on payday he might buy me something on the way home. But he just walked along, watching his feet, ignoring me.

"What's wrong?" I asked him. He looked up. He wasn't depressed at all, he was smiling.

"Found another one," he said.

In red chalk on the footpath, were the words, YOU ARE AN INDI-VIDUAL.

"Is that a rule?" I asked.

"Doubt it," he said. He was really happy. "Yesterday I found one that said, YOUR PARENTS ARE FAR FROM PERFECT!"

"Maybe you shouldn't read them," I said. "You don't know who wrote them."

"It doesn't matter. The words are there."

From then on I always walked looking at my feet but I never found as many as Jim did.

Three months now until I take the big dip. Sara has been gone for ages, but her mother still goes to school to pick her up every day.

"Sara is in the Blue Stream. When she emerges, you will have a beautiful adult child to share your home," the Principal has told her.

They don't say how Sara can be more successful at avoiding accidents than her sister was.

Mum caught me the other day; she has no understanding of privacy. Neither does my brother.

"Privacy is far from Godliness," he said, standing at the door, when he heard me shouting at Mum. Luckily I had put my clothes on by then or I would have died. Mum sat on the bed and we had a talk.

"You feel a bit funny?" she asked. It was vague, but there was no way I could describe it.

"Yes."

She made me stand in front of the mirror and we looked at each other. Clothes on, thank god.

"You enter the Stream looking like you do. In the next seven years, your breasts will grow, you hips round. Hair will grow, under your arms and there." She pointed.

"Vagina, Mum," I said. Once I realised how embarrassed she was, I felt better.

"Yes. Your sex organs will increase in size—your vagina, uterus, clitoris."

"Is that a clit? The boys at school ask to see it sometimes."

"Well, don't show them. You'll grow in height and weight, perfectly, because you'll receive the right diet. And there are hormonal changes which are happening already. That's why the boys want to see parts of you they don't have themselves. It's a very difficult time, darling, physically and mentally painful, and if you weren't in the Stream, you might do things you'll regret later on."

"Like what? What did you do to regret?"

"I'm not really supposed to tell you. You're not supposed to have any ideas when you begin."

"Please, Mum." It was sounding worse and worse to me. I didn't want to miss out on the pain, I wanted to regret things.

Mum said, "The changes in you create the unrest. If you float in the Stream till the changes are over, you'll be perfect. That's what they say."

"But is it true?"

"Yes, of course. It's mostly true . . . for most people."

"Do you think it's true for me, Mum? What do you think?"

"We'll see," she said. She said we'll see. Maybe I'll stay here, maybe I won't have to go into the Blue Stream.

Something terrible has happened, something scary. A woman was walking along and four kids like me grabbed her, they hurt her, raped her, and they killed her. Kids! Some were eleven, some were twelve. One was ten. And there were girls there, as well as boys. They told us only teenagers committed gang-killings. So what are these kids then? It's really scary. The newspaper thinks that thirteen is too old now. But they can't drop us in the Stream earlier than that. There'd be no kids. We've been told we aren't allowed to hang around in big groups, just one or two. Too bad at school where we all used to sit on the oval and just talk about stuff. Too bad about going anywhere you might see someone you know.

My mother told my father she was taking me to the dentist, because I couldn't enter the Stream with cavities.

"I'm proud of you," he said, his eyes unfocused. He is drunk a lot these days.

"'Nother drink, Dad?" my brother said, "nothing drink?" They laughed, the two men. Mother and I went to the station.

"I want to ask some questions about the Blue Stream," she told the man.

He made us watch a video about teenagers and then the office was closed.

Jim still screams when he wakes up. He keeps thinking he's emerging from the nothingness.

Jim and his Friends had to go to a meeting with the new Screamers and the old. It was for their twenty-first, instead of having a party. Barry couldn't go, because all the toilets he looks after were flooded, and they needed them for a conference.

When Jim came back he took my hand. He pressed something there. Red chalk. He went to his room. I didn't see him again.

June told me about the meeting, how all these Screamers from their year got up and said how wonderful the world was, and the new Screamers screamed and stared, and some of the old Screamers cried. She said Jim cried. She said she didn't cry, because she knew it was reality and that is how it is.

There was no scream this morning and I knew. My mother knew too. She left my father snoring in their bed and got in with me. We pulled the covers up and she held my hand and told me a long, long story. Each story started another, and I helped. We told stories for three hours until my father woke up. He opened his door, walked into the hall, saw us sitting up in bed. Saw Jim's closed door. Made me love him by understanding. He closed my door.

We heard Jim's bed being dragged and had a sudden hope–perhaps he was asleep and Dad was trying to wake him. But we heard something heavy land on the bed.

Dad opened the door.

He came to us, took my hand and Mum's, and said, "I think you should look at his peaceful face," and we did. He was Real Jim on the bed with the marks of his own socks around his neck.

All his grief was with us now.

In the papers that day, the meeting was called a triumph of the human spirit.

GREAT MOMENT IN THE HUMAN RACE, it said, ALL THINGS TAKEN INTO DUE CONSIDERATION. GOOD ADULTS GREET NEW ADULTS.

The number of Screamer accidents was not reported. Mr and Mrs Thompson came over to discuss Jim and the meeting.

"Terrible thing," Mr Thompson said. "Such a shame for Jim to suffer his accident so close to the success of the Program."

Laura said, "Funny how those socks knotted themselves." Her father, without turning to face her, pointed a finger directly at her. She stared. She said nothing else.

"All in all, a good birthday party," Mr Thompson said. "All things taken into due consideration."

It will be my birthday soon.

I can't tell you what will happen in my future; and once I'm there, I may not remember my past. From witnessing Jim's year of Screamers, I fear for my own life; I only hope I can conform. The only ones alive are the ones who are conforming now, and will do forever. The others have accidents. Screamer suicide does not exist. Why would they kill themselves when their lives are plotted for them, their behaviour planned and ordered? They have no worries. The adults say the strong human beings are left, but I say they are gone.

Dad's really angry with Mum. She won't share her drug.

"No one'll know, unless you tell them," he snarled, all angry and red-faced, standing over her as she sat on the couch watching the TV that wasn't on.

"Everyone will know," she said. She doesn't seem to mind the drug, but I don't want them to give her any more. She looks like Mrs Thompson now, like a photograph, barely moving, barely anything on her face. If I could steal her drug to give to Dad I would.

I woke up early this morning, excited because it was my birthday, but worried about the Blue Stream, no matter what the beautiful lady said.

Mum and Dad came into my room with a big tray of cake and lollies. For breakfast! Other years I couldn't have those till after eggs. There were two presents.

"One for now, one for later," Mum said. Her eyes were clear; I could tell she hadn't taken her drug. Dad sat on the bed and grinned stupidly. I thought maybe she had a plan.

I opened the present for now. It was some old book I can't even read because I won't have time.

"Thanks, Mum," I said anyway. The other present I saved for later. Then I had to get ready for the Stream.

The guilt in my mother's eyes was the worst. Seeing it, I knew she didn't have a plan; other than to say goodbye. She had tried hard to keep me, and she had failed. So I suppose that's the end of me not going into the Blue Stream.

Mum did her best.

We went to many places, even the headquarters of these people called "Freedom Stream". But they had no plans of action—they talked a lot, that's all. They still sent their kids to the Stream.

Finally we caused a bit of fuss at the Minister's office. We got taken away by police. Mum got taken away and I got a talking to, by the beautiful lady with her hair in a bun, soft and fluffy around her face like a princess.

"The Stream is a place of beauty," she said. It made sense that she would know, she was so lovely.

When Mum picked me up she looked beautiful, too.

She didn't take her drug because she wanted to know, to experience the farewell, feel the pain.

I wept for an hour in her arms, saying goodbye. I didn't know if she would be there when I returned. It would depend. If she had a moment's selfish thought, she would have an accident. She wouldn't want to see me. But I would want her, need her to be there as I emerged from the womb so unlike hers.

I couldn't say I love you.

I always thought the Blue Stream would be out in the country, in the open, just covered with a perspex bubble to protect the floating, growing children inside. Where else would you find such a Stream? They even showed us pictures from a plane of the Blue line stealing across the land. But they took us to this big old building; there were heaps of them, all these huge old buildings I'd never noticed before.

There were no signs. We shuffled in the gloom. Barely able to see each other. The adults smiling, being kind, making jokes, saying, "See you real soon," as if we were supposed to laugh. The other kids were mucking around, excited, because it was their birthday, just like me. All born on the same day. They all shouted about the Blue Stream. I could only think of red chalk, and I wanted to remember it.

We entered through a small door, one at a time, so the ones outside had no idea what was inside. We expected a bus or something, an underground rail link to take us out to the country and the Blue Stream.

But inside, it was a huge room, even bigger than the pictures, a roof so high the rafters faded into a Blue. The whole lot of us fitted side by side, and there must have been a hundred. It was dark, at ground level, you could hardly see the next person, only the adults in their luminous suits, marching up and down, taking the roll about fifty times and refusing to answer questions. The only light came in a Blue glow from the plastic rectangular boxes held suspended above us. Ten wide, ten long, ten deep–one chained under another, a whole warehouse filled with a piece of art no one would like. The walls Blue and glowing.

The kids all shut up and gazed; the boxes way above were filled, the ones below were empty, inviting.

"What is it?" one kid asked, "Where's the Stream?"

"This is the transport there," one of the adults said and the rest laughed. I would have screamed but wanted my calm. Panic would remove control of my mind; my memory.

The perspex boxes above us moved, whispering slightly as they settled lower. It was like a ride at the fair *(Fun Activities to share with the family, number six)* or like a game where you had to end with the boxes in the right place.

Around me, kids were crying and trying to run away, but there were too many adults. They began a soft song,

"You sink first,
A cold, fresh shock,
And as you rise,
You begin to float,
And float, and float, and float."

Over and over they sang it, as we waited for our box to reach the floor and each kid was picked up and laid down and the next box moved along.

They called my name, and I climbed into my box as it was lowered to the ground.

They didn't have to lift me.

I lay down and breathed deeply like they told me.

Waited for the Blue Stream

Waited for nothingness.

I wake up screaming.

But I remember.

THE HANGING PEOPLE

———

Meg saw the hanging people for the first time three days after her father's funeral.

Parking four houses down from her Auntie Annie's place, she walked the tree-lined street; smelt meat, old meat.

There was no debris or rubbish on the ground, so she looked up. And saw the hanging people.

She grunted in shock. She was not a screamer, not a squealer, shouter or moaner of names. She was quiet. So she grunted, walked quickly to her aunt's house and pushed open the door.

There must have been a riot, a revolution, and her wealthy aunt, in her lonely large house, would have been a certain target. Meg Archer expected to see men with guns, men feasting on her aunt's jam. But the hallway was bare of humans. Just the telephone table whose legs Meg had kicked during many long childhood conversations. She was never chastised for this, although the table was antique and the scars she made irreparable. She had been a frequent visitor to this home when her grandmother was alive. Her parents loved to drop her there and disappear into the night, off to do their business, then return as the sun rose, red-eyed and pale, too sleepy to tell her where they'd been or ask her what she had done.

Those were dull times for Meg, but she was always a kind child and tried not to let her boredom show, because her aunt and grandmother would spend every moment thinking of ways to treat her. They would sit in the drawing room and eat dinner off their laps, away from the table. They talked with mouths full and laughed throughout the meal. Meg's mother did not allow these things to happen at home.

Meg could stay on the phone as long as she wished at Grandmother's house. It never rang except for her. Their friends didn't call and there were no urgent messages. They did not expect calls, so the whole house hadn't to remain silent in anticipation. Auntie Annie never worked. She wove exquisite lace and gave it to charities, looked after her sick mother's needs, and was always there when Meg needed a sympathetic ear. Auntie Annie listened and clucked and tutted to hear about what the teachers were doing, and, later, about bosses and workmates, about homeless clients who refused help.

Meg was often alone with Annie. Grandmother had some mysterious job, some private thing the family did not discuss. It took her from home for days at a time, then gave her weeks of holidays. It killed her, eventually.

Her aunt, frail now, with age and grief at her dear brother's passing, clasped Meg's hand in her dry one.

"Are you all right?" Meg asked.

"I'm coping," she said.

"But have you seen outside? There are people hanging from the trees."

"Like monkeys, you mean, dear?"

"No, like by the neck till they are dead. Like dead."

Meg could hear hysteria in her voice. Auntie Annie was so calm.

"Aah," she said. "I think your father saw ghosts when your grandmother died. We've always been a sensitive lot."

"But those people are there," Meg said.

Auntie Annie walked to the window and gazed out. She stared for a long time then turned to blink at Meg. "A cup of tea, then," she said.

Meg looked out at the street and the people swung in the wind, heads bowed, fingers stretching in tight skin like amateur sausages.

Meg left her little flat empty to stay with her mother, thinking two people grieving are better than one. But it was hard there; her father's scent still in the air; her mother's helplessness and the always-present wreath of cigarette smoke. Meg was a disappointment to her parents for never taking up smoking. The idea of selling poison to people repelled her, although her family's business had helped her find friends. Her father had run the family-owned cigarette company and Meg had been very popular throughout school and University, because she had such a supply of cigarettes, all free, and she wasn't greedy. And her parents didn't care if you smoked at their place and if your parents smelt smoke on you later you could blame it on Meg's house.

Some parents thought it was wrong, but no one said anything. The cigarette company was old, established generations ago, and it had made the family wealthy. They were a strong family who ignored criticism.

Before her father, her grandmother's brother had run the place. He was not right for the job. He developed a chronic cough and let the company fall into insolvency. Once Meg's grandmother died all reason left him, and Meg's father took control weeks later. Soon the company was thriving again.

Auntie Annie made cups of tea and they sat in the dining room with saucers on their laps, biscuits crumbly and sweet in their fingers.

There were a lot of photos in the room. "Are they all dead?" Meg asked.

"They were alive when the photos were taken," Annie said, then, "What will you do?"

There was the question of the company, but Meg had always known the answer.

"I think we may sell, what do you think?"

Annie took her hand and squeezed. "Make your ghosts happy," she said.

Meg looked at all the photos, thinking Annie meant them. "I can't keep the company going for the sake of history."

"That's a choice for you to make. You can't escape, dear, just don't think that. Look at your grandmother. Poor old Mum." Meg had never thought of her grandmother as poor. "She thought she'd leave all that behind and look what she ended up doing."

"What? I never knew."

"Your grandmother took the job just before you were born. Fifty-eight, she was, one of the oldest, just as you're one of the youngest. She was such a brave woman. She did what she had to do, learnt quickly, and went out on wings of mercy."

Annie poured more tea. It was cold, now, so Meg went out to make more.

"But what did Grandmother do?"

"Nothing any of us wouldn't have done, given the chance." Annie's voice took on a tone Meg recognised as her own, the one she used to blindly defend the family company. "She travelled from place to place with her little leather bag."

Meg knew that little bag. She had long been curious about its forbidden contents. Annie told her where it was and she gathered it, excitement growing at the thought of knowing what was inside.

Needles. And some small empty vials. Meg was disappointed. She had not expected anything in particular, but certainly something more than this.

"Those held morphine, once. Your grandmother had a silken touch."

The days passed slowly after Meg first saw the hanging people. The hours seemed drugged, the air thick. Meg found her limbs sluggish, and she could not run from the things in the trees. Aunt Annie barely moved; she spent her days in the drawing room, drinking tea, waiting, Meg thought, to be needed. Her mother smoked, moved things from one pile to another, then formed a third. Meg went back to her own flat occasionally to rest her smile of support, love, strength.

The smell of corpses was in her nose, her clothes. She saw them lining the streets, men hanging black in trees, sexless bodies in the gutters. She did not feel threatened by them. She felt sickened and disgusted. She was ashamed of that disgust; she was proud of her open heart, her helpful heart.

As she shopped she could smell them; bodies propped by the frozen vegetables, bullet wounds clear.

She found a hanging man in her mother's shower and reached up to grab him down. She turned to find her mother staring.

"What's that you've got? Armful of air?"

Meg remembered dark nightmare times, towards the dawn, when she cried in vain for comfort.

"I'm stretching, that's all. Stretching."

Meg thrust the man's body at her mother, watched its ragged shirt catch on her pearl buttons.

"I'm going to see Auntie Annie," she said, and ran from the house, leaving her mother dancing too close with a long-dead partner.

She worried about her aunt. Annie was beginning to smell; she clearly was not washing. She ate very little. Meg said, "There are more bodies now. They stink."

Annie nodded. "Your grandmother saw them until she went to work.

She'd come in from the garden shaking like aspen and tell me not to go outside. But there was nothing to see. Nothing to smell.

"She was known amongst circles, and those circles spread. She would rescue people, for a price. Rescue is never cheap. But she was helping people; that's what the public never understood. That's why they hated her."

Meg felt the sheath of her skin buzzing. Small things returned to her, her grandmother's long absences and the secretive nature of her death.

"She didn't survive jail. How could she? She was seventy-four when they put her in there. And they didn't understand her there, either. She was only helping people out of their misery."

Meg gazed into the medical bag. Morphine. Sleepy, simple death.

"What did she do? What did Grandmother do?"

"She answered calls from people whose parent, child, friend, relative was beyond help. She went to tortured bodies and to trapped souls and released them with her gentle touch." Meg could remember her grandmother's fingers stroking her forehead. She drew her fingernails through the hypodermic needles, allowing them to prick and pierce her.

"I'll come back to visit tomorrow," she said.

The corpses swung from the trees. Meg reached out to one; her hand did not go through the solid meat. The body swung at her touch. She pushed it again. It swung higher. Her hand itched; small flakes of moist flesh clung to her palm, her fingers. She wiped her hand on her jeans.

Annie had a picture of Meg's great grandfather, her grandmother's father. When he died, her grandmother had seen the hanging people. He was in his War uniform covered with medals. Meg had never known what the medals were for—she'd assumed they were won in battle.

Her mother snorted at this. "Not him. Never saw a fight, that one. He was such a good hunter they made him head of the court martialling crew."

Meg remembered trips to the attic at her grandmother's house; the frightening sight of those staring creatures—a tiger, a deer, a lion and others. They had been banished within a day of The Hunter's burial. His children were afraid to destroy them altogether. He had been a fearful man.

Meg wondered how many he had executed. Many, it seemed, because his chest was covered with glory.

———

Her mother asked her to go through her father's desk, sort the rubbish from the worth. Meg relished the task. Her father had been a private man, and she lusted after knowledge, was keen to delve into his secrets.

She found pages of his neat writing, the beginning of an autobiography, or more accurately a history of the company. She realised he would never like to give anything personal away.

It was The Hunter's father who started the company. The Company Man. He had used the money his father, The Salesman, had left him, and reclaimed respectability for the family. It was clear to Meg her father had worshipped The Company Man, had wanted to emulate his work, his life.

The words were passionate, summoning images of her father Meg did not want to see.

"It is said that all great things come from small ideas," Meg's father wrote. "The Company Man's business came, he said, from a vision he experienced in the grief of his father's death. These are the words of The Company Man, describing for us his epiphany:

"'As I walked alone, contemplating my future, head down and eyes on the path, I ran into an unexpected obstacle. On raising my eyes, I saw the body of a hanged man swinging above me. In terror I ran, in a most ungainly way, to my wife. She did not see what I saw.

"'I took solace in a rolled cigarette, except my shaking hand meant the rolling of it was an arduous task. I wished at that moment I had had the foresight to have cigarettes rolled and waiting. Then I wondered at what it would be like to have the relief there, ready for the smoking, without having to do the work before.'

"These words to us from our founder show us where our company came from," Meg read. She put down her father's words and thought about her family line.

Meg asked Auntie Annie about The Salesman.

"He sold firearms, I believe. And was very good at it. There was some reason for his having such a lowly job, which his son did not intend to carry on. Some need for the family to start again, some disgrace long since forgotten. Funny, these things."

"Do you know if he ever saw streets full of hanged people?" Meg asked.

"You all do, darling. All of you in the line."

Meg was having trouble sleeping because the bodies were under her bed now. It was hard to work because the queue was long with the homeless and the dead people.

She went to the cinema, thinking the dark would shut them out.

At the end of the row, leaning against the wall, she sat with her feet resting on the body which lay on the floor amongst the popcorn and plastic. She could feel it shifting like jelly and wriggled her feet to settle them. There was a person next to her, but she did not ask if he could smell the decay.

She stared ahead waiting for the movie to start, sniffing the perfume on her wrist to cover the smell of the body and gazing ahead to a neck of such beauty her pulse quickened.

He had short hair, so his scalp glowed. His T-shirt was low around his neck; he seemed to be aware this feature was his best.

It was softly downed, smooth, lightly brown and she wanted to kiss it. Not to see his face or touch his body, just kiss that beautiful neck.

As she stared, she could see a welt forming around that lovely neck, but the lights dimmed, and though she squinted she could not see his flesh in the dark.

Meg finally told her mother about the bodies and her mother said, "Your father stopped seeing them the day he took over the company."

Auntie Annie said the same thing of her grandmother—with the first flap of her angel's wings, the bodies disappeared.

Meg finished sorting out the desk but didn't tell her mother about the papers she had found. Her father had given her the greatest present—the story of her family.

The position of Executioner had, for ten generations, been passed from son to son. This was a great privilege, and her family was wealthy because of it. They remained anonymous and received their gifts secretly.

They prospered.

Until the generation before The Salesman. No sons were born, merely three daughters. As the father lay dying, they discussed what the loss of the commission would mean.

"No more free food, gifts left for us at the gaol, no respect." There were two married sisters but the eldest had never had a lover. At thirty-two, it seemed she never would. She had always dreamed of taking her father's job; waited for the moment he would offer it to her. But the position of Executioner was always a man's.

It was also secret. The leather mask worn had seen many sweaty faces, many running noses, tears, eyes. It covered the features completely.

And she was a solid woman and strong, and she had the stomach for it.

Her father agreed she would have the job.

For eighteen years the deception continued. She became a 'he' and wielded her hangman's rope.

Then discovery, by a small accident of fate. Her arms were only ever bare as she rolled her sleeves to the heavy work of execution. All other times she kept them covered. But she had foolishly bathed another woman's son, her arms shown naked. Someone recognised the birthmark there and the talk began. The family were disgraced.

By this time she had married, her job giving her the strength and power to find a man. Her son, The Salesman, was nearing manhood.

He had to watch as his mother became the first execution of the new Government. The family had lost the commission.

Meg read back to the first Archer, so named when names described profession. He was in a position of power. With his bow and arrow he put to death those deemed unworthy of life.

The Archers fought in wars and received medals for bravery. They invaded countries and cleared away the native shrubbery. They were good men and women, church-going and gentle. There was a place for them in heaven.

Meg could not eat because each bite was flavoured with rotting flesh.

She tried to work, tried to house people, but she found her sympathy had gone.

Her fingers were sore and she could see why. Thin festering scratches stretched across them, yet she could not remember being near brambles or barbed wire.

Then she thought of her grandmother's medical case, the deadly needles which rested inside.

She ordered fifty hypodermic syringes through her work, saying she was taking up voluntary work. This was true. She had decided to follow her grandmother, but the work she did would be free. The family would not get richer through her efforts.

Carrying her case full of syringes (her grandmother's case, with the needles left behind, blunt and old fashioned) to the streets, she called, "Old needles for new. New needles for old."

They trusted her, because her clothes were clean and her hair neat, she wore a name tag with her photo on it.

She swapped her fifty needles then swapped them again and again. She passed out her glittering jewels and did not wait for thanks.

Those guilty of failure, of self-abuse and of alienation were the ones she served.

She did not pause for more than a day, because the dead would begin to swing in the trees and her womb to ache. Meg knew soon she would need to make an heir.

Meg was ready to have a baby.

BONE-DOG

In the porn industry, models don't usually get to choose the venue for photo shoots. I guess "Fat Slits" has to be a bit more flexible than other magazines; some of us just can't get too far from home. They agreed to send the photographer to me, agreed to my price; their attention brought tears to my eyes.

When I heard the photographer's van at the end of my long driveway, I walked slowly to the vast tree stump where I sometimes display the gifts Bone-Dog brings me. I had the tree cut down and turned into doors—very solid doors tha will never slam shut and lock me inside the house.

I like my doors open.

I could see the photographer's lips twitching as he walked towards me. Controlling his laughter. Bone-Dog growled deep in her throat. I motioned her away.

"I'm Melody," I said as I gave him a beer and he drank it in one. He was not a talker. He wiped his mouth with his shirt; I could see silvery snail trails on the sleeve. This was a man who did not bother with a handkerchief. He was bony, too. I hate bony, skeleton showing through.

"Where do you want me?" I said, winking. He squinted, as if he wasn't sure what he'd seen. I couldn't be flirting with him. Not possible.

"Just there'll be fine," he said.

I waited until he was set up, then let my robe fall.

He didn't actually shiver; he was protected by the camera lens.

He lifted his head, though, as I began to arrange my bones. I know so much about bones I can hear my own glide and click as I move. Naming them is easy. All you need is a good memory. My memory is very good.

He lifted his head and stared.

"Oh, yeah," he said. It's nice when their voices sound like that. I leaned against the stump. It creaked a little.

His breathing reached me. He wasn't looking in the lens, but he was clicking, shooting me.

I arranged my bones this way and that for him. My fans would love these ones.

I like to get fan letters. It keeps the postie coming, every day, and if I don't collect my mail from the box he'll tell someone. That keeps me safe from being locked inside the house with my Bone-Dog. Even though I've taken precautions, I don't want to be locked in.

"Your film's run out," I said. He stepped from behind the camera and towards me. He reached for me. Touched me, stroked my forearm, the childhood scar there shiny and puckered. Blood and fat and bone and I screamed when it happened.

"Ha ha, scared of blood," kids said.

I had to tell them the truth. I said, "No, I'm scared of bone."

I wanted more photos afterwards, but he was ashamed and out of film. He stumbled about packing up; he almost stepped on Bone-Dog.

"Sorry, little fella," he said, glad of the distraction.

"She. Baby."

"Baby the dog?" he said. I nodded. I liked him for seeing her. He couldn't have known how kind that was. Not many people admitted to seeing her. Hearing her rattling. It's not in my head. That little dog found me, sniffed at my ankles and followed me home. At my feet, snap snap, bones jumping like a little dog.

It would be a good set of photos. He had seen Bone-Dog; he understood me.

He bent to pat her but she trotted over to me and squatted at my heels.

"Pretty, isn't she?" I said. "Prettier than me?"

He nodded. Shook his head.

"Another beer?" I said. I wanted him to stay. I wanted to suck his fingers, lick his ribs.

He shook his head. "Gotta develop these." He lifted the camera. I saw his elbow flinch. He wanted to snap Bone-Dog.

"You're out of film," I said.

Bone-Dog was on her haunches, ready to bite. Snap snap go her teeth. I can hear it even if she's not with me. Snap snap of a little sister wanting her bones back.

He leaned down to pat her.

"I wouldn't. She doesn't like strangers."

He ignored me. Leaned closer. Stepped back when he saw, it became clear, that she was a Bone-Dog.

He sucked breath. She leapt at him, bit his little pointing finger off and spat it out, sucked clean of flesh.

The wound didn't bleed. I could smell burnt flesh. He stared at his cauterised hand. He walked backwards to his truck, "You should control that thing," his jaw snapping, and he left me with her.

There was plenty of food but I didn't feel like eating. Sometimes, after I have my photo taken, I don't feel like eating. I want to stop being a fat woman. Bone-Dog lay at my feet, all bone, skeleton, and I went to the kitchen and made an eight-egg omelette and ate it standing there.

We've lived here many years, the perfect place for us. Paid for with porn. Bone-Dog doesn't approve of my work, but she is happy to sleep in the house I paid for, sleep in my bed, refuse my shameful food. She found the place herself, bringing me the paper and staying so quiet as the real-estate man showed us around I almost forgot she was there. It was a quick, eager sale; most people were put off by the old graveyard, partly uncovered, so close by. Not Bone-Dog; she loved the sense of all those bones, so close. I allowed myself the fantasy that our mother was buried there, and in the early days would visit with offerings of food, laying it at the collapsed brick entrance to the graveyard. I haven't been back for a long time, but I remember the mess of it, the jumbled, forgotten nature of it.

I slept until the moon and Bone-Dog woke me. Looking out my bedroom window I could see the bones in the yard, how well I've lined them up. They shone silver in the moonlight. If I stared long enough my eyeballs quivered and the bones jerked and danced.

Those bones, so carefully laid out. "Thank you, Melody, for being so careful with our bones," their thin voices said. Whistling like the wind so Bone-Dog howled at the noise. "Melody, Melody," their voices tuneless. Melody and Baby. My little sister was Baby because Mum hadn't thought of a proper name yet.

I called her all the names I could think of but she didn't blink. Dolores. Jemima. Janina. Godliness.

Bone-Dog leapt at my feet. I reached down to pet her and she snapped her jaw together. She hadn't forgiven me for letting her die. She thought I let her starve to death. She thought I let her bones be jumbled up, and that I should have escaped earlier.

Bone-Dog thought I liked being locked in that childhood house, but the smell of it has never left me.

I have a very sensitive sense of smell. A hint of rot and I have to leave the room, waste the food. Mould on bread, rotten meat and vegetables, sourness of milk. Fresh food is all I can abide. The smell of rot is a warning. Do not eat this. Do not be near this.

Bones left in the sun for long enough will lose their smell of rot.

My mother left when I was five. Went out for a run to get back in shape. Gotta get back in shape. I was old enough to stay by myself. She deadlocked the door so we would be safe and she ran away, her smooth long legs tan against her shorts, her shoulders muscular but slim, the keys hooked to her waistband.

"Back soon. Gotta get back in shape," she said. I'm still not sure it was an accident. Perhaps she left us there because she wanted me to be thin when she got back. She ran away, a long run, because she had not been since Baby was born

It was a hit and run driver. I hit and ran at school, once I got my weight back. I could hit hard and run fast for my size. I still can. I can run and surprise people so their jaws drop.

It's not good for my ankles, though. The driver hit and ran and moved her body to a river or a lake.

They didn't know who she was and no one claimed her. I knew who she was; I saw her once on TV and told my little sister. She stared at me. She didn't blink. She didn't move after the first three days, just lay there. She was one month old.

There was food in the fridge. I liked to eat. There was some cake and chicken and cheese. There was beetroot, pickles, potatoes and one carrot. There was plenty of food. There was chips and chocolate and lemonade.

I gave the carrot to my sister but she wouldn't eat it. I didn't want to eat, either, once the things started to rot. I put off opening the fridge because of the terrible smell, but the house smelled bad, too.

I didn't eat very much. I chose from the fridge the least rotted thing and ate that. I gave a little to my sister every day, an offering to her to make some noise.

It was quiet in the house. I could reach the kitchen sink with a chair. I couldn't use the can opener.

Watching my sister was like watching a TV show. A slow one. She slowly changed. The smell of rot was terrible. I never got used to it. I watched her every day, watched her change.

I was only five.

I cried a lot, but no one heard. My Dad was gone away and my little sister was a mistake with a stranger. I had no aunties or uncles or grand-parents.

I cried a lot.

Our phone wasn't connected, Mummy said we didn't have the money for it. I have one in every room. I have a huge freezer, well-stocked. My cupboards are full of tins, and in each cupboard I have a can opener and a fork. In case my legs break under my weight, I can crawl around and eat until someone saves me.

Mummy said, "Don't leave the house. You stay here till I get back."

But I knew I had to be naughty the day I opened the fridge and all that was left was a piece of green sausage. Very hard and I couldn't chew it. I knew I had to be very naughty and find a way to leave the house.

I tried doors again. Then the windows. The only one we had without locks was the one in the toilet. Mummy didn't want any men coming into the house or ringing up.

I couldn't reach the window. Even standing on the toilet, and the cistern was slippery.

So I covered the cistern with the mat from the bath by standing on the toilet seat. Then I put Mummy's tool box on the seat so I could climb onto the cistern.

The window opened when I pushed it. People asked me that. "How long did it take to open the window?" I learned to lie, to say it took days. I learned to say I had tried to get out from the moment Mummy went away.

I walked along the road in the direction I'd seen Mummy run. It took me so long I was sure I'd see Mummy running back, and she'd pick me up and carry me home. She'd have icecream and apple pie and a piece of bacon to eat on the way home.

I love a fresh-killed pig.

I walked. My sister was in my knapsack and I could smell her, but it wasn't so bad outside. There were other smells.

I walked until I came to a house but it was a stranger's house. I couldn't go there. I didn't know, but I put the knapsack on upside down, and my sister's bones with her flesh still on them dropped out along the road. They could never find them all.

So I sat on the wall and had a rest. I told my sister we would have some dinner soon. I didn't know she'd already gone out of the knapsack.

I sent Bone-Dog away. "We need ear-bones. And this one is missing some spine. And we need three thigh bones," I said.

Bone-Dog snarled. She liked to bring what she liked to bring. I had no say.

She rattled up the street; I worked hard while she was gone. I cooked more food for the freezer. The X-rays I pasted all over the kitchen windows cast a greyness. When the sun was out their shadows bone-danced on the floor and the table, keeping me company as I cooked.

She was gone a long time. I sorted out the bones on the lawn, reshaped them, rearranged. Then she returned and dropped her offerings at my feet. A finger bone and a shin bone and a jaw and a skull.

She pushed the bones towards me with her nose then trotted two steps, three, wanting me to follow her, to say how clever she was. She jumped and leapt, bones slipping in and out of joint.

Bone-Dog brought me a small foot bone. I placed it in the pile.

Bone-Dog snarled.

"I'll put it in place properly later," I said. "I'm tired now." Bone-Dog whined. She knew more than anyone that bones should be together.

Bone-Dog snapped at me all night, hungry for my bones. I could smell rot on her. It gave me nightmares of being locked in the house, my skin scraping off as I climbed through the toilet window, my sister waiting below, quiet in the knapsack.

I awoke to the stink of her in my throat and I kicked out, rolling her smash onto the floor.

Her old bones scattered, rolling under my bed, into the corner, into the hallway. I heard a hungry moan. I lay there, knowing I needed to take her bones and spread them far and wide, give myself some space. But the thought of such activity made my heart crash. It took the bones ten years to come together the first time.

I was fifteen. I wanted to leave school because no one liked me, and I needed a job, money to get away from my foster mother. She was one of those skinny women who find obesity frightening. That house always smelled of packet chicken noodle soup.

Bone-Dog appeared on the day which became my last at school. She found me, snap snap, and expected me to know who she was. She bit through to bone on my ankle, luckily, because the kids were going to lock me in a box and see if anyone missed me.

Bone-Dog saved me. She didn't want me to be locked up ever again.

I have the first bone Bone-Dog brought me on my shelf of special things. Up there with the prizes I carried in my pocket when I climbed through the toilet window; a rock; a little doll; a very small can of fruit.

The first bone was a finger. I didn't see the significance of the offering for a while; it was only when Bone-Dog brought me another finger bone, a thigh bone and a smooth elbow that I wondered if she was bringing our mother's bones together. If perhaps my fantasy had been realised and we were living by my mother's grave.

But we still haven't collected a full set. She doesn't listen to me when I tell her we are missing the pelvis, a toe or a knee. She brought me a man's pelvis, then a child's, then distracted me with shiny old bones, meaty new ones.

I felt bad, pushing her off the bed. I'd taught her a lesson, though; she brought me the bones I'd asked for. She jumped and leapt, bones slipping.

I had assumed Bone-Dog and I had the same plan in mind. But when she finally brought me a knee-bone and I made a low cry of joy she blinked at me.

"Mother's nearly finished," I said. "Only a couple more pieces." She blinked again, then bared her teeth in a slow snarl of outrage.

I realised I had misunderstood her. She wanted an orderly bone-yard full of skeleton companions, not a bone-mother.

"It can't hurt," I said.

She jumped and leapt, bones slipping.

"All right, I'll follow you," I said. Big sister martyr making up for disappointing little sister. And I thought perhaps I could find the final pieces to our mother's puzzle myself.

Bone-Dog looked at me. She knew I had two hundred and six bones in there.

And she was hungry. She never forgave me for letting her die.

She looked at me, choosing which bone she wanted first. I laughed at my paranoia.

She nipped at me, her skull clicking. Herding me to the gravesite.

I didn't want to visit there, but she was keen to show me. She wanted me, big sister, to be proud.

She was very patient. We had to rest a lot. I hadn't walked more than one hundred steps, the distance to the mailbox and back, in years.

I took a brown bag of food with me and ate snacks on the way. I offered her some, as I always did, and she turned her snobby nose up.

"You should have eaten what I gave you," I said.

There were many bones, though just four gravestones. The others were all unmarked, mixed up, in piles. Perhaps bastard children were buried there without a stone, and murderers, adulterers, the ones they chose to forget.

So many bones.

It was quite a hike; my bones screamed.

Bone-Dog grinned at me, a snarling hateful grimace, and I knew she sought revenge for her stolen life.

"Go away," I said. I had no name for her. "Leave me alone. I don't want any more bones."

She leapt at me, her bones growing, an adult skeleton leapt at me. I turned to run, tripped, fell flat on my face in an open grave. I didn't sink. I was too fat. I stared down into the darkness, smelling the rot, the wood, the flesh, the bone.

"Help," I said. I could hear nothing but my air sucking in and blowing out. I could not control it.

God, the stink of that rot.

"No," I said. No. And Bone-Dog danced a victory jig across my fat back.

SMOKO

Smoko. I stood up, stretched, picked up my smokes. "You'll need a jacket," Jillie said. She sat opposite me, caught my eye when she could, told me about the sex she had as if that would make me want her.

"Don't feel the cold," I said. I winked. They love a wink, these humans. They don't know that dragons blink one eye at a time. It's one way we recognise each other.

Gavin was there ahead of me. He was always there, expecting me to acknowledge him because of what he was, not what he is now. I'd rather talk to a human than an ex-dragon like Gavin. Jillie joined us, and a couple of the other girls, standing there sucking on their smokes as humans do. Somehow they never notice we blow into our cigarettes. Lovely to get that heat out. Otherwise there'd be small fires burning all over.

Dragons don't die of lung cancer. They don't get sick at all; only sick with love, when one of us falls for a human.

"What do you think of the new girl?" Gavin said. He nodded to the other side of the foyer.

She was lovely. Could have been a dragon. I convinced myself she was, because I wanted her to be. I motioned with my cigarette for her to join us. She smiled, walked over. I liked her confident step, the absence of nervousness. She accepted a cigarette, and I watched to see if she blew. She was so dragon-like.

She sucked. Disappointing, but it was okay; just meant superior caution during sex.

Humans damage so easily, and if you get them pregnant, the kid'd have to die in the womb or be killed soon after. None of us liked those jobs, but half-dragon, half-human? Human would soon take over, and dragons would be dead. They're so scared of us, they'd hunt us down. We have to burn our half-breed spawn.

"Andrew," she said. "That's your name, isn't it?" I always feel a heart-stopping moment, having to share my name. Does this human know the secret? Will they call me by my human name while I'm in dragon form, transforming back to human and trapping me that way forever?

"And you are?" I asked.

"Alison." She held out her hand; I turned it and kissed the palm. She flinched from the heat of my lips. She shivered a little. It was cold for her in the foyer.

"I'm Gavin," Gavin said. I stared at him. "Fuck off," I thought. "Fuck off." Humans like Gavin who've once been dragons are very boring. They've lost their spark. They're the sort of boring person who raises their eyebrows and smiles as they speak, as if that makes them interesting.

Alison paid Gavin a little too much attention. She was too kind. I had to admit she was no dragon. I snorted, a little steam from my nose. It made us all laugh, hunch over and snort, weep sharp tears.

When I lifted my head Alison was gone.

Alison was far too cool to hang around my desk at finishing time like the others did. Waiting for me to say I felt like a drink, where I felt like drinking. Their eyes are so transparent. I can see into their brains.

Even with both of us pretending we didn't care, we ended up in a dark corner of the pub, alone. It was all I could do to stop from sucking her down. She smelt so cool, I barely scented her blood.

"You don't talk about the normal things, do you?" she said.

"Like what?"

"Like where you live, where you went to school."

"I'll find out where **you** live soon enough."

"Sure of yourself."

"So are you. I like that."

She swayed into me. "You smell good," she said. "Like a bonfire."

"Love a bonfire," I said. "Let's go, huh?"

We left the pub and walked. I felt like a fool. I never walked, never walked and talked. I felt like an idiot.

The park was empty. The moon was thin. She stumbled as we walked, and I clutched her, feeling the ice in her veins.

"Let's lie down," I whispered. She sank to her knees where we stood; I lifted her up and carried her to a place where the grass grew soft.

We lay there on our backs for a while. I was scared of breaking her.

"Look, a shooting star," she said. "That means good luck."

It made me smile to think of humans taking our truths and turning them into myths.

"It's a meteor," I said.

I kissed her on the neck and stood up. Didn't say a word because I had no good excuse to give her for leaving.

"Are you going?" she said.

I winked. "I'll see you Monday." I burned a little pile of leaves nearby. She liked the smell. It was a little gift to her.

I drove to the outskirts of town and put the keys down where I'd find them instinctively. I entered my stinking cave. Then I changed.

It felt glorious. Shaking off that soft skin, my thick hide stretching and filling. My vision cleared. Night is day to a dragon.

"Welcome to the world, child," I roared. I lumbered to the mouth of my cave and blew flames in a circle until the trees around me flared. "Welcome, Dragon Child, child of fire." I moved through the flames, rolling about to warm myself. The little suburb below rested. Somewhere in the world a dragon baby would be squalling. Dragons everywhere were burning a welcome.

"Welcome, Dragon Child, born with the meteor. May your life of fire be eternal." I roared and a roof below began to crackle and burn. I watched as the family emerged from the flames and the trucks arrived. I heard wailing. As a dragon, I cared little for the lives I risked. As a human, in those moments of transformation, I felt sick to my stomach at what I had done.

Alison didn't speak to me on Monday.

"What's up?" I said. I didn't care; I asked because that's what you did. It didn't matter what a human thought of you, so long as they did what you wanted them to.

"Thanks for leaving me in the park on Friday."

"Sarcasm. Never quite saw the point of that." I winked.

"There's a point," she said. I spent the week being nice to her, leaving little burnt offerings on her desk. A packet of scented candles. A note with burnt edges like a treasure map. It worked. We didn't go to the pub on Friday. We went straight to her place.

She was marvellously soft and delicious. We spent the weekend in her bed.

I brought home steaks and threw mine on a plate. "How do you like yours?" I said. I washed blood off my fingers. I liked mine blackened.

"Rare," she said. I couldn't figure it. She curled over when she laughed, so her knobbly backbone seemed like dragon spines. She acted like a dragon, but she wasn't one.

We watched the news in bed. Alison hated the news. She said it had no relevance. I said, "But you never know what you're going to find out. Who you're going to recognise."

"I knew someone on the news once. I didn't like it," she said.

I didn't really care. Dragons are always in the news. The quick-sighted will inherit the earth.

"It was my brother," she said.

"What did he do?"

"He died."

"That's a shame," I said. I didn't connect with death. I never loved anyone who died.

"In a fire," she said.

Now that was interesting. "They say you don't feel any pain in a fire. Warmth and light. It's supposed to be very comforting," I said. I held her, hoping this was what a human would do.

"Is that what you tell yourself?"

"When?" I said. Alert now, because her tone was vicious.

"When you see on the news that a baby was killed in a fire. Like my brother. He was three weeks old."

He may not have been one of ours, I thought. Though if a dragon had been the father and a human the mother, the baby boy would have to be killed.

"You didn't have the same father, though?" I said. I had to be sure.

"Oh, no," she said.

I flicked the channel. A cooking show. I felt for her thigh and clawed her till she closed her eyes and let me in.

My dragon friends laughed at me. "Too much time with a human," they said. When I took Alison to a dragon party they left, making a point; outcast. She smoked as much as I did. I hoped her lungs could cope.

Gavin always had cigarettes. He was one of those. A loser. A named dragon.

Alison took me to the place where she lost her virginity.

"Everyone has a special place, Andrew. A place they feel safe."

She stared at me.

"Not me," I said. Never tell a human where your cave is. No matter how much you love her.

That night in her own place she was possessive. Wild, dragon-like. She moaned as we joined. I didn't listen to her words, but I realised afterwards what she'd said.

"Make a baby in me."

"You wouldn't want to fall pregnant to me," I said as we lay together.

"Why?"

I laughed. Nervous, don't ask laughter. I thought of some of the halves, born to humans. I had killed three myself, slice with my tail then burn the place down.

Dragon mothers are okay. They simply abort.

Three weeks after I met her, we lay together outside. We lay that way every night. I came to know her breathing as well as my own.

"Look, Andrew," she said. "A shooting star."

"A dragon baby," I thought. There was something in her voice I couldn't catch. Relief?

I kissed her.

"I forgot, I have to go do something," I said. I saw her nod in the half-light. I kissed her again, deeply, but her tongue didn't greet mine. She slitted her eyes at me as I left.

I felt pain lifting, my skin thickening. My stomach rumbled and my eyes saw further, saw through rock.

"Welcome to the world, child," I said. I loved being a dragon, the hunger of it roared in my belly. A dragon can fly, burn, warm himself with farts and burps. A dragon can terrify; even the gentlest, nicest dragon loves to frighten. A human needs evil to terrify. I turned to walk out to start my burning and saw Alison. Dragons never get cold but I felt chilled to my centre.

"Alison?" I thought. I backed away.

"Andrew." She named me in my dragon form. My brain hardened, my thoughts roared. My skin began to shrink.

Even as she destroyed me, I wanted to be inside her. Dragons fuck so fast and hot, your brain can't catch up. You don't know what you've felt till it's over.

"That's for killing my brother," she said. Was he one of mine? Was this vengeance or dragon hunting?

She turned to go. I roared and I burned her. Did she think I'd let her walk away? Even as a human I could rip her to shreds. She got me because I knew her; that stilled my flame for long enough for her to say the word. It's a rare dragon who's caught that way. Most are so quick to kill intruders not a word is spoken.

Gavin was caught by a woman too.

I burned her. We changed together. I changed to a human and she changed to a dead girl.

I wept my last dragon tear, had the sense to catch it in my T-shirt.

The whole cave stank. Dragon shit glowed in the corner. The smell of burnt flesh made me retch.

A-POSITIVE

Not long after my father killed my mother, I removed him to a special home.

"I'm taking you somewhere nice, Dad. They've got big TV and lots of food."

"Why can't I stay with you?"

I thought of the shit in the seams of his trousers, the smell of him. He was so helpless. Such a child.

"It's for the best."

I carried his empty suitcase to the front door.

"Got my Agatha Christie books in there?"

"Yep."

"And my photos? And my postcards? And my pyjamas?"

"All there, Dad."

I patted him. "You'll love it. I'll visit often," I said. I couldn't wait to see him settled in his new home.

The house was mine at last, and I didn't bother with a garage sale, didn't sort a thing. I called the Salvation Army and told them to take the lot. Everything. All my belongings were those of the man I used to be.

They marched up and down the stairs with load after load, and they were friendly at first, making jokes.

After a while they were dead silent, and they worked quickly.

They wouldn't look at me.

They carried out boxes of clothes, books, ornaments. Clocks and crockery. Glasses, flags, beakers, needles, syringes, stainless steel bowls, drips, magazines, photos. Papers they would burn or read. They carried out furniture.

They carried out bedspreads, sheets, towels. Toaster, fridge, TV, stereo.

"Shower curtain," I said, and they even took that. I went on inspection when they finished; they wouldn't come in.

I brought out one last armful of things; toothbrushes, soap, a hula hoop, jewellery, a bucket still crusty with blood, a pair of shoes and a teapot. I passed these over the threshold and waved my past goodbye.

It was still there, though, in the walls, the carpet, the ceiling, the smell of the place. So I hired a wallpaper stripper and a carpet remover and a floor polisher and I bought some paint and that was a full month's work for my girlfriend and me.

Then it was time to go see Dad. The pathetic little marks he'd scratched into me were gone, the memory of his light weight, too. He was always a small man. Smaller than Mum, although that made no difference to their happiness.

They married soon after they met, then spent fifteen years living the life. They never wanted kids. Kids would interfere. Kids didn't travel well or eat well and they were no good in restaurants. They cried and were dirty. They couldn't speak for years and when they finally learnt it was only to abuse you.

Mum and Dad planned to remain childless.

As I was growing up, people often said, "Were you an accident?" because Mum and Dad were so old when they had me. I eventually gathered that "accident" meant "unwanted", and I truly did not want to know the answer. Thinking they were comforting me, my parents said, "No, you were the most planned baby ever," and told me why I was born. I realised then we were not a normal family; that not everyone shared blood with their father.

My parents exchanged fond glances as they told me the story of my birth. I always felt they cared about each other so much, one day they would both love me together. I was well-treated, properly schooled, impeccably fed, but the giggles and the games they saved for themselves.

"You were planned for very carefully, because your father got sick after a lifetime of being healthy. We just didn't know how to cope. We couldn't do the things we used to; he tired so easily."

"So you had me to keep you company at home," I said.

"Not quite," Mum said. "We went to so many doctors, and none of them could tell us how to bring him back to life. After weeks of tests, all they said was, 'It's middle age.' It really was a terrible time."

Dad was silent.

"So we started trying the other doctors, the ones you didn't see at hospital. Now they were a funny lot."

Dad smiled now. "They had me naked for the night air, eating raw meat to clear the toxins, swallowing by-products I wouldn't like to discuss. And there was always the sex, of course."

"But none of it worked. He was still lethargic, so tired. He drooped about the house, driving me mad."

Mum always hated it when I was tired and weak. "Get a move on! Show some life!" She poked at me. She thought I did it on purpose.

"And then there was the doctor who made us young again," Mum said.

"And caused you to be born," Dad said.

"So you had me to keep you young?" I said.

"Yes."

"It was his blood that was the problem," Mum said. "It was old and tired. That's all. I would have given him all of mine, but we didn't match." Again, the fond smile. They sat together on their couch. I was on my chair in the corner; I had to twist to face them.

I said, "But you do match." It was one of the rare times I impressed them.

"Everything but our blood," Dad said. "My family were no use; they either had different blood or they were diseased. And the hospital wasn't interested in helping us."

I didn't know much about Dad's side of the family. There was a big fight years ago, around when I was born, and they didn't talk anymore.

"Is that why you hate them?" I said.

"One reason," Dad said. He and Mum had only ever needed each other.

"We were often at the doctor, begging him to help us," Dad said.

"Demanding, really," Mum said. "How could we live like that, with death? We couldn't."

"Lucky you didn't die, Dad," I said. He wasn't much of a believer in luck. He always said, "Luck is what you do with your opportunities," which was okay if you got opportunities. If your parents took them all, how much luck could you expect to have?

Mum said, "The doctor told us it was a shame we didn't have a child, because it would probably have blood which wouldn't clump his. That was when the planning began."

Dad wanted a transfusion whenever I was able to provide one, so I have never been strong. As soon as I felt rich with blood, I'd be drained again. It was all they asked of me, though. I had no chores; no cleaning, cooking, visiting, politeness for me. Just that look in Dad's eye, that need, and the pain, and the life going out of me. Our special room was called the theatre. I thought that was normal. "I went to the theatre," people said. When I realised there were two kinds, I no longer boasted about having one. People only laughed, anyway.

I always knew when it was going to happen. I'd be the centre of attention, have favourite meals. We'd go for a drive one month, shopping another. I could never enjoy these special days though. I knew what was coming. And all day Dad would pinch and squeeze at me, wanting me pink and tender.

I never had an imagination, so I had nowhere to go while the transfusion was taking place. I wished the ceiling was a story book, all the cracks and lines making rabbits and bears. All I ever saw were cracks and lines. I knew them very well.

Dad liked to hum along to a bit of music in the background. I still hate anything classical. There was always that silence, between the movements, when I'd hear Dad's bad blood drip drip into the bucket, as mine was slowly entering his veins. It was perfect, that rhythm, and I imagined I could hear it over the crashing cymbals and roaring chords of Dad's favourite music.

Mum's favourite was the garden and she threw the full buckets over the flowers. I couldn't understand why she never answered when people asked her how she kept it so nice. Why didn't she tell them? So I answered for her. Just the once.

"Dad's blood," I said. I was locked in my room that day, all day, and the shock of being a bad boy kept my mouth shut for a long time. I liked it better as Mum's good boy, Dad's blood boy.

It was a private, quiet life. My pleasures came when they took their excursions. Dad would fill up, jovial and magnanimous as he took my strength, and Mum cooked my favourite casseroles and desserts for the freezer.

I was left to pretend the house was mine. Sometimes I dreamed a crash, their caravan folding in two and their blood pouring out when rescuers freed them.

And then things changed.

"Poor Old Girl needs to save her energy," Dad said, though he was the pale and shaky one. He liked to joke that people thought Mum was his mother. "Old Girl," he called her. Never thought to let her have a go at me.

He lost his license, was the thing, and she'd never had hers because he did the driving. They took my pleasures away. Now, they never left the house. They sat quietly with me, listening to the blood pulsing through my veins.

Dad wanted blood every three weeks then. It got so I couldn't bear those nights at home, all three of us waiting for the others to talk, and almost the only thing we had to talk about was the next visit to the theatre.

Sometimes they discussed grandchildren as if I wasn't there. Never, I thought. I knew how they would treat a grandchild. They thought my blood was getting old. I'm not one of those types who feel better when they do the same things to the next generation of innocent children.

I began to go out at night, leaving the house without a word, slamming the door like a teenager. I wasn't sure what people did, out. I tired very easily, and would sometimes just sit in a place where there was a lot of noise and absorb the energy.

I found there was an undertow in the city. It dragged me, without a fight, to kindred spirits. Damaged people without armour.

I went to one of those bars where people are whipped and manacled, because I knew about receiving pain. I'd been strapped down, pierced, drained, all my life, but I'd never liked it. They gave me a whip to use but I wasn't strong enough. Under the lights you could see my thin arms. It was very warm in there although I'm usually cold. You could see how many times I'd saved my father's life, a record of tracks.

Someone was impressed. It was a woman, with a black cowl over her face to cover the criss cross scars there, her body shrouded, her voice low, her fingers cool. I wouldn't take her offered drink, but allowed her into my car. I agreed to drive her home.

I stayed with her for two days. It was the longest I had been away from my parents, and I felt breathless without them.

We ate pizza and drank wine, and I told her my life. She was sickened. Sickened, a scarred woman hiding in black.

She said, "Why do you agree to it? You're an adult."

I had often tried to answer this question, alone, in the dark, thinking terrible thoughts in the middle of the night. When I was young, it had all seemed so normal; when I realised it wasn't, I was embarrassed, like an abused child, or one in a strange religion. Now, it's the guilt, mostly, and the fact that I've never lost my need for approval. They liked having me close by, and I was too weak to move away. I didn't finish school, which Dad found irritating. He said intelligence was only a matter of looking and learning. They learnt how to give transfusions, didn't they, by watching? Mum going to hospital once and watching the whole thing. It was Mum who did it; Dad hated the sight of blood. He always kept his head turned away.

I didn't need a job either. They gave me plenty of money. I never wanted for anything.

"I don't know," I said.

I began to suffocate in my girlfriend's arms. She was draining love from me, swallowing it in breathless gulps. So I returned home.

I had never heard my father raise his voice; now he screamed, screeched, called me a killer. I said, "Who am I supposed to have killed?"

"Me, me," he said. He took my wrist and tried to lead me to the theatre.

"No," I said.

"What do you mean?" Mum said. Her face looked dark, damaged.

"I'm not giving blood anymore. I need it all for myself."

My father wailed. My mother cried. "Where were you?" Mum said.

"With my girlfriend."

My father stopped wailing to snort.

I went to my room.

Each day my mother grew fearful, my father begged and drooled, and I yearned for my girlfriend. So I went to my girl in black. I never imagined my mother was in danger. Their blood didn't match.

I stayed away for two nights. She wanted to meet my parents. I said, "Soon." We went for a drive in the country, to the old boarding house where she kept her mother and we watched her mother take a bath.

It was very quiet when I returned home. Quieter than usual; I could hear no pottering. The house seemed darker—colder. But I could be inventing. Could be the house was the same as ever, and it was only afterwards I turned it into something else.

I found Dad lying on his bed in the theatre, waiting for his transfusion. The room smelt so very clean compared to the world outside its walls.

Dad told me the story. He told it in a wheedling tone, he told me the truth, hoping it would make me help him.

"You hadn't been here for weeks," he said.

To him, I only existed in the theatre, or when we were preparing for it.

"And I was very ill. So I wanted your mother to do that one small thing for me. Just once. It's not like I ever asked her before."

He led me around the house, indicating a wall, a room, making me look at nothing.

"But her blood was no good for you."

"That's what she always said. But I thought, maybe she's lying. Maybe it was always good. And when she said no, no, no, all I could see was red. She was cooking the potatoes how you like them, in case you came home, and I said I'd do it. But I saw red.

"I just scratched her, I thought, so I could see the blood, see if it was OK, but it wasn't."

And neither was she. My father wept and snuffled in a corner in the kitchen, denying what he had done, not looking at the proof before his eyes.

I had no time to prepare myself. I felt greater grief than I could have imagined; this woman had cared for me, kept me alive, kept me clean and fed.

We were always good at secrets. We took Mum's body away to the country and buried it. We were the only ones who would miss her.

Dad never got another drop of blood. He was probably addicted to it; he suffered. He seemed to get old very quickly. Was it Mum's death, or having to live with his own blood?

Dad finally paid attention to me. He followed me around like a little lamb, and I loved ignoring him. He didn't complain, just shook his head and sighed.

He became quite tender towards me, remembering things which never happened, emotions we never shared. Then one day he reminded me of the truth.

"Sometimes you just have to be patient. We had to wait those first few months while you grew your own blood, to take the place of your mother's. I didn't want anybody else's blood. Only yours." He said it casually, as if we had all been involved in the decision. I think he thought he'd talk me into going back to it.

We had a lovely time alone, Dad and I. He'd talk and I wouldn't listen. I cooked food he disliked or couldn't digest, and I locked the door of the theatre and kept the key on a nail out of his reach. I never washed him, till he hated the stink of himself. I sprayed him with after shave and perfume, toilet deodoriser, and laughed as he cringed from me.

None of it was enough.

It was never going to be enough. I wanted him used, drained, sucked out.

I took my girlfriend home to look at Dad.

We stood outside his bedroom window as the sun rose and watched him struggling from his bed to greet the day. He slept naked; I wouldn't help him into his pyjamas.

My girlfriend thought he was perfect. She helped me get the suitcase down from the cupboard, and watched from the car while I cajoled him out of the house. We laughed all the way there, her hand on my thigh. We felt committed; both our parents would be in the same home.

It brought tears to my eyes. It was only a small place, just a few mothers and fathers, ancient things; this one guilty of sexual abuse; that one of beatings; that mother nagged still, her purple tongue swollen from some unprescribed drug. My girlfriend's mother had her skin scrubbed in the bath. And scrubbed. And we could visit any time. We could watch it, stare at them, hate them even more.

I dropped him off and went to my own home. He saw something he didn't like before I left; his own greedy need perhaps, in someone else's eyes.

I said, "You'll fit right in, Dad. They'll love you."

He fought like a demon to come back home with me.

My girlfriend and I visited often. We joked about our parents falling in love; everyone loved Dad there. The other residents and their occasional visitors. People loved to make him bleed, because he hated the sight of it. They pinned open his eyes and made him watch as they cut off a little toe and sold it to the highest bidder. They took his blood, plucked his white stringy hair, shaved his body. We watched from the gallery, my girlfriend and I, and we talked quietly about love and revenge.

You just have to be patient. You just have to wait until they're old and helpless.

Dad was in good company. One old man was daily raped and forced to perform orally. He liked it at first, I was told, but soon learned fear. A woman was hit every time she opened her mouth and sometimes when she didn't. She soon learned to bite her tongue.

In the dining room, hungry old people sat in front of food they hated. Some of it was mouldy, all of it was cold. They had to eat what was in front of them.

All the rooms were small and dark.

I felt unwonted tenderness when they let Dad wander the grounds in his nightshirt, a small figure with a painted face, laughter drawn in red around his mouth. He stroked and patted every part of his body. I imagined he was memorising it for the day it would be taken away from him completely.

THE MISSING CHILDREN

———

"Come in from the storm, chilluns," I said, smiling. I try to make it fun when I order my children around.

The elder looked into the blue sky and rolled his eyes. The younger continued with her water painting on the deck of our house.

I looked across the lake and saw the glow of a coming storm. I closed my eyes and shivered, sick with memory. Just one memory; a storm, a flash, and then my new life in the Lake George community.

Children go missing during storms. Everyone knows that. Children never go missing on sunny days.

I threw a piece of carp on to sizzle. "We'll be eating inside," I said. Children are always hungry.

"We can't eat till Dada gets home," said the elder. I willed Parse hurry then, speedy boating, because I wanted him here with the children and me.

"Hello, is anybody home?" I heard.

Parse thinks it an amusing greeting; I find nothing funny about being always here, always in or around our lake house. The others from the past are like me, confined to our homes while our children swim in the lake and roam free. At least the others from the past are mostly in pairs. I look at Parse, so much older, so much of the future, and I curse myself for my teenage rebellion, for my insistence I marry this man instead of one of my own as decreed.

My intended mate, Matthew, lives alone on the edge of the lake. He can reach out of his bedroom window and touch the shore. He likes to stay connected to the land. The adults who brought us here see Matthew as terrifying because he loves the toxic earth which killed so many of them. He doesn't mind the terror; it suits him to be left alone.

Matthew learns all he can. He is becoming so wise he frightens people. I make a point of sending the children to speak with him, learn what he knows of strange places and of dreams. He tells the story of Sarah and her partner, who disappeared. We, the children of the past, believe they are safe somewhere on solid ground, that their children build castles and dig holes in the dirt. They eat food grown in the earth.

The others say Sarah and her partner are buried alive. They say you should never reject Lake George, because the lake is sensitive, passionate and vengeful.

Only Matthew and I know he is my children's true father. Parse thinks some miracle occurred to allow him to breed; I know his seed is useless. Parse is a good provider, though, a good man and so very happy. Not bitter like many of them. Matthew is bitter and brilliant, and loves nothing but the sight of solid ground. And he likes to teach the children.

No one must ever learn the children's lineage. We would be buried alive, all of us, to cleanse the lake of our sin.

"One law for us, another for them." That's written in the book. To stop us saying, "But you do this, why can't we?" They don't care about just one partner. We, the children of the past, are punished if we stray.

When I was young I dreamt of a strange place, full of hard surfaces and fast moving boxes and the smell of rot. The other children dreamt often, too, and we would whisper together on the lake's edge, conferring, comparing. Parse watched from his porch. He lay on his belly, trailing his fingers in the water of Lake George. He stared at us. We ran and climbed the trees. He didn't know about running.

I don't walk on solid ground any more.

Most people don't like the lake's edge. They are wary of the movement of the ground, so used are they to the sway and rock of the water. When I was young it was the best place for children to be alone, to talk about our dreams.

We dreamt of living on solid ground, not on the lake. We dreamt of other water, vast expanses stretching further than the world's edge.

"Lake George is the Grand Water," Parse said. He was the youngest of the adults, and the one most willing to talk to us. The others mostly watched, as if they were scared of us.

Parse was lax with the rules, too. He would let us climb and play, where the others said, "Careful," so often we thought careful our names. Now my children are called careful, too.

I dreamt of other people, a soft woman who hugged me, a man who smelled of work as these people never did, other children.

We did not speak to the adults about our dreams. I don't believe they ever dreamt; they were too sensible. They didn't like stories.

We did. Sarah in particular; she loved to tell tales.

She could swim silently as a fish, and moved from lake dwelling to lake dwelling, clinging under the boards to hear stories not meant for children's ears.

Sarah was the one who alerted me it would be my last day at school. "You're a woman, now," she said. "That's it." Childhood is for work and learning, they say, adult-hood for play. I was fifteen; none of us menstruated before then, though Parse said the adults of the past sometimes started at twelve.

I served the carp and we ate, companionable, joking. The children love Parse, though they think him a little foolish.

My son said, "Mama thought it would storm tonight but I told her otherwise."

Parse looked at me, his understanding bringing tears to my eyes. Later, Parse tried to tempt me into swimming with him. It's his form of love-making; to swim with me is his idea of bliss.

"I can tell you about your past while we tread water," he said. If only he'd been so eager when I was a teenager. We would sit with him as he spoke, the other children and I, waiting for a slip-up, a hint at the truth. If we splashed his feet with cold water he would sometimes drift into a dream-like state and tell us more and more.

Parse sighs loudly when anyone has sex. He loves to sing, to drown out the noise. As a teenager, I said, "Parse, why don't you do what they do? Aren't you capable?"

He shrugged. It seemed a strange gesture for an adult to make. "I don't like it, Eloise," he said. "When I was fifteen they made me go to every dwelling and try to make children with the ladies there."

"Every house?" I said.

He nodded. We gazed together over the vastness of Lake George, the hundreds of houses.

"They thought it might work because of my youth. It didn't. That's why they decided to go back and get all of you."

This was more information than anyone had given us. I fidgeted, not wanting to break the spell but desperate to ask questions. Parse gazed at me.

"Things might be different, now," I said, lowering my eyes. I poured water from my cupped hands onto his feet.

"There's so much to tell you," he said.

I caught the eye of the other children and gestured them to come over, to be quiet. We listened to Parse tell the story of our other world.

Parse said, "Years ago, many, many…"

Matthew interrupted. "Before we were born?"

Parse smiled. "Ah," he said. "That's a funny one. Let me tell you the story and you'll see what I mean. We have all the technology we need. We cannot go any further. We don't need to work because all is provided. Our lake is kept clean and revitalised, our lives entertaining. But we cannot have children. When we die, it could be the end of humanity. To think all that equipment, the mechanisms of the lake, running click click, food produced, electricity buzzing, serving our bones. Perpetual motion serving beings who are not eternal.

"Our fathers…" He stopped. His brow wrinkled.

"So what happened?" I said.

"It's a little confusing. I don't know. It was a traveller. She came to us and told us news of other survivors. Other small communities. She had lost three fingers and one eye, and she was covered with scars. No one trusts strangers.

"She said that no children were being born. She told us she could bring us children for a fee. The rulers understood, they said, but I don't. Because what she did was to travel four hundred years into the past and take you from your families. There was a storm each time, I remember. Lightning. I was quite frightened." As if his experience was worse than ours.

We all cried, tears for the families we could barely remember.

One of the adults saw us and rowed over to intervene.

"Here comes Mr Lex," I said.

Parse stopped talking. Blinked. A look of terror came over him. He gazed onto the shore, as if imagining himself there, buried beneath tonnes of earth and dying.

"Not upsetting the children, I hope, Parse," Mr Lex said.

I thought quickly. "We're crying at the bravery of our forefathers."

"History, then?" Mr Lex said.

"History," I said. "Parse was telling us how the dwellings came to be built on Lake George."

Mr Lex smiled. "And how was that, Eloise? I need a refresher course."

Parse stiffened beside me. He would make a terrible rebel: No guts. And no faith. Of course I remembered the story.

"A long time before we were born, people lived on the land. The lake was used for swimming and sometimes food was found. Water was for travelling on.

"Then, the Powers that Were decided to empty the world of people for their own playground. They brought war and disease, and they created vast open fields to play in. They poisoned the land. But they did not kill everyone. Small communities were left, strong, healthy, resilient. Our forefathers were The Canberra Survivors, a small, disparate group. No real connection between them; all ages, both sexes, different ethnicities. They never identified what helped them to survive when others did not. These brave survivors decided to reject the poisoned land and build on the clear and majestic Lake George."

"Very good," Mr Lex said. "You forgot to mention the lineage though, child, which gives me my ruler's hat. We must never forget our roots."

"Who were my parents, Mr Lex?" Sarah asked.

I was angry with her for a moment, thinking she would get Parse into trouble. Mr Lex stared. He realised his vanity had caused him to make an error of revelation. "We do not question our parenthood here. We are all parents." He backed away.

"But what's my lineage? Will I be a leader?" Sarah asked.

"Oh, I don't think so. Do you?"

Not long after this, I became a woman and Sarah disappeared. I had my rebellion and married Parse and fell pregnant to Matthew.

Now I have two children of my own. We have all we need; our lives are full of laughter, we eat well, we are fulfilled. Lake George cares for us all.

My only fear is that one day, someone from the future will come and steal my children away.

IN THE DRAWBACK

If he flared his nostrils and breathed deeply, the drummer boy could catch the deep salt tang of the ocean, its seaweedy stink hinting at vegetation and food. He glanced down to where a group of men were collecting firewood. They worked in silence; no voices reached him. But they were companionable. Compatible. The drummer boy knew that if he joined them they would be agitated. "Be quiet," they'd say. "Stop your fidgeting," and they'd ask him to fetch something from the caravans, something difficult to find and unneeded.

Sitting on the rocks, he gazed out at the water, far away in the distance. He stared without blinking and chewed on a piece of salt fish until thirst drove him to stand. He blinked then and saw it.

"There's something out there," he said. "Hey! Hey! There's something out there! Something big!" Thomas, down on the beach collecting wood, stopped working and, shielding his eyes, stared out. He stared for some minutes, then shook his head.

"There's nothing there," he shouted through cupped hands. "Maybe a tangle of ropes if you're lucky. Go claim it for yourself, boy, bring it to show us tonight."

The inhabitants of Sunlit Waters rarely looked out to sea. Months could pass without anything being revealed and they grew bored watching the drawback. They had found many treasures in the past; old boats and bone, rubbish, bits and things discarded and lost over the centuries. Once, they had anticipated the revelations and scavenged the goodies, looking for clues to the past.

But the drawback was slow. The drummer boy knew that, yet still he never failed to be amazed by it. "The water will never touch that place again," he'd say to the others. "It won't come back." The men shook their heads, used to it and bored. Decades now, the water had been drawing back. Long enough for it be normal.

The drummer boy walked out on the sand with his sack over his shoulder. He found some smooth glass for Miles' collection, seven plastic lids for Tom. He found a circle of material that he guessed was once the neck of a t-shirt. He filled his bag with little treasures and walked on.

As he approached the pile, his step slowed. It was nothing; he could tell that now. Just a tangle of bottles and the sort of seaweed that looks like human hair. He wrenched the bottles out; everything was useful in some way. They knew that at Sunlit Waters.

There was something smooth, though, right at the water's edge. Smooth and brown, like a rock, but shaped unnaturally even. The drummer boy's bag was heavy and the light was falling, so he left the mystery. He knew it would be revealed when the tide went out.

Three of the men had been to the city to shop. There would be a feast tonight. Food was always shared equally, salty food to make them thirsty. They would sit together in the games room and make what conversation they could. There would be no fish, and they would pretend not to hear the crash of the waves, clearer in the night but still far away.

The walls in the games room were covered with mould from the roof down to where the tallest man could reach with a scrubbing brush. From there, mould spread in patches and stripes. The smell of it was dirt and vegetable in one. When the men first entered the room, they breathed though their mouths, but soon grew used to it.

They sat around a massive metal table, circular, scratched and dented. A find from in the drawback.

The drummer boy sat on an upturned boat in the corner and thumped his feet against the wood, thumping thumping until the men turned and noticed him.

"Be quiet, boy," one said.

"There's something out there. I know it. In the drawback. I saw a glimpse of it today."

"Be quiet, boy.'

And he was, for a while. The men who'd been to the city spoke of the noise there, the low hum which made them all queasy.

"It's busy, though. Colourful with women. And they laugh in the city. You know, funny ha ha."

"Did any of them speak to you?"

They shook their heads. "They looked at us as if we were crazy," they said. "And their faces are thin, like this." The man sucked in his puffy cheeks and the others laughed.

The drummer boy glanced at their faded clothes, the salt sheen on their skins. Pale eyes in brown faces.

The men drank wine, great mugs of it. The drummer boy found a mug for himself and filled it. He sipped the thick red liquid and felt nothing. He sipped again and again until the numbness set in.

"Look at the boy!" someone said, and they all laughed at him, slumped in his chair dribbling vomit onto his chin.

He lifted his head and saw their faces, disgust showing through the drink.

"I'm not a boy," he mumbled. Thomas spat on the floor.

"You're the closest we've got, so wear it," he said. They all sat back, their feet up to ease swollen legs.

The drummer boy went into a frenzy then, whirling and drumming on every surface he could find; the table, heads, bottles and glass.

"Attaboy," they said, being nice to him, wanting him to keep playing the child because they missed children so much, they missed their little darling over-protected faces.

"Hey!" the drummer boy shouted. He started on a run to the cliff's edge, then turned to climb down, slipping and losing his grip in his eagerness. He reached the bottom and ran towards the path through the tea tree shrubs, terrified that whatever he had seen would sink and disappear before he could show the others.

"There's something out there," he shouted.

Everyone was in the caravans. Thomas slammed the door of his, bored with the news. "It's history," he said. "Who cares about what's done?"

Miles had been tending his flowers but grabbed his coat and nodded. "Time was, everyone'd join in," he said. "Time was, you'd be left behind the pack if you didn't hurry."

Fred shouted at them, do it yourself, find it yourself ya buggers.

So Miles and the drummer boy walked alone. The drummer boy knew the sighting was his, once confirmed by Miles. He would receive the greater share of whatever bounty was found. Why else would he sit and watch on that lonely, windy cliff top?

The flat expanse of sand stretched out before them, almost unchanged over many months. Only wind and the occasional scavenger bird digging for worms changed the landscape now. Once the water drew back it did not return.

Far out, near the water's edge, they could see a great mound.

"Is it a ship? It might be ship. It will be full of treasure if it's a ship," Miles said. He loved trinkets and shininess, loved anything that glittered, even if it fell apart in his fingers.

"We won't know until we walk out and see," said the drummer boy.

They walked.

"It's not a ship," the drummer boy said.

"It's a whale," Miles said. They smiled at the thought of a whale, unseen for decades, suddenly showing itself. "A shark, then."

"We'd smell if it was a shark. We'd smell the stink of it and the birds . . . " They glanced up, watching for circling seagulls. There were a small few, as always when people walked. People on the move meant food to a bird.

"Anything dead would stink. It must be some kind of ship. From space. A space ship that landed and sank and they never got out," Miles said.

They were silent as they approached the giant mound.

It was a man. A huge man, as big as four men. They could see his heels. He was face down.

There was a massive chain around both ankles.

The drummer boy and Miles stared at the man until they shivered. "You run get the others," Miles said.

"You go. They won't believe me."

So Miles went and fetched the men to come before the tide returned and covered the titan to his heels again.

They crowded around the huge man. The tide was out to his head, but they knew it was on its way in again. They stepped closer, took off their shoes and rolled their pants up to stand over him and look hard. His clothes were rotten, still damp from being covered.

"It'll be a year before the drawback reveals him," Fred said.

"We can see him when the tide's out," the drummer boy said. "We can get the other caravan parks to help us drag him."

"Let's just leave him for now," Thomas said. "There's no hurry. He's not going anywhere."

"But what if the tide takes him?"

The chain around his ankles, corroded almost to dust, sank into the sand.

"What's at the end of it? It may have been protected by the sand," Fred said, screwing up his eyes.

They brought spades and large digging shells, and slowly removed the sand. It was still very wet, and filled the hole they dug like quicksand. Working quickly, they revealed glimpses of what lay beneath.

"It's a rock. The chain is caught in a rock. They must have used some massive force to press this rock."

"The woman on the hill says once they all were tall. Strong, like this one," said the drummer boy, tapping on the rock with his sticks, tap tap.

They found skeletons about him. Weapons. A buckle.

"Why are they skeletons and he is flesh?" the drummer boy said.

The giant had remarkably little stink about him. It was almost pure brininess, so salty the drummer boy could barely breathe.

"We're not going to be able to turn him on our own," Miles said.

Many years ago, a whale had beached itself and two or three caravan parks had joined to turn, cut and remove the meat. Better to share than to have the carcass left behind. They still had the whalebone cutlery, the needles. They would never kill a whale; they didn't need to kill anything. The shore was always littered with dead fish as the drawback continued. The older men said the fish was saltier now. Chewier. They talked of soft-fleshed fish that melted in your mouth.

The giant's skin was white from being under water.

They poked and prodded, tore off bits of the rotten cloth to use back at the caravan park for stopping drops.

"Someone needs to tell her," said Fred. "She'll want to know."

"I'll do it," said the drummer boy. He didn't mind visiting her on the hill. There was a smell in there the men didn't like. A dried fishiness and they didn't know if it came from her or the things about her

"She'll give you treats tonight and someone will come fetch you in the morning," Thomas said. The men laughed. Tears came to the drummer boy's eyes.

"Baby," sneered Fred. The drummer boy knew he didn't fit in. They wanted him to pretend to be a child but hated him for it. Despised that he made them think of children.

The drummer boy walked back to shore and up the hill to the caravan belonging to the woman, Petra. She wore a floral dress and had him do her hair. "A lady has to look after her hair," she said. The men didn't like to touch it. It was thick and greasy like seaweed, and their fingers felt coated with grease for days.

As he did her hair, the drummer boy told her of their discovery. He said, "They want to wait for the drawback to turn him over."

She shook her head and tiny specks flew off. One landed in the drummer boy's eye. "Nonsense. They'll drag him out. They'll get the neighbours to help and drag him out of the water. What are they waiting for?"

"I think they're frightened of him."

"Well, they should be. They know my stories. The terrible time of ancient dreams. Once there were many people like him. Men and women so tall they used caves high in the cliffs to store their treasures. That table in the games room was a gong," she said. "Can you imagine the size of the mallet? You could dissolve a limb to liquid with one hit. It was used by the giants."

"What happened to them? Did they all die?" the drummer boy asked.

Petra shook her head. "No one knows." She pointed to her most prized cup, a huge thing with a piece like a bite out of the rim. "All we know is, they were here."

The drummer boy had explored some of these caves. He could not reach them all. Inside them he found perfect spheres, papers long past reading, shiny bowls and things that glowed. Petra salvaged nice things, remains of the past she didn't like to use. Mugs on hooks, cracked and yellow. A little stack of books, pages glued together from their time in the sea.

The drummer boy collected remnants of toys. He had the head of a plastic action figure. The axle of a toy car. Seventeen mismatched building blocks.

Petra fed him a delicious soup and made him talk about things he didn't want to talk about.

The drummer boy said, "How do you know the past?"

She said, "It's the books and the things we find and the stories I re-member. I try to pass the knowledge on but they don't listen. They don't care about the terrible time. They don't want to learn from the past. A great wave begins with a sudden drawback. Something must follow." She muttered, losing her point, and it was frightening to the drummer boy to learn she didn't have all the answers.

All the caravans were falling apart, long past their holiday glory. Rusty. A metal smell about them all. A mustiness. The flooring all white, sanded away by years of walking.

She said, "Did you hear about the fire at Tree Shady Park?" He shook his head, horrified to think of the children who may have died there.

"It's alright. No one died. Places can be reborn, too. They can drown and be reborn. Changed." She squeezed her eyes shut. "You tell Thomas to get the others and drag that thing out of the water."

The next morning, the drummer boy told Thomas of Petra's instructions. The men spent half the day discussing how it would be, then sent runners to the other caravan parks to ask for help. They agreed the apex of low tide was the best time.

Thomas said, "Drummer boy, you guard tonight. No one is to begin without we're all here."

They left him a campfire. He boiled a pot of water and dug his fingers in the sand to collect pipis. He cooked them and ate them, hot and tasty, straight from the shell.

He could not remember a time when he felt happier.

He collected a pile of rocks and threw them at the birds swooping down seeking a beakful of meat. Rocks landed with a splash in the wa-ter. The ones on sand sank down, and some landed on the giant's back.

There was something almost delightful about hearing the bones of this titan clunk, and the drummer let a few more rocks fall until there was a small mound on his back.

He slept, curled sitting up in a ball, and was woken by birds. In the distance he could see the groups walking towards him.

He walked to the water's edge, which pulled rapidly to the shoulders of the giant. The drummer boy washed his face and wet his hair, slicking it back out of his eyes. Then he saw movement.

He turned, thinking one of the men must have run forward.

"We won't begin," the drummer boy said. There was no one there. It must have been a fish, he thought, lifting out of the water, or a low-flying bird.

As the men approached, he quickly removed the rocks nestled on the giant's back. They looked shoddy in the daylight, weak and pathetic, and the drummer boy was not proud of his actions.

As he lifted the last rock off, the giant's shoulder twitched.

The drummer boy shouted and stepped backwards. He fell over, landing in the sand and wetting his trousers.

He wriggled backwards away from the motionless giant.

"He moved," he shouted to the men. "He moved his shoulder."

They snorted. "He didn't move. He's probably caught a fish in his shirt."

"It's only the parasites. New food for them all. Word will get out and they'll come from everywhere to feast," Tom said.

Miles said. "Time was, we'd shoot those birds."

The giant lay on his stomach, his arms beneath his body. It took the men from three caravan parks in shifts to drag him out and turn him. Others had heard the news and were travelling up and down the coast.

This was something which never happened and it made most of them uneasy. They were not comfortable with community. Community insisted on modes of behaviour, saying the right thing.

Providing for visitors.

Thirty men heave ohed on one side, twenty tugged on the other. The giant's flesh was surprisingly firm, the drummer boy thought. He marched around the grunting men, tapping his slow rhythm as they worked. He felt proud of his drumming. He did not miss a beat, he would not, he would drum and drum and drum while the men toiled to turn the giant over.

Other bodies they'd found were either dissolved to bone, or the flesh turned greenish and jelly-like. Usually you grabbed the arm of a revealed body and your fingers sank to bone. You could slide the meat off the bone and collect it in a bowl. Even the dogs wouldn't eat this sludge, though the woman on the hill swore by its efficacy as fertiliser. She sold the vegetables grown on this stuff (she called it sea sludge) for a higher price, saying it cured ills of the mind. She said that when you defecated next, your shit would contain tiny worms, too small to be seen. These worms drawn down from your brain by the scent of the sea sludge in your belly.

The drummer boy would rather keep his sadness than eat anything grown from that stuff.

The giant's body was not like that. His flesh was firm. The ropes they used dug into his shoulders, and the drummer could see the flesh reddening.

"That can't be right," he said. "His flesh should not change colour." The drummer boy drummed one-handed and pointed at the markings on his back. "Why is his skin marked?"

They shook their heads. "Who knows? Let's turn him over then worry about it."

The drummer boy marched around and around. The tide was coming back and would cover the giant to his ankles this time. The men rested and debated whether to come back as the tide drew back.

"If we wait a year the water will draw back, anyway," one said. "There's no hurry."

But as he spoke the carrion birds circled above, rawking down at the people stealing their food.

They set back to work. It was tough going, and they took it in shifts, collecting water and cooking pipis and fish to eat. They all talked, theorised about the man.

"So, did he walk out into the ocean, dragging or carrying his rock, until he could no longer walk?"

"Or did they drop him off a boat and he couldn't move?"

"And who dropped him? And why?"

Finally they had the leverage to turn him over.

"One, two, three," they chanted, and with a strain and a push, he was over.

Water lapped at his hair, softening it into baby fineness. His arms were crossed tightly and he held something there, an armful of something. His wrists were chained. His eyes were closed and his mouth was so tightly pressed he looked like he had no lips. He was terribly scarred, marked.

"His lips are sewn together," someone up that end said. "And his cheeks are puffed out. Has he got jewels in there?"

They had heard tell of people who were buried with their jewels or money in their mouths, their lips sewn shut to scare off thieves.

"Shut up," someone further down said. "Shut up and look at his arms."

The drummer boy pushed through the knees of the men. Some of them were weeping.

"It's children," he said. The giant held, close to his chest like he would not let them go, five small skeletons.

"Children!" the men said. They began to wail with fear and sorrow. "It's children!"

They all stepped back, wondering what to do. Where to go from here. They stared at the children's skeletons.

"They'll need a proper burial," said one. "At least that."

There were nods, agreement. They were good at burials. There were thousands of bones in the dirt behind the caravan park, all carefully laid in a stack and words said over them.

The woman on the hill trundled down on her electric car. When she saw the lips sewn, she spoke. Her eyes were closed, chin to neck, voice muffled.

"They did it at sea. Did it once to the master of a captured ship." She waved her arm at the sea, as if they would find evidence of this under the waves. "He moaned so much the pirates sewed his lips together and tossed him into the sea."

She tossed her arm and her fingertips flicked at the drummer boy. "Don't you remember we found that boot once, with a needle imbedded?"

This was proof to no one but the drummer boy and the woman. The men hissed, "Shut up! Shut up!"

The giant was covered with sucking, biting things. One burrowed into the eye of his penis, which they could see through his torn pants.

The drummer boy stared at the giant till his eyes watered.

"I saw his finger move," he said.

"Be quiet now, boy," said Fred.

And then they all saw it. One finger flicked stiffly. Then another.

Then his shoulders shook.

The men ran, shouting. The drummer boy behind them, not as fast in the sucking wet sand.

They stopped a ways off and stared back.

He couldn't be alive.

They watched as his fingers unclasped. The children's skeletons tumbled about on his chest as he released his grip, and he lifted his great hand and swept the bones off like crumbs. His shoulders shook and the men ran shouting to the cliffs as the giant slowly sat up.

They watched him through binoculars from the cliffs. Petra was there, and the other women, too. He took hours to stand, his movements slow and careful, as if his body reawakened slowly. He seemed so human when he stretched some of the men murmured, "We should talk to him."

Then he lifted his hand to his mouth and touched the stitches there. He looked towards the cliff and began to walk, each huge footstep sinking into the sand and being lifted out with a sucking noise they could hear from the beach. The ancient chain broke away.

He thundered on. He searched the ground as he walked, fingering the stitches.

"What's he looking for?"

"Something sharp."

They moved further back as he approached, wanting to run but wanting to know as well.

Then he reached down and lifted up a shell. He'd found his sharp object.

He was close enough now they could see the barnacles clinging to his ears.

"Stop him," Petra said. Her voice came in gasps. The drummer boy had never seen her scared.

"Who is he?" the drummer boy asked.

She shook her head. "I don't know. I don't know."

"But who sewed his mouth? How?"

She slapped him, the fat fleshiness of her hand softening the blow.

She looked at him sidelong. "I don't know," she said. She began to shake, to quiver, like her body knew what was coming.

Feeling the stitches with one hand, the giant used the sharp with the other and soon his mouth was loose. He bent over and spat a mouthful of rocks to the ground.

He dropped the sharp.

His nose screwed up, his lips kissed out then peeled back in a grimace. His teeth were smaller than they could possible have imagined; like an adult with baby teeth.

There was the beginning of a sound, a low-pitched noise which made the drummer boy feel sick to his stomach. The giant opened his mouth wider, wider, and his jaw seemed to dislocate itself as he stretched his mouth out so wide they could see deep inside his throat. He began a noise, one long echoing note which shivered the drummer boy to his core.

One man began to cry, then another.

The woman wailed. "We don't want to hear it," but the giant stepped closer, closer, and it filled their world and that of everybody nearby.

To a man they began to weep. The drummer boy was filled with such complete sadness he saw no room for the future, but he was used to sadness. Used to absorbing it, ignoring it.

Miles fell over, dizzy, disoriented. He wailed, "I'm drowning! I'm drowning!" though water was nowhere near. The drummer boy felt his vision blur and he reached for Petra. She was slumped in her electric car, vomit covering her chest.

The giant stood, his head back, mouth open, as men turned to jelly about him. Far out on the waterline, whales beached themselves and those still capable of seeing shouted in surprise at the sight.

The drummer boy heard crashing, cracking, and he saw the cliff collapsing onto a dozen men below.

Men cried salt tears and the drummer boy watched as they staggered towards the water, seeking out the drowning in droves. Thomas lead them, striding as if he was in control, but the drummer boy saw him falter in every step. Petra rolled till her wheels stuck then she threw herself down and crawled like a worm out to the water.

How did the ancients stop him? the drummer boy thought. How did they sew his mouth without dying on approach? Did they numb themselves? Sacrifice themselves for the children?

The children. There was a small family of them in Tree Shady Park. The drummer boy's stomach pained him so much he couldn't swallow. He had to spit it on the ground. He wanted to run to the children, gather them up and take them to safety.

The giant wiped spit from his mouth and was silent. He looked around at the deserted beach. The drummer boy thought, He sees me. I should run to warn the children, run my fastest and beat him there.

The giant stepped towards him. The drummer boy thought, no. No. I'll lead him away. I must lead him away.

So he began to run. He ran. The giant stepped after him, walking slowly, each step ten of the drummer boy's.

The drummer boy ran inland, rhythmically, counting the beat in his head as he ran. He knew the giant would catch him. There was no doubt of that. But the further he could lead him away the better he would feel.

He ran for a full day before he sank to the ground in exhaustion.

The giant stepped forward, picked him up and held him close. The tenderness of it crushed the drummer boy's ribs and made him wish for just . . . one . . . more . . . breath.

AL'S ISO BAR

I feel such an ache in my bones, but I will not complain. This pain means I am alive, when so many are not, and if I can be kept from the grave I have nothing to complain about.

I move my limbs slowly, so that nothing is shocked into stiffening and refusing to move. When that happened once I pretended to contemplate some unseen fancy while the world pulsated and probed around me until movement returned.

I move into the bedroom where he waits. His head and shoulders are propped up by a mountain of pillows. His arms are spread over the sheet, which covers his thin frame. He drums his fingers, beckoning me.

"Again?" I say. I cannot bite my tongue.

"Will it take your mind off your next husband?" he asks, and I climb painfully into his bed to perform my duty.

He tastes bitter.

It's probably wasted energy; this old man is past impregnating me, though he wants to hope: "Just one more, before I die."

Pity makes me acquiesce.

I curl up to keep his small spurt of seed inside me, curl up, pull the blanket up to my ears.

He shuffles about, makes scrunching sounds in the bed. My eyes are closed; I don't know what he's doing. Tearing sounds, like he's tearing strips for papier mache. To make a smooth young man's mask perhaps, to fool me into keeping him.

Rip rip rip rip. I don't open my eyes because I don't want to see his face, don't want to see his secret face.

He stretches his legs out and his toenails scratch me. I clench my teeth, screw up my eyes, move my legs away to the edge of the bed. His toenails are ridged and yellow; they are like mountains when he wears slippers. He blows his nose in the kitchen sink and I dropped a piece of apple there once, picked it up covered with his slime.

Apples are good for pregnant women.

This one will not take, I'm sure. He cannot will me to fall pregnant when he has lost his potency.

He shuffles papers, screws up papers and the sound chills me. Does he have to do that here? Does he have to make me hear it?

He has cleaned up the mess by the time I awaken. Or someone has; there is the scent of lavender in the air, so the housewoman may have already glared at me in my sleep. She thinks I'm lazy, fat.

That is how I need to be.

I'm not at all hungry, not at all queasy, I feel nothing and I'm glad. I'm tired of my husband, tired of the old man stink of him. I stretch out, prepare to rise. One slipper is ready for me to slip my foot into; the other has been kicked under the bed. I stretch for it. I see, on his side, one white ball of paper and I suck in air and dust. Cough. I glance at the door, listen to the silence, cannot reach the paper from my side. I glance at the door, listen to the silence, walk around and collect the paper. It rustles a little. I spread it out and place it between "Foods to Avoid" and "Preparing Baby's Room" in my latest issue of "Perfect Parents". Why I read these rags I don't know. One of the women's groups subscribed me to make a point, but I can't remember which group so the point is lost on me. I read the things anyway, out of boredom.

I go to the bathroom, am given my daily pregnancy test (negative) and wash myself carefully.

The house is very quiet.

My husband has gone somewhere, the housewoman is vacuuming upstairs. With the magazine under my arm, I take my carrot juice to sit in the sun.

I feel safe in my little spot. The windows are high so people can't see in at me. There is only one door, at the end of a long hallway; I have warning if anyone comes.

Even though no-one is watching I sit up straight. If I let myself slump I'll surrender to the tiredness that threatens to overwhelm me.

I settle into the soft chair. I feel distracted, my nose twitches.

"Galena," I shout. "GALENA!"

"Yes, Leah?" she says. She is younger than I am but ugly; no man would choose her over me. She hates that. I see her liven up when a new husband arrives, her lipstick becomes redder, a vaginal invitation. They don't notice her. She can only make an impression with her perfume, its noxiousness reminding us all she exists. She has been with me a while and will have to leave soon. She is beginning to be curious. Why is she aging when I am not? We eat the same food, she is thinking.

She calls me fat but I'm not. It's all breasts. She says my hair is fair but it's not, it's blonde, long and straight. Hers sticks out oddly and has a metallic scent that disturbs me.

"You'll have to take off your jewellery," I say. Her hand goes involuntarily to her chest; I suspect her locket rests beneath her jumper.

"I'm not wearing any," she says.

"I know you are," I say. "I can smell it." She sighs and walks away.

"Wait," I say. "There's metal in this room, too."

She shrugs angrily at me. She should be grateful for her position but she isn't.

At least our small conflict provides me with something to do in between.

"Can you look for it, please?" I say.

She kneels and crawls around the room, using her fingers to search. She finds it; a ring binder pushed to the back of the couch.

"This?" she says, waving it at me.

"Yes, yes," I say, waving back at her. "It's giving me a headache, would you take it away?" She smiles then, knowing from long experience I'm not pregnant. I realise she had been testing me, placing metal there on purpose so she would know. Metals only disturb me when I'm not pregnant.

She says, "Your husband will be having lunch in the study. Will you join him? Finger food," she adds with a smile. Cutlery sets my teeth on edge.

"Sure," I say. I didn't realise it was that time. I can't wear a watch for the wild rash it raises on my wrist.

As she walks away I flip through my magazine. There is the rescued sheet of paper; I need to dispose of it before I am discovered.

"Al Dempster. 36. 12 unknown offspring, 10 unacknowledged, two estranged. No personal attachments. Owner/operator, Al's Iso Bar."

What was wrong with Al? What precluded him from candidacy? His age? It made no difference, really. He would be old before long with me anyway.

I brave a blinding headache and shred the page.

My husband is already eating when I reach him.

"You must be hungry after such a busy morning," he says. I smile at him. He scowls. He is always angry with me. He didn't know what he was getting into when we started. He rises, pushes my chair in when I sit, pinches me. He's pathetic. He hates what he is doing but isn't tough enough to stop it.

There is a small pile of paper, face down, next to his plate. The shortlist? I won't give him the satisfaction of asking about it. I don't want to acknowledge the fact this old husband is picking his replacement. I hate farewells. I want him to leave as on a normal day and never return. I just want him to go. Al Dempster, I think. What's so bad about you? Why were you rejected?

Lunch is smoked salmon, rollmops, anchovies, brie. It's raw egg mayonnaise.

"They told me the results this morning," he said. There is a hint of despair about him. Last night was his chance to gain eleven weeks of life; he failed.

"You know sometimes it doesn't show till the day after," I say. I feel some small regret; this man was young, vibrant, when he came to me. He made me laugh. Once he dressed up as Galena and spent the day fussing and stamping about the house. I laughed and laughed. I remember our nights early on, when it felt good, and how much he missed my body when I was pregnant.

"You did very well," I say. "What was it? Eight? Nine? I don't think ten."

"This one would have been ten," he says. "I wonder what they would have been like."

"No," I say. "Don't you fucking dare." I poke him. Bony, thin and old. "How dare you? Selfish senile fuck. Selfish! What would people say, what would they say?"

"I only said I wonder," he says.

"'I only' means nothing. It means everything. You think I don't wonder? I don't. I can't. You think I don't wonder?"

He screws his face up at my nonsense.

"I would have liked to leave a child behind," he says.

"You aim low," I say. "You're in the history books, your name is in there, next to mine. You are listed on nine separate occasions as aiding in the discovery of precious metals. You've saved lives. And you would have liked to leave a child behind." I stare at him. "You would have been a bad father."

I walk away. My mind is full of "Go Go Go Go." I don't want to see him again. He disturbs me. I imagine him swallowing safety pins, small metal objects, just to give me a headache.

Damian, our police, is checking the cupboards.

"Can he go now, please, Damian?" I trust Damian. He loves me from a protective position; he cares for me. He underwent chemical castration for me.

"I don't think he's finalised his choice. We should probably wait until it's down to one."

"Then I need to be away from here. How long? An hour?"

"Logistics are complicated at this stage," he says. "There's a lot of coordinating, organising, employing. You don't want to know."

"Tell me," I say. Damian has let slip before, small details he knew I shouldn't know. "Tell me the truth."

"Maybe he thinks no one is good enough. No one as good as him. But he has to choose someone."

"That's not what I meant. Tell me about the others. Why can't I help to choose? Why can't they just choose whoever came second last time?"

I know he won't tell me, but I'm hoping he'll try to distract me with the offer on an outing.

"Look," he says, "why don't you get away for a few hours? You need a break; you've been pushed too hard. Wear the gloves, the mask, don't try to catch a train or you'll collapse." He fumbles in his pocket for paper money. I know that's emergency funds for me. There is no limit to what he can spend on me.

"Stay in the city at the new hotel overlooking the lake. It's almost metal-free. Try not to have too much contact with people. I'll come and collect you when he's gone and the new one's here."

"Thanks, Damian," I say. I kiss him.

I forget him. I have no time to spare; just hours before I'll be taken back. I walk as quickly as I can, but it is not comfortable for me. I can't be in a car either, the metal.

I ask for directions, actually speak to people. I overhear strange conversations; I hear one woman say, "I've had my fill of funerals."

I find my way to Al's Iso Bar. Clouds whirl on the window, a weather map painted there. I finger the notes in my pocket. I think, "I'll just go in, buy something to drink. I'll deal with the headache if there is a metal bar. I'll drink something blue, or green. I'll drink some red wine, or a beer."

I push through the door. The place is empty. The bar is wooden. Good. I won't be distracted by that.

It's very warm inside. I shrug off my coat.

"It's a constant twenty one degrees Celsius," I hear. I turn around and this, surely, is Al.

"Perfect inside temperature. Outside I'd prefer it a little warmer, what with the wind factor. Can I get you something? Cocktail?"

I look up at his carefully prepared list. He smiles. He reads them through to me, chuckling, can't help himself, he thinks he's so funny, brilliant.

"There's a Snow Bunny, that's a White Lady with some ice. Sweet sixteen Degrees, that's your Malibu based cocktail. Summer Hummer… very chilled, that one. Russian Cold Front—drop of champagne makes that one. Peach Haze—if you haven't had your fruit yet today. Champagne cooler speaks for itself. Shall I go on?"

The concept of choice stuns me a little. Usually my food and drink arrive, perfectly planned and prepared, every nutrient met. Some bad food allowed when no baby present. Like brie. Coffee only rarely. Alcohol never.

"What's the most alcoholic?" I say.

He laughs. I can't tell anymore about natural attraction, but I guess he approves of me.

"They'll all do it for you. You look like a Sweet sixteen girl to me."

I smile at the compliment.

"That'll do me, then."

He prepares it painstakingly, tut-tutting at his mistakes, starting again twice, tipping the mistakes into another cocktail shaker.

"Don't worry, I'll call it a Tornado and sell it off later," he says. "We get pretty full during happy hour." I wonder how he copes; he seems very slow. I don't know how to talk to him, what to say. "Did you know you were nearly my husband," would sound insane.

"So, have you been here long?" I say, thinking he would tell me he'd applied for a new job and we'd talk about why he didn't get it. Was it age? Alcohol intake? He seemed very nice.

"It's quiet at the moment. They're all a bit scared, you know, of dying."

"Dying of what? Is this place dangerous?"

"No, no, you know, this killer. There's been fifteen dead, my age, some of them and younger. No one knows who's doing it and they just seem to die. No evidence, they reckon. Nobody seen. Doesn't worry me. Nobody'd waste the effort knocking me off."

I sip my cocktail. He watches.

"Haven't seen you in here before."

"No, I don't go out much."

"Kids?"

I shake my head, drink a little more. Where would I begin on that one?

"What about you?" I ask.

"Yeah, don't see 'em though, bit of a shame but what can you do?" He shrugs.

I think of my husband at home, his parental regrets and I think that Al and I may have been happy together. His lack of sentimentality was attractive.

"You don't miss them?"

"Course I do—well, not enough to do anything about it, know what I mean?"

I feel sudden blinding lust for this man, more than I had ever felt for my husbands. Finding him myself, perhaps, or the uncertainty of it, the unlikelihood of it. I have no idea how to proceed, so I put my attention to his décor.

There are posters everywhere, posing questions.

"Which city experienced 322 days of rain?"

"What is the driest place in the world?"

"Where did the heaviest hailstones fall?"

"What is the coldest place in the world?"

I look around the room. "Where are the answers?" I say.

"You have to ask me," he says. Stares into my eyes. "Just ask me." I wonder if anyone has ever asked him. To tease him, I laugh and say nothing.

"Maybe later," I say, though I wonder if I will have a later. Damian might be tracking me down right now, seeking to draw me back to my place. They were anxious; it was almost five months since I had last found metal for them.

The door swings open and an old man comes in.

"Hey, weatherman, what's the forecast?"

Al pours a beer and places it on the bar. The old man doesn't pay. Al says, "Looks like rain for a couple of days, then clearing to fine for the weekend."

The old man chuckles. "He always says that, figures he'll be right some of the time."

"That's it. Right as often as I was before all this." Al lifts his arms to encompass his world. "I used to be a Weatherman," he says, loving the word which is almost meaningless to me.

The old man shakes his head. "Quiet in here," he says, nodding at me.

"It's this killer. The blokes are scared to go out," Al says, wiping the bar with a cloth that leaves streaks.

"Not me," says the old man.

I can't stop staring at him. What was it about my old men? They were so bitter. This one seemed unruffled, happy enough.

"I've been getting the young lady here drunk on cocktails," Al says. With an audience he feels safe responding to me. I have another cocktail, Al has another beer. He gives me some peanuts fresh from the pack. He makes me laugh, and I don't know who he is.

"Bathroom?" I say.

"Through there." He points. Does he watch me walk? It feels that way. Does he follow me? He stays with the old man. That old man. I peek through the door and see them leaning in together. Laughing. Al catches me watching and waves. I know Damian will be here soon. He will find me. I don't want to be found here, with Al. I don't want them to know I have any information at all.

"Al," I say. I beckon him.

The old man laughs, flaps his hands, go, go you lucky bastard.

"You right there?" Al says. Up close, without the bar between us, in harsh lighting, I can see his flaws. His nose, red and pockmarked. His cheeks veiny. His eyes yellowish. His knuckles bruised.

But he smells good, real, and I say, "My husband is very old," and he pushes me up against the wall and kisses me. There is nothing romantic, nothing considerate about it. He bites my neck and I yelp. He kisses me again and I grab at his belt, at him.

"Incoming," shouts the old man and we turn, he is in me and he comes and that is it. His eyes widen in surprise as he lets me down.

"What happened?" he whispers. It's my scent. I don't tell him that. What I smell like is baby-making.

There is silence in the bar. We can hear nothing through the thick dark door. I am suddenly terrified that Damian is there, finding me, and I don't want that, I want to run home myself.

"Back door?" I say.

Al shows me. He looks dazed and I think I would tire of him very quickly as a husband.

"Come back soon," he whispers.

I smile. I wonder briefly what he would say if he knew what will become of his sperm. He would shrug, perhaps. It may put him off sex, that's what happens with some of them. It's like some primal thing; producing offspring is the ultimate aphrodisiac. When the prospect is taken away, some of them go limp.

I run home. When I arrive Damian is there at the door. "I thought you'd be back," he says. "You're amazing."

"In what way?" I say. I'm a little out of breath. I feel sweaty, stinky. I need a bath.

"They've picked him. He's on his way now. The other one's gone; they're just packing up the rest of his stuff now."

I nod. "I'd better prepare." This is my wedding day, after all. There will be no guests, and Damian and Galena will act as witnesses. Still, the wedding feast will be good.

He's not bad, my new one. Quiet. Says he likes to read; they all end up reading, we've so many books and so little else. I can see now they know more than me about husbands. I might have chosen Al and then where would we be?

I hope my new one's seed turns out okay. He is a kindly lover, patient as I move slowly to stop my limbs from stiffening. He is sweet this morning when I wake up feeling queasy. Just the thought of all those cocktails makes me sick.

They give me my pregnancy test and there it is. My new husband is thrilled and I see no reason to tell him about Al. The next baby will be his, and the next.

They keep me safe in my cocoon-like home until the eleventh week of gestation. Then I start to shake; that's how it always begins. Someone is watching and I am transported to my other house, my metal house.

Maps there, and charts. Pens and compasses. Weather maps (Al) and tidal charts. These things mean nothing until my body begins to absorb the foetus, then lines spin and whirr. I pick up a silver fork, then a gold chain. I pick up a chunk of sulphide, a small zinc-based toy car. I pick up some tiny lead balls, a sheet of aluminium, a silicon chip. I breathe deeply; the air in here seems thick. These things mean something to me and as my body eats my bellied-baby, I can see where to find them.

I can see where the precious metals are and I tell the people in suits watching me. They treat me with something to take away the pain and my new husband bathes me and feeds me ice cubes made out of orange juice. He doesn't speak for a long time, then he says, "Did we lose the baby?"

I almost cry at his innocence. It gets me every time. They all figure it out, eventually, or an approximation of 'it'. They all learn to despise me. But what can I do? It's not my fault. My body does what it does.

Sometimes I try to be sad but it doesn't work.

My new husband goes shopping with some people to buy me a gift, congratulations on being pregnant again. I ask Damian to let me out for a while; I need space. He is so good to me, so understanding. He lets me go.

I wish I had a friend to go to. Sometimes I wish that. Last time I was out I had somewhere to go so I go there again. People look at me and I wonder what they see. My face is not famous. My name is known and the names of my husbands. They age so quickly, become obsolete so soon.

These people don't know the gift I give to them.

The sign is yellow. Weathered. It says "Al's Iso Bar is closed. Due to untimely death of owner." I look around for someone to talk to, someone to ask, but I don't really need to know.

My husband is happy, fertile. None of his competitors remain to try to claim his place; he can rest easy. Adrenaline, apparently, leads to infertility.

But now I'm wondering, if they kill off the failed suitors, what happens to my ex-husbands? Prison or death? And what will happen to this one, because I like him. I'd rather him not be dead. Can't they be useful somehow?

I'm curled up in bed. Warm. I sleep well with the light on. I need to; he reads all night long, and I'm waiting for the day when he starts to tear the papers, scrunch the papers, finding my new husband for me and killing off rejected suitors with a scrunch of his hand.

THE LEFT BEHIND

I am a judge listener. These things I heard and saw; these things I do not judge. I will tell this tale a hundred times, and it will be told, because it is our history, our lesson.

It is our law.

The judge and I sat in the sun discussing the nature of our people. Rather, he sunned while I sat carefully shrouded. The judge loves the sun. His skin is as thick as an elephant's hide. He's one of the few who enjoy—can stand—the pure sun's heat. He forgets about the others, sometimes. He likes me to get up early to watch the sun set. We both miss the times when day was day, night was night. Before we were nocturnal.

"Our people are basically good," he said, and coughed.

"No," I said, because he likes his listeners to argue with him. "We are no different from the ones who left in the rockets. We are just slower in our reactions."

"Why, then, do you and I sit idle, while the world turns?"

"Well, then, it is because there is plenty for all. Take away the space, the shelter, the food and drink. How soon would we be looking for an escape? And a scapegoat?"

"Ah, Lydia," he said. He smiled at my word play. He rolled his chair over to share my shade. He is a very dark man, with muscles strong across his back and brown eyes which seem to fill his face.

He could crush my thin white body so easily, push me into the sun and watch me squeeze my pale, weak eyes closed. But long ago I stood strong against him, and he would never consider testing me again.

He stared down at the shoes on my feet.

"Leo is working beautifully, I see." I smiled at him, giving him the benefit of the doubt—he was not being deliberately cruel.

"His hands are becoming independent of his mind. There is no prejudice in the shoes he produces." I coughed. "You see," I said.

"Your husband is a very clever man."

"Your husband is a very clever man," I thought. I am long since trained to repeat it all in my mind.

We sat in silence for a while. It was a very quiet place, the river gently drumming past. The river runs right through our town. Before the rockets left, it was dammed and channelled; it was stagnant. Now, we let it go where it will, and our water is sparkling.

I thought of the judgement he had made the evening before. It was the first for a while, and had made his brain active again.

Three people came to us to say of a companion, "He does not bathe. His matted hair becomes clogged and irritating, so he does not wear clothes. His body is covered with hair, and we must work closely with him."

This was a very hairy man. He could not speak, but his eyes were large and kind like those of the judge.

"And you are perfect?" said the judge to the spokesperson.

"I am now," she said. Half her face was strawberry birthmark. She kept her fringe long to cover it, like a curtain drawn aside. The judge did not speak. She coughed. "Comparatively," she said.

"And you?" said the judge to her companions. "The two of you, despite appearances, are perfect?"

The complainants realised they had made a grave error, that they were in fact the defendants and had been from the beginning.

"Have you heard, listener?" the judge said to me.

"I have heard and seen. I saw a man, worthy to this community, who works hard at a fire to keep our horses shod. I see four people who are equal. I hear three people complaining; in their voices I hear the roar and whine of a rocket leaving the earth."

The judge smiled. He says my listenings are poetical.

"That is what I hear also," he said.

Leo, my husband, had found his way into the room and sat up the back, nodding. He loves to hear me speak.

"Sentence is: three bear suits to be worn for a month."

The hairy man laughed aloud, and spluttered, and clapped his hands.

The judge said, "I hope you are not deliberately distressing your companions. The world doesn't like to hear of such things."

The hairy man hung his head; a chastised beast. And that was our work for the night.

"I'll have lunch with Leo," I said.

"All right, but meet me in the garden afterwards. I want to discuss the case." The judge coughed, and went to his own meal.

Leo and I chose the restaurant. It was the last time I would enter that place; I would not be welcome by twenty-four hour's passing. Leo held his coat over me to keep the moonlight away, because I had forgotten my umbrella and it was bright that night. He is so careful of me, though I tell him my pregnancy has not made me weak, only nervous about how to tell the judge. I can't put it off forever, hard as I might wish I could.

The new owner came to us to speak the menu. "No, I didn't lose them cooking, we have lamb or pork or chicken or beef." I couldn't groan to her face without hurting her feelings, but I did not feel like meat for lunch. I ordered chicken, Leo ordered beef, and she dexterously laid cutlery on the table.

"Why the opening statement?" Leo said.

"She has no fingers on either hand," I said.

"Who would care?" he said.

"She does, it seems." I reached across to hold his arm. "Thanks for coming. It's nice to see you there."

"I came because I couldn't wait to give you these. And I know the judge likes to keep you late with his ideas."

He laid upon the table the most beautiful pair of shoes I had seen in my lifetime. They were made from leather so soft he must have been working it for days, and he had cut them perfectly. They kissed my feet like warm mud. I could not speak for the tears in my eyes. He is somehow embarrassed by the beauty he creates. He always tucks his work away when I approach, makes his shoes while he waits for me. He doesn't know I sometimes quietly watch him.

"You don't like them?"

"They are beautiful," I said. I kissed his eyelids and we sat in silence until the food arrived.

"Chicken," the waitress said, "and beef." She coughed over our plates. When she was out of hearing, I sighed. "I'm so tired of meat, meat, meat. When can we go back to well-rounded meals?"

Leo smiled. "You will miss it when the animals' lungs fail and you have nothing but potatoes to eat. It's best to make the most of it now. And imagine the colonists. Perhaps they have no meat at all."

"Then they should have taken the animals with them. Not just those sperm and egg iceblocks."

Leo laughed. "You're sharp, all right, Lydia."

I made the joke later to the judge and he, too, thought I was clever.

"But there was no room for us, let alone the animals," the judge said. He, of all the people I knew, was sorry to have been left behind. But what would he have done? If he hadn't been left behind, he would never have become what he has. They would never have let him.

"And who do you think they would have taken on their rockets, if they had a choice. You or the cow?" I had intended a joke, but the judge did not laugh or speak.

"Judge? Have I offended you? Please forgive me." He was with me in the shade; he took my hand and we watched the grass sizzle.

The judge said, "I was one of the foolish ones, Lydia, who imagined I was to go. I packed my small bag with things I considered precious. I remember not what; that bag remains in my home, unpacked. Once they had turned me away from ship after ship, I realised anything I had considered precious enough to take to a new world would be worthless here. And I am not lacking in anything, so I was correct in my assessment. 'No, I'm sorry, your name does not appear on this list,' they said, and I waved my family ahead. 'I'll see you there,' I said. I watched thousands upon thousands enter the ships, and eventually it became clear I wouldn't be going and why."

"This is our new world," I said. My heart has been so much happier since they left. I repeated his words in my head, squeezed his hands and wanted to comfort him. We were interrupted in our thoughts by a messenger, red-faced with bad news.

"Only it's the Barwin baby, judge. Only it's been killed. There's blood all over and we need you to take a look." He seemed to bend in the wind, he was so tall and thin, but his voice was strong and clear. His cough was very mild.

The judge's grip tightened on my hand. "What is it, judge?" I said. I would never have guessed his answer.

"I have come to fear this," he said.

"What, though?"

"Murder," he said. I did not know what he expected me to say to such a thing, so I said nothing, then; "It is strange," I said, "but I dreamt about children yesterday."

"As did I," he said.

"But it was a good dream. Positive," I said.

"Sometimes those are the most frightening," the judge said. Sometimes the community dreams together. We have not assessed why this is so, unless it is some atavistic draw to those in the rockets. Does something happen to the rest of humanity and the echo reaches us? That night we dreamt we were shrinking to the size of dolls, and the children grew like giants, and they kept us safe and warm. We were looked after. I found the dream comforting. Another time we dreamt a single rocket returned, and landed safely in the sea, where it sizzled, bobbed, cooled. We all bathed in the warm waters and waited. We took out boats to draw the rocket ashore, and we released the door.

Out tumbled skeleton upon skeleton, bones grey, tumble bumble and we all woke up sweating with fear.

I did not reach Leo till very late that morning.

"You are tired," he said. "Your feet drag."

"What have you been doing?" I said, though I could see his hands were full of leather and needle.

He set these aside and said, "Oh, just listening. There were songs from over there, and the trees rustled, and I heard mice, I think, scampering. Almost as entertaining as a television show." He smiled, waiting for me to laugh. I made a little huff of air because he couldn't see me smiling.

"I barely remember television," I said.

"I remember it," he said. There was uncommon bitterness in his voice, and I knew he was thinking of all the television he'd heard, not seen, and how the world had revolved around it before they left. We didn't turn it back on, once they'd gone. Television went the same way as the printing presses; too much effort for too few people. It was only the generators we needed, for our rare, precious light.

"And how was the singing?" I said. It was a joke amongst the two of us that we had not heard a lovely voice in a long time.

"Not so bad," Leo said. "Though they still hesitate between each song, as if waiting to be stopped. Have you eaten?"

I didn't speak. The thought of food made me sick.

"What is it?"

"Tonight. I . . . I was listening."

"To what?"

"A child was found by its mother. Dead." I coughed.

Leo's voice was careful. We ourselves had lost a child, in the womb, out in the wilderness soon after the rockets left, before we realised there were others.

"A child?" he said. "But children die quite often."

"Yes, but children rarely have their throats cut. Children rarely bleed to death."

Leo pressed his fingers to his lips. We did not speak. Understand, this was the beginning of it. This was the first murder since the rockets left. We had no law of our own to deal with it, and we disliked the law of the rocket people.

We sat under the stars, not long before the sun rose and we would have to go inside, and Leo said, "Tell me what you see."

"True or imaginary?"

"Imaginary." I told him a saved-up memory, an image he'd heard many times before. We both loved it.

"You and I are lying on the top of a cliff. We are facing the sky. The whole world is abuzz."

"Abuzz with noise, but each noise is clear," Leo said. This was his part of the story. "The hum of the rockets has been heard for three days now, like buses warming up for a long trip. The smell of their fuel is in the air; the plutonium they warned us about." He coughed. "They told us if just one rocket failed, the explosion could hurt all of us. But they thought, what's it matter? They had a joke; do you remember it, Lydia?" I had passed into the house and returned with tea he had prepared. This was his special part and he told it perfectly every time.

"The joke is, what do you give a deaf, dumb and blind kid for Christmas? And the answer is lung cancer."

"What sounds did you hear?" Sometimes he remembered too well what it had been like amongst the able.

"There were rockets warming up, children crying, adults shouting. Doors slamming, cars starting, cars crashing. Sirens and shouts, pleas and cries. Then explosions as they left. Then silence."

"No one will ever forget that silence," I said. "And the sight that followed. For a week, the greatest fireworks display ever seen. The sky full of light and flashes, as the rockets slowly vanished into the distance. Such light we couldn't sleep. And then the sky was dark.

"And there was a shower of sparks one night, an explosion of light and a shower of sparks, and the last rocket was gone."

"And we felt nothing for the people who died when that rocket exploded, because they were already separate from us. Alien," he said. Their very departure damaged the ozone layer more than decades of their existence could have. But they already found the world unliveable. What would they say now? As the rockets left, we felt great fear, and great courage, at being left behind. Later, we would change the words. We would say we chose to stay.

"And what do you truly see?" Leo said.

"I see my lover, with a cup of tea, waiting to be kissed."

He reached for me, kissed me deeply, sweetly, without lust.

"What will you do tomorrow?" he said.

"We will try to find the baby's killer."

I was tired from unhappy sleep but I rose to be with the judge.

"Don't forget shoes for the postman tonight," I said to Leo. He grunted. He is not good in the evening.

The judge is at his most positive at that time. In the evenings, he believes the earth can heal itself, that the others left too soon. That is his belief. He was subdued, though; I felt sure he had slept badly too.

And there was the terrible work ahead of us.

I thought we would speak to the mother first, and her neighbours, but instead the judge bade me take him to the school.

We have just five children of school age, and they are precious. They learn their lessons in a brightly-lit glass schoolroom. People spend their nights looking in, watching the children.

The judge and I watched for an hour. The deaf teacher smiled and corrected work as they ran about him. Every now and then he would rise to write something on the board; not one of the five paid him the slightest mind. He coughed for their attention; they mimicked him cruelly.

All five were healthy and strong. They could see, hear and speak. They had all their limbs. They jumped up on a desk and leapt off onto one another, they squealed, they stuck their tongues out at their observers. One amongst them was a teenager; he had known the world before it changed. He directed the children—he seemed more a teacher than the good man at the front of the schoolroom. His mother had hidden him when the rockets left; she couldn't bear to lose him. He was her eyes.

Their education is very casual. They learn a little of old world history and geography, and they laugh, as we once did at outdated ideas.

They learn mathematics, geometry, engineering, naturopathy; anything to aid their survival.

And ours.

Some of us wept quietly as we watched. So many had been submitted to a terrible torture before the rockets left, a terrible, barbaric thing. I was lucky to have only lost a child; some of these women had their wombs torn out, to stop them committing the sin, taking the risk of bringing another like them into the world. As if we were monsters.

The judge wept too, as he watched.

"You miss your children," I said.

"Oh, yes," he said. "Oh, yes." One of the children in the schoolroom defecated and smeared it onto the window before us.

"They would be almost grown by now," the judge said.

I moved him away; took him to see the mother. We had wasted enough time.

"I had such hope for her, such dreams," said the mother. Her voice was dull, flat. I, too, spoke like that for a while.

"She was perfect, wasn't she?" said the judge.

"Oh, perfect. It's what we've got to hope for, the kids," said her companion. They sat holding hands, two enormous women. I wondered who tended their needs. I wondered, briefly, how she had shifted to give birth. Then she rose with agility, made tea in a flash, spoke to us in that flat voice. Sometimes I feel I am a little insane. I cannot let go of prejudice; I can't let it all go.

"What do you think happened?" I said. She passed tea around, and a rich, fatty cake.

"We just came home and found her, didn't we?"

Her companion nodded. "Some animal must have killed her."

"What sort of animal did you think of first?" I said.

"The human animal, of course. Nothing else would be so cruel, to take a mother's child away."

"People here aren't like that," the judge said. The women stared at him malevolently.

"What would you know?" the mother said. Each word came out like a tiny explosion.

"I know something," the judge said. He was agitating them both.

I said, "How old was your child?"

"Oh, she was two, little precious, perfect, perfect." She coughed. Unconsciously she was aping the judge's language; she stumbled over the word perfect, because it was not commonly spoken.

"And was she a good girl?" I said. I knew of the child's tantrums and her attacks.

"She was an angel." I saw small cuts on the woman's arms, a scratch across her face. Her shins were bruised. She coughed.

"No trouble? I'm just thinking that perhaps someone lost their temper with her."

The mother's eyes widened at the suggestion.

"It's possible."

"Maybe," said her companion.

"So where had you been previously?" said the judge. "And who was minding the child?"

"She's very capable," said the mother.

"Yes. She tells us what to do half the time," said the companion. The two chuckled together.

We did not speak for many minutes. The companion had a coughing fit and a great fuss was made to soothe her throat. I glanced at the judge and he winked at me. He practised the art of silence; he thought that silence and guilt could make a person yabber. But nervousness can do that, too. And guilt isn't the only cause of nervousness.

Neither of the women yabbered and finally the judge rose.

"We are very sorry for your loss. It is a loss which will affect the whole community, because each child is ours and precious."

It took all my strength to keep my hands from covering my belly; some early protective instinct.

"We will complete our discussions in the open court," I said. There was no police force in our community; there was no need for one. Earlier, some attempt had been made, a protective force, it was said, but no one wanted to join.

So the judge and I were alone in our work.

The judge insisted we should go to the theatre, a strange choice, I thought, but I did not say so; he was certain it was clever to find the people together, talkative and happy. People disliked being asked questions. Invasive questions often meant hurt to some, although there was nothing to be ashamed of anymore.

For me, it was a chance to enjoy some entertainment, a little guiltily. It was so much easier being there without Leo; I could watch without describing, though from the mutter about me, others were not so released.

The play was a new one, penned by one of us, and the audience recoiled, laughed, shouted and snorted, as required. It was a fuller play, clearer, than anything I had seen before the rockets left, and the actors were so smooth, so without ego, I was lost in the performances. It was a full house and it struck me as I gazed on the faces about me that none showed strain; none were there from condescension, duty, or guilt.

The playwright had polio, the actors were blind or limped, they were all damaged in some way and none of it mattered. Oh, God. The terror if the rockets ever return.

We saw the grieving mother and her companion during interval; they sat with the fingerless restaurant owner who came to my side and whispered, "My restaurant is not for questioners."

"I am only a listener," I said.

"Then you are a fool to yourself," she said.

I could not speak back. Because she was right; we do not like to be questioned. We like to accept creation and its beauty. We accept our luck, that we are here and they are not. We don't seek answers to why, who, how or when. We tacitly agree that questions led to the world's destruction.

So it irks them when the judge and I make them face answers they don't want to face.

I was entranced by the play, the actor's faces. I jumped when the judge spoke. "What is the audience saying? Are you listening?"

I had thought I was listening to partners describing the play. Then I listened beneath the words, and I heard the mutter. My ears are fine. Like those of a clever pink rabbit.

I heard, "strong," and "danger." I heard "mother" and "sacrifice." I heard the words, "the children will do it," and the words "grow stronger" and "every day." All mutter, mutter, below the surface.

"Everyone is talking about the play," I told the judge. It was the first time I failed to do my job correctly.

I was home late again that night; the sky was light. Leo was already in bed, but he left a candle burning by the front door so I could find my way in. It was close to burning to the ground; he had been in bed for a while. He trusted me to be home in time to blow the candle out, and if I wasn't, he would blame himself for the house burning down.

I let my clothes slip to the floor and slid into bed with him. His body was a furnace; I felt burnt by its touch.

He sighed as I fitted myself to him. The sigh stopping my loving hands and roving fingers.

When the rockets first left us, and Leo and I thought we were alone, before we joined another pair, and the four of us joined eight, and we became a community, Leo and I slept under the sky and made love every night.

I had imagined this to be heaven; a life spent with my lover, the person who understood me completely, as I understood him. But I found myself desperate for a new opinion, a new subject to discuss. Leo felt the same way, I'm sure. He sighed sometimes, like the sigh he gave when I snuggled beside him, as if boredom had filled his lungs and expelled the air.

I did not rise when I should have in the evening. I stayed with my husband, and told him all I had heard.

He said, "It is clearly the mother, then?"

I said it was, but the reason why was not so clear. We lay together in our dark bedroom, no chink of light allowed in. Leo loves the sun, like the judge, even at its hottest. He raises his head to it, and he sees orange. Orange is the only colour he knows, apart from black. Our little joke is that I describe everything in orange or black. He can't stay out in it too long; he's like most of us. But the burn of it on his skin makes him almost see. He said once, when we had made love three times and drank so much tea we were up and down to piss, he told me he had not expected the sun to burn like that in his lifetime. Or his child's. It should have taken so much longer.

We were in the community by then, and the doctor said we were safe to have another child. The doctor was once a doctor's son, but he learnt enough, hearing his father work, to practice now.

He was a very small man, who sat on your knee to look into your throat; he had spent a lot of time under his father's desk, or in his coat cupboard.

"I wanted to know how others suffered," he said. "Because I had aches and pains, I was so small. I dreamed of being complete."

I liked to visit the doctor, though he was a very busy man. Those tiny hands running over my body, that child's voice saying, "Hmmm. Hmmm." He told me there was every chance my baby would be born without damage.

"After all, you should hardly be here, yourself," he said, then scribbled at his pad. He was blushing, like a child with a crush. He subscribed rosemary to me; he was scribbling directions to find a marvellous bush. He was always so busy, "All these lungs," he said often. "If only people didn't have to breathe."

So Leo and I began to try again.

I did not feel like facing the evening's work, so I gave into luxury and spent some hours reading. Such worlds of knowledge in books; unabridged, they present to me information I could never have received from any electronic media. I smell the pages, hear the smooth slap of air as I work my way through. Obsolete, yet more than adequate.

I read aloud to Leo, stories of adventure at sea, tigers, hunters, love against the odds. It was a marvellous evening. I felt my baby was listening, so I chose happy stories. I didn't want salt tears in my womb.

The judge destroyed my comfortable mood not long after I collected him. He felt we had wasted the night, and was not interested in hearing what I had learned about the function of lighthouses.

Our first visit was to the bed of a new mother in a home just doors from the court. The doctor was concerned about the welfare of the baby, and the judge wished to see for himself. I had avoided such situations; I did not want to be led to questions I didn't want to answer. What would I say if the doctor mentioned my pregnancy?

The woman's child lay crying in its box in the corner of her bedroom. She lay with her back to it, her eyes staring at the wall. I went to her; the judge went to the baby.

"Look at you," he said, very softly. "So strong, so perfect." He turned to woman.

"Is he sighted? Can he hear?"

The woman didn't answer. I leaned close, said, "Did you hear the judge's question?"

Her gaze flicked from the wall to me and back. "The doctor said there's nothing wrong with him."

The crying increased; she raised one webbed hand and placed it over her exposed ear. "He said I was very lucky."

"Would you like someone to help you care for the baby?" I said.

"Oh, no," she said. "I can take care of it." She coughed.

In retrospect, I wonder if I deliberately didn't listen to her.

"What do you hear, Lydia?" the judge said.

"I hear a tired woman who loves her baby," I said. "I hear a partner downstairs who can care for both for the next two weeks. We can return then."

"We will."

We went then to our empty courtroom; there were no cases to hear. Neither of us were sure where to proceed with the murder investigation—we had studied law for entertainment, and now we had a system, but not the spirit. I did not want to ask him his findings; I was afraid they were the same as my own. And we had no jails. We had no execution apparatus. We had no desire for these things. Yet, what would warre do with a woman who killed her child? Exile was the only option; so cruel. It was lonely out there.

I said, "You know we will do anything to keep our world safe."

The judge shook his head. "We cannot allow it, Lydia," he said, and he talked and I listened, and no one came to see us. When at last he began to sleep, I covered him with his rug and left him there. He hated to be moved while he was not conscious. It made him feel helpless.

I told Leo about the new baby and its mother's dislike. Our baby kicked at me, kicked, kicked, and I said, "Our baby seems very strong." I placed his hand on my belly. He smiled.

I saw his face was marked.

"What happened?" I said, my fingers stroking him.

It was a fresh cut, long across his eyebrow.

"Oh, Leo. Did it bleed?"

"It bled," he said.

"Did you fall?"

"Oh, no. I visited the school, just wandered my way over there. I was feeling anxious."

"Can't wait, my love?"

"Something like that. By the time I made it to the school, it was their lunch break; I could hear the noise on the oval. I followed the noise, stood behind the rail and someone described them for me. He said they were running about, collecting piles of things—he couldn't tell. Then he said, my goodness, rocks. The children each picked up a rock and the teenager said, 'Ten points for a walking stick,' and they threw their rocks. Then he said, 'Fifty points for a dwarf,' and again they threw the rocks.

"The man told me this; I thought it was a trick. I would trot away and be laughed at for my cowardice. So I stayed.

"'Five points for a squeeze-eye,' the teenager said. That was me; that was those of us who can't see. That's when my eyebrow was split open. My new friend helped me home. And there it is."

"But what did everyone do?"

"We just stood there and accepted what they offered us." I cleansed his wound; it was not so bad.

"At the other school, the children are learning well, I've heard. Well-loved children. Who don't attack the elders," I said. In the next community was a school for the children who weren't so perfect, to quote the judge.

"Perhaps that is the place for us, then," Leo said. We did not discuss the kicking mule in my belly, though I imagined travelling to that other place, when we were three.

I was awoken the next night by the messenger.

"We must fetch the judge," he said. "Only another baby has died."

I said, "We will go there first." We went to the home we had visited the night before. I bade the messenger wait outside and entered alone. The baby's throat had been cut carefully across. It was in its box still; the weapon on the floor. The mother was dusting the room, fluffing the bedclothes, opening windows to let in the fresh evening air.

The father sat in an armchair in the corner, watching. His large ears seemed to turn at every sound; he did not speak through his tiny mouth. I thought he sat forward in sorrow and went to comfort him, but saw his hunch pushed him into the position. I patted his shoulder and went to the mother.

"Can you tell me what happened?" I said.

"I woke up and the baby was dead," she said. I saw no sign of tears.

I thought of our new world and how long it had been since I was laughed at. I thought of the judge, his love of strength, perfection, and the truth. And I carefully folded the knife into a piece of cloth.

"We'll go to the judge now," I said to the messenger. I coughed. I knew he would be sitting where I left him, in the court, but let the messenger take me to the judge's home. He lives alone.

"Only he is not home," the messenger said.

"How very odd," I said. "Let's check his place of work."

And there was the judge, where I had left him.

"Judge," I said, before he could speak and accuse me of neglect. The messenger breathed closely behind me. "There's been another infanticide." I shook his arm with deliberate roughness. Shook free the knife, which fell to the floor. The messenger bent to it with a gasp.

"Leave it," I said. "Evidence."

I often wonder if my actions were misguided. If perhaps the killings should be blameful, not lawful. Perhaps the mothers should have been charged with murder, not the judge with treason. But Leo says it is inevitable; what the rocket people called survival of the fittest. And that is good. I would not like to die famous for such a thing. Everyone was happy to accept that the judge was a danger to our world. It made their own actions seem noble.

Leo and I are settled in the new community, now. We were welcomed here; Leo for his shoes, I for my knowledge, my judgment. I will not be judge here, though; they will have to find their own scapegoat. Babies are dying here, too.

We feel safe.

Here, we are away from the memories, the guilt. And I do feel guilty; I will never forget the sight of the exiled judge, painfully rolling himself away. He did not stand against my accusation. But he said, "You cannot fear that which is superior. Otherwise you must fear all creation." This seemed telling only in my favour, but it didn't make me feel better about sending him away.

There were times, before we arrived in this safe place, when I feared the child in my womb, and thought perhaps I would better serve my people by not allowing it to be born. Because what if this child was born perfect, and came to believe it was better than us? What if it began to miss the rocket people, people it never knew, and to despise us?

The mothering instinct was more powerful than these things.

But you, my daughter, were born with a twisted leg, and you are safe and so are we. So I tell you this story, again and again, so you will never forget the wonders of being alive.

I was a judge listener. These things I heard and saw; these things I did not judge.

TIGER KILL

———

Tara's gown was so tight she couldn't breathe. Karl would make her leave the dress on, later, when she would lie back and take it.

She followed him into the dining room.

The only other woman at the table laughed like a man and didn't cringe from their crude talk. There were seven men at the table. It was the only table in the room.

Tara noticed the thickness of the linen tablecloth, wondered what it would be like to sleep on. It was changed after every one of the thirty courses. Cutlery and plates didn't clang when collected. A distraction was performed in the corner of the room as the table was cleared each time; a naked woman bending over backwards to grasp her toes; a dwarf gulping beer from a glass taller than he; two children kissing and touching each other intimately; a cat forced somehow into a large bottle, with just enough room to turn around around aroundroundroundround; a naked man with idiot eyes and an enormous penis which reached, engorged, almost to his fat, pink, hairless nipples; a woman with festering cuts who held her arms and legs for display like a fashion model, showing maggots at their chewing work; a tall, oiled, hairless girl scoring herself lightly with a sharp blade till she shone with a thin coating of blood; an old man weakly stamping wine grapes, a foot in either of two transparent buckets; a man, drawn and grey, dancing a jig, his raised arms revealing hairless armpits, his shrivelled genitals thumping against his thigh, each leap a day less to live.

All these distractions so the diners would not notice that linen leaving. Tara fingered the material under the table, wishing her knees were bare so she could feel its texture there.

In an avuncular gesture, Karl gave her a ginger lolly, dug from the corner of his coat pocket. This to gum her mouth, keep her silent on this important night.

As they talked around her, mouths full of octopus legs, lettuce soup, deep fried salt and pepper periwinkles, china tea, wine, she thought of the story of Little Black Sambo, such a racist story now. Little Black Sambo begged his mother to make pancakes for his breakfast, and she agreed, if he would run to the stall for butter. "Oh, yes," he agreed. Such a treat.

But on the way back he was spotted by the man-eating tigers. They chased him up the tree, and the sun melted his butter all over their heads. This made them angry, so they ran around the tree faster, faster, around, around aroundroundround, trying to make Little Black Sambo dizzy, fall off.

But it was so hot, and they ran so fast, the lovely butter yellow fur of them began to blur as they ran faster. They ran so fast they turned into butter which Little Black Sambo took home to his mother.

"Such lovely butter," the mother said.

"Oh, yes," Little Black Sambo said, as he sat down to his plate stacked high with springy, hot pancakes.

Tara had loved that story as a child; had always wished for that plate of pancakes to be hers. As the next course came out on a sizzling hot dish, she wished again for those pancakes.

Karl took her plate and piled it with the grey flesh. The other woman had not smudged her lipstick. She seemed to suck the food in without using her lips or chewing. Tara watched the woman eat the meat and did not ask what it was.

"Like it?" the men asked Tara one by one. She had not swallowed the single mouthful she had taken. It sat on her tongue. She smiled around it.

They waited for her answer. It was a trick, of course. If she said yes, the meat would be bear, or cat, or human; the naming of which would make her stomach heave. If she said no, it would only be beef, done in a special way, and she would be the foolish one.

Karl would not let her go to the toilet, although the meal went for many hours. It was a test of strength. She thought perhaps the irritation in her bladder could be mistaken for sexual desire. Perhaps that was the purpose.

She swallowed the meat and did not answer the question. The plate was so large it must have carried the entire animal; what could be so fleshy? They ate sago broth with opium and honey, stir-fried ginger, caraway seeds, coriander, carrots, peas, spinach, cabbage, potato and onion. They ate tomatoes stuffed with avocado and truffle and pimento. Each course came out, the table cleaned between each, and the entertainment went on in the corner of the room. The men ordered the servants about loudly, each trying harder to be more demanding. Karl told them such servants were called tigers, once and that ladies' attendants were called pages. The men began to say, "Hey, tiger," to the servants, because it was the only way they would tame such a creature, by giving its name to a servant.

Tara and the other woman didn't call their attendants "page."

As the soup was being prepared, the man who claimed to have caught the tigers came to their table. They all knew he was the hunter, and they wanted to hear the story of how brave the tigers were, how the man nearly died.

"The tiger becomes obsessed with the animal it kills. It doesn't leave the slightest taste, and will eat the internal organs, the eyeballs, the hooves, the strings and bows of that beloved creature."

The hunter watched Tara, took in her position, her breasts, the colour of her skin.

The hunter moved around the table as he spoke. They ate quails, tossed the bones over their shoulders, and the crackle of the bones seemed to be his jungle floor, his boneyard.

The hunter circled the table, making them twist their necks.

Karl scraped the last of the sauce from the central bowl. Somewhere teeth crunched on gristle.

"The flesh may rot and still the tiger will stay. Near that meat it will live, sleep, for as long as it takes."

The next course arrived, each person given a different portion, some a little more, some a little less. She watched them stare at each other's plates and covet that extra mouthful. Asparagus spears with hollandaise sauce, radishes always within reach, and phallus-shaped bread, which they tore with their hands and did not take the time to butter.

"The tiger will not share with any scavenger. A deer may last six days, a buffalo perhaps weeks. Because the tiger has to work so hard, it has to spend its life hunting. So a large kill is like a holiday. He doesn't want to cut it short."

"So all a hunter has to do," Tara thought, "is watch the vultures overhead and find that tiger's feast. And there will be an over-fed, rested tiger, protective of his feast, not expecting danger. All a man has to do is take the prey with a full stomach."

Even at just a mouthful of each dish, her belly was swollen against the tight metallic shine of her dress. Her mother had worn a tight dress too, and her grandmother. They wore tight dresses and remained silent. They lived with legs ready to spread and died on a whim.

"Oh, yes. Until the tigers learned that man knew their habits. Then the holiday was over. Then it was just a mouthful, a single meal from every kill and then away to find more food. A tiger needs thirty cattle a year to live. How much do you think a man needs?"

No one knew. They were no longer listening to the hunter. The other woman had begun the story about a recent assignation, how foolish the man had looked. Each man at the table imagined how he would impress her. They became anxious for the Tiger's Penis Soup, wanting its juices, its life-giving, ever-growing goodness.

The hunter pulled a chair behind Tara. She alone was interested in how the tiger died. As the soup reached the table, the man Karl wanted most to impress said, "I've heard that when a man or beast dies, his soul enters his penis. So we gobble the tiger's soul."

The table laughed heartily. Tara opened her mouth wide at Karl's prodding; as if she, too, found this a delight.

She wondered, but did not ask, where the soul of a woman goes.

The soup cost thousands for the nine of them, the rest of the banquet the same again, and then there was the wine. They needed two tigers' penises for a tureen large enough for ten. It is rare to find two males together in the wild because they like to keep their space, and their females, to themselves. The soup is considered to be an aphrodisiac.

The stock is chicken, a fresh chicken straight into the pot, cooked over day-long heat, strained through muslin. Most delicate. The flesh is discarded, given to the cat or used for the spring rolls.

And then the soup was before them, presented in a gold-edged porcelain tureen made by the finest potter. The hunter presented the lid, allowed steam to reach the noses of those at the tables.

"Just the smell," he said, breathing deeply.

"I paid for that steam," Karl's boss said.

To Tara, it smelt like boiled meat.

There was silence as they swallowed the soup. They waited, each mouthful, for the promised erection, the promised desire, and they winked at each other like young boys pretending to have sprouted pubic bush.

Tara swallowed her portion, did not bite the secret ingredients but let them slide whole down her throat.

Later, she would think of the tiger's penis as Karl pretended virility. It was so long, twisted. She would feel his tiger's dick reaching up through her intestines to her lungs, where it would squeeze, squeeze, would not let her breathe.

The other woman sucked the fingers of the man to her left. The man to her right licked her lips, her chin, her cheeks, with a rough tongue.

"What about the rest of the tiger?" Karl's boss said, "do we get any of that?"

"Oh, no," said the woman serving them. She was a short woman, dressed in heels which made her tall. "That tiger, he's thrown away. No good. Skin with a bullet hole, stained, all that. Once, a tiger would have been all used up, when people believed in such things. His meat would be swallowed for the stomach trouble. His fur used for ladies' clothes. His brain for curing laziness, sure enough. His gallstones to give better vision. And his tail, in the bath, makes your skin soft.

"His eyes will stop convulsions and all his fangs, his claws, his whiskers, make a powerful love charm." She laughed. "People were so silly. Now, we just take him for his penis, for the soup. And how was it?"

Tara could feel the hunter's hot breath on her neck.

The man opposite Tara gave the waitress a squeeze, a pinch, a wink. "Just lovely. Lovely."

The next course was brought out, a mountain of batter pieces, holding surprises Tara didn't want to receive.

As Karl reached for another lychee, she realised how big his hands were, like baseball mitts or paws, broad, short fingers, a vast expanse of palm.

The hunter whispered to Tara, "Once the tigers couldn't be caught by taking their food, the hunter would set up a Tiger Kill."

Only she was listening. Only she could hear.

"The hunters tie a nice deer to a tree and wait. They rustle and make noise, because the tiger hears well. He sees well, too, but his sense of smell is poor, unless he is hunting the prey of love. If the creature stayed perfectly still, well-hidden, quiet, the tiger wouldn't find it. The moment the creature tries to run, the tiger leaps."

They ate quince tart, pears stewed with ginger wine and steeped with mint, honeycomb with bee's wings still attached, vanilla and chocolate icecream, then at last the meal was over. The men went to their rooms where women had been summoned. The other woman went with Karl's boss. Tara went with Karl.

He lay on the bed, his stomach a pink balloon. When he shut his eyes, she locked herself in the bathroom and relieved herself.

"Out you come," he said. She could tell by his playful tone he was naked.

Then his tiger's penis was at work, his fingers were about her throat, he was squeezing, squeezing. She reached for a weapon and grasped his belt. Lifting it high, she struck his back with a thick thwap, but he enjoyed the sting of it.

She became aware of a figure standing over them. It was the hunter. He raised his club and hit Karl on the side of the head, knocking him off her, away from her.

"Thank you, my dear," the hunter said. She grabbed her shoes as he crouched over the body, nestling the penis in his hand. As she left the room, she heard the thud and click so familiar to her; a brother's knife; a father's; a lover's knife.

So as not to disturb the hunter at his work she closed the door quietly behind her.

Tara didn't use the lift because she wanted to feel the strength of her muscles. As she descended the stairs, she rubbed at her make-up so it ran in streaks over her face, brushed out her curls with spread fingers. The

hunter could not be expected to spare her again.
Next time, she would be ready.

THE WRONG SEAT

After her death, Moira Braddon caught the six p.m. Sunday bus, a three hour trip, every week without fail. She sought sense amongst the passengers who travelled with her; looked for signs they had been affected by her death. She wondered which of the women it could have been, which of the women who travelled every week could have been in an aisle seat and fallen victim instead of Moira. She was lost and confused; she hated these people because she meant nothing to them and she loved them because they were everything to her.

She loved the man who had been sitting in her seat when she had climbed on the bus at five to six. It was her seat; the ticket said so. As an experienced traveller, she knew that booking in early and boarding late meant a good window seat and less crowding. Yet Moira, weak after a soul-destroying weekend, smiled at the man who had the window seat. She sat in the aisle seat and the man settled comfortably.

She would have loved someone to talk to, perhaps to make laugh, about her disastrous weekend. But she couldn't tell her travelling companion. She couldn't tell anyone. There was no one who would listen to her, not avidly. Not with interest, because her single status was of concern to no one but herself. Twenty-eight years of age and even a dirty weekend was beyond her, her trip away a failed attempt at romance. An embarrassing failure; she had over-estimated his interest. She had taken kindness and pity for lust, and built up the relationship in her mind until a late trip on Friday night and an appearance on the door step seemed a logical, inevitable step.

She had stayed at the hotel the full weekend out of pride. At his shocked (appalled, really, even terrified) face, his inability to pretend to be happy, she lied. "I've come to see a friend, just thought I'd pop in to say hello."

"Hello," he said. "Nice to see you." He did not lid his eyes in lust, although her silk shirt clung about her breasts and was tied to reveal her smooth, brown belly.

She wore the silk shirt all weekend, only left her room to buy snacks from the foyer, and watched videos and snacked until it was time to check out at ten in the morning. Then she wandered town all day, pretending to have someone to meet, waving and smiling at people who weren't there, so that others would think she wasn't alone. It was beyond understanding, her lack of popularity. She was pretty enough, and tried so hard not to let people down. No matter what they wanted she smiled and said yes, yet remained lonely.

She climbed on the bus at five to six.

Uninterested in the movie playing, an old adventure story, shown on a TV so badly magnetised the colour was three diagonal bands of green, grey and red, she watched it all the same.

The man next to her stared out the window. Once, Moira laughed at a joke in the movie. She leaned to him, so they could laugh together, but his face pulled into a wince of irritation.

She watched the movie and waited for the trip to end.

It was someone on their way to the toilet who killed her. Leaned over and slit her throat. He leaned over, and she smiled at him, thinking he was about to kiss her and wondering why, but still happy to be kissed so spontaneously.

At first she didn't realise what he had done. She felt a coldness across her throat, thought it was his touch and thrilled to its alien nature.

She opened her eyes but he was gone.

She gurgled in surprise. They were very close to home. She was in pain, but didn't understand why. She touched the man at her side, wanting him to look at her, tell her what was wrong, but he shifted his arm away.

He grunted irritably at the noise she was making, the snuffling and the dripping.

She felt for her handbag, absurdly wanting to show the driver her ticket before she asked for help.

The bag was gone, and she felt cheated. That was all this was about? A small amount of money and some over-used credit cards? She thought about the letter she had written to a friend, detailing graphically and falsely her sexual activities of the weekend. Her killer would read that and think it true, perhaps, then regret killing such a woman. Or he would laugh at it, remember her eager, reaching face and laugh.

The man who killed her got out at the first city stop.

She stood up just as the driver was going around a corner, lost her balance and pressed her hand onto someone's shoulder. They hissed.

She discovered standing and walking were not possible anyway; she was weak.

Her breasts were slick with blood. She felt constrained, and tugged weakly at the buttons of the shirt till they slipped out of their holes.

She spread her shirt open. The man next to her glanced at her, but saw perhaps a dark singlet. The unhealthy glow of the flickering street lights did not aid vision. And if she could not understand her state, how could he?

She wondered if they would call her Moira Braddon, or if her name would become The Passenger in Six B—or Six A, as her ticket said.

When the lights came on as the bus rolled into the depot, the man who had taken her seat looked at her and shouted, "You stupid bitch," though how it was her fault he didn't say.

Nobody wanted to stay around with a dead body on board. They were off the bus and waiting for their luggage before Moira could sneeze. They collected bags, and left. Names were a matter of record, addresses the manager took, apologising for the inconvenience. People were annoyed, then. They felt guilty at first, then when they were told how inconvenient it was they were annoyed. They went off into the night, home to where no bodies lay.

The man who had not known she was dying was allowed to go as well.

Moira caught the six p.m. bus the following Sunday because she was tired of hanging around the depot. She wandered up and down the aisle; she didn't know what to do. She sat on the laps of people who had window seats and stared out. She kicked the back of the chair in front but the person did not wake up.

She would have liked to see her funeral but she seemed confined to the depot and the bus. It would have been a dismally attended affair; she couldn't pretend otherwise. Her mother would have cried and the others would have waited till it was over and left. She always wanted to be cremated but hoped her mother hadn't listened. It didn't seem as final, now, being popped into the ground.

She caught the Sunday bus again.

Each time, there were familiar faces; passengers from the trip where she died. She never saw the man who killed her; he was somewhere else now. She wouldn't see him again. She wouldn't close her eyes for a kiss. She forgot him; and he had touched her in a way no one else had.

Finally, the man who had sat next to her was on board. He had a window seat again.

She leaned over the woman in the aisle seat—a middle-aged woman reading a book with deep interest. She stared at the man who had let her die; who hadn't noticed her vanishing.

He stared out the window. Moira twisted herself around until she could see directly into his eyes. She looked for some image, a picture of herself snapped there, or some reason for his inactivity. His nose wrinkled. He glanced at the middle-aged woman as if imagining the smell came from her. But her nose wrinkled too. "Must be the toilet," she said, although the occupied light had not shown so far on the journey.

Moira was distressed to learn that she smelt. She had always been very clean, her clothes and her body. She didn't catch any buses for a while but found she was very lonely at the depot. She would just begin to enjoy the warmth of a person and they would catch their bus. At least when she journeyed with them she could have them for longer.

After a while, she didn't care about her stink. She would sit next to people who had an empty seat, sit there and talk to them as if they were real. Some would breathe into a palm to see if it was their breath.

Moira grinned into their faces, waiting for them to notice her.

She left her shoes behind and wore her stockinged feet. She climbed onto the backs of seats and waved her feet under their noses.

She grew to need those looks of disgust, because they meant she existed.

Walking naked up and down the aisle, she bent and breathed into the faces of the sleepers, breathing into their dreams, giving them nightmares of cesspits and poison.

She liked to lie down in the aisle as they got off. The people walked over her and she raised her arms to let them smell her sweat. They climbed off quickly when she lay there, like they had when she had died on the journey, when she was carried off on the last night of her life.

It was good when the videos were running, because she could watch the screen, and the people's eyes were open and staring. She tried to see herself reflected, but they always blinked too soon.

Whenever the man who had ignored her death was on the bus she spent the whole trip with him. He always had the window seat, and it took her a while to realise that he was staring at his reflection, not the dark world flashing by.

She sat between his toes, or stood leaning over him. He began to get used to her smell.

He usually sat alone because people would ask to move. They thought the smell was him.

She breathed into his ear. She said, "How was it my fault? Why blame me? Didn't you see him? Why did you let me bleed and die? I bled and died without you turning your head. Didn't you smell my blood? Where are you going? Where are you going? Where do you go?" She followed him to the door of the bus and waved him goodbye like a lover. He always took a few steps away from her, stopped, took deep lungsful of air. He sucked air that didn't smell of her, and she wandered up and down the aisles of the buses, her breath redolent of rotten teeth, the air in her wake like diarrhoea, her underarms like years of grime.

The last time she clung onto his back like the old man in the sea, wrapped her legs around his waist, her arms around his neck, hoping that she could go with him that way.

He pushed other people aside to get off the bus, seeking the air outside. He pushed hard, rudely and blindly, and as he ran down the steps the other passengers collectively pushed back. He was thrown from the bus and landed with his head against a pole; he did not move.

Moira looked at him and thought, "Enough."

Then she left, before he could rise and give chase.

SKIN HOLES

I can sit up in bed now. William says it won't be long before I'm about. I have a big window to look through; today I saw a man sitting in shoes, no socks. The skin on his ankles made me stare until he caught me and stared back. The skin there was rough and brown, like a tree trunk. Like two little trees were growing straight out of his shoes. That skin looked tough. That skin you could pierce and pinch without causing any pain. I envied that skin, ugly as it was.

I would never have even skinned if it wasn't for William. I was eighteen when we met; well past the age when people usually begin. But I never liked the idea of it. Then I met William and we fell in love. He loved me as I was for about two months, then he started pinching my flesh, lifting it off my bones and smiling. He was well holed himself. It surprised me he went out with me, sometimes, because he was so fine, so thin, and I was so plain and dull.

I met him at the bus stop after a busy day at kindy; the kids had been noisy, boisterous. It took the whole day for the teachers to calm them down, then off they went, quiet as mice with their parents. They didn't like me to help with discipline. I just gave out the play doh and rolled out the sleeping mats. And gave the kids hugs. They all loved hugging me. They said I was soft. I didn't have any rings, either, no rings to stick into them. They were happy in their little school. I hope they miss me. I hope they remember me.

I was happy at school for a long time. I wasn't clever and I wasn't pretty, so everyone liked me. Then, after a while at High School, everyone started to skin and hole. I wasn't allowed, didn't want to anyway, and they started to hate me then. I didn't finish High School. Mostly because of that.

I always daydream at the bus stop—everyone else reads; books, magazines or papers. I hate reading. I think it's really boring; it takes too long. I'd rather wait for the movie, or get someone to read aloud to me.

"What?" said the guy standing next to me. I was trying not to look at him; he was too beautiful.

"What?" he repeated.

I had been fantasising about giving a thank you speech on stage for an award of some kind. I looked very thin on stage but I had no holes.

"Nothing," I said. "Sorry. I was talking to myself."

"You said, 'Thank you, thank you.' Do you usually talk to yourself?"

I laughed. Nervous and shy. The bus came past, jam-packed full.

This beautiful creature said, "Do you wanna share a taxi? My shout."

There've been other times when a choice was clear before me—the safe way, leaving my life as it was or the risky way, sending my life spinning out of control. I could see the choice clearly here. I had always chosen safety; this day I said, "Okay."

He seemed to like me a lot. He thought I was funny and he made love to me often. It wasn't all that good the first time. It was strange to have someone looking at my body so carefully. I was used to what it looked like. He kissed my toes and my shins, then he sucked his breath in.

"What's wrong?" I asked. It could be anything.

"Don't you shave your legs?" He sounded distant to me. I always send voices away when they are hurtful.

"My skin is very tender. A razor or wax hurts too much. Even woollen clothes scratch sometimes."

He nodded, but stopped kissing me.

He was a beautiful lover. I only had one short affair before him. Very short. Meaning once, in my parents' room while they were shopping. It was horrible, and he was a horrible boy. Compared to him, William was a prince, even though his bones left bruises on my flesh and the rings all over his body pressed and left marks like ringworm. It took me a little while to ask him to remove the ring from the head of his penis, just when we made love. But he did it.

"Only for you, Valerie," he said. That was the night he started pinching my flesh. He stroked my hair as well.

"Such soft, dark hair," he said. It was the one thing I had which was lovely, compared to others. They had limp hair, lifeless. Mine shone and was healthy.

He didn't talk about himself much. He spoke mostly about the people who loved him. How he had helped them because of that love, changed them. I promised myself I would love him that much too.

And he did change me, a little. Mum and Dad began avoiding me; they didn't want to know what I was doing. Mum just fed me well, and I ate what she gave me, so long as William wasn't there. If he was I'd say, "I'm not hungry," and he'd squeeze my thigh. Later he'd give me a reward; a massage, or he'd talk to me about what I could become.

He made me feel different inside my body.

I can remember the night I decided to skin. We went to a party with his friends. They were all so thin, and they were well holed. They were funny, witty. They did all sorts of things some people might find offensive. Not me. I don't mind what anyone does. Mum and Dad partly taught me that but they'd add, "So long as you don't hurt anyone." William and his friends say, "Where's the fun in that?" I know they're only joking. That's the sort of thing they joke about. I could never think of remarks like that. They tried to be nice to me but they just aren't used to fat people. I was sixty kilograms and for a height of one and a half metres, that's pretty huge.

I never felt fat inside, or when I was home with Mum and Dad. They're both big-sized and old-fashioned. They were proud of me, the envy of their friends because I stayed at home most of the time. The only thing Mum got mad about was my posture. She said I walked like I had a hunched back. It's all right for her. She doesn't care what people think. She walks around with her breasts pointing out, even though breasts are ugly. Curves are ugly. Boys' bodies are sexy. When I walked with my shoulders curled to my chest, my body was not so noticeable.

I had avoided skinning and holing for so long because I hoped it would pass as a trend. It didn't though, and it wasn't just the young. Parents were doing it too and I was becoming part of a shrinking minority. People used go to work or school during the day, just little dents in the skin to show where the rings went, dressed respectable and nice. Then the sun would go down and the clothes would change, they'd strip off and put the rings back in for all to see. Now people leave them in, the holes don't close up that way, and they're all doing it.

I can remember when I was little, people only had holes in their ears.

I used to like eating my lunch in the park. I liked sitting there, watching the other people; it's like TV. I can watch it as much as I like now; William got me a little one to put by my bed. I used to only watch it at other people's houses because Mum and Dad threw out our TV. They said it only shows the new world, not the one that makes sense, the one they know. They read lots of books instead. I hate reading.

All these thin people in the park walk around instead of eating. Once, while I was waiting for William to arrive, I had a cheese sandwich. It was delicious, with fresh bread and that thin cheese. Usually people ignored me, pretended I wasn't there, fat thing, a blob on the grass. I was up to my second half when this true thin guy came up.

He said, "How can you eat? People starve around the world and you stuff yourself to obesity."

"It's only one sandwich," I said. He was even thinner than William. I felt like if I shouted, my air would blow him away.

"It's a week's food for some, you glutton."

I stood up and walked off quickly. He was too weak to follow as fast.

He said, "Glutton!" into the wind. I hid around the corner till I saw William. He did not want to hear the story, for shame. He was ashamed of how I ate. He gave me a particularly cruel lecture about myself, and I was so upset I said, "Why do you even go out with me then, if I'm so horrible?"

He calmed down then. He said, "I'm the only one who can save you."

"People love to attack others," Mum said when I told her about the man in the park. "And they love to justify their own stupidities. Once it was that if you didn't eat, the food was wasted. Now they want you to starve." I also told her what William said, about saving me, and she just gave me a tight squeeze.

When I hugged Mum or Dad, no bones clanged and jarred.

I got my ears pierced on the spur of the moment soon after I met William. One in each ear. I didn't like it much. William smiled when he saw it and seemed pleased. He was the expert on how to avoid infection, so a few times a day (whenever he thought of it, really) he would wash his hands carefully and sit me down. Then he would slowly spin the earrings through the holes, so that each part of the metal saw daylight.

I never told William, but the feeling made me sick. It hurt a little, because the flesh dragged with it, but it wasn't that which was so horrible.

It was the metal inside me, spinning, taking space in my body like it belonged there. That's what I hated. But William loved doing it. And my ears didn't get infected. But they didn't make me feel beautiful, either.

I spent some lonely times with William. I felt very lucky for a while, then I began to feel like a weight around his neck, a ring in his nose. A couple of times he made excuses why I should stay home, not go out with his friends, and I knew he was ashamed of me. When, at that party I hated so much, I heard him telling his friends that I was going to skin soon, even though we hadn't discussed it I knew I would have to do it in order to keep him.

The only skins worth going on are the speed ones. The others drop the weight off but your skin shrinks with it, so there's no point. You've got to lose it in a few weeks, so the skin hangs loose and is easily pierced.

I didn't tell anyone except William what I was doing, especially not my parents. I took a little holiday and went to William's house. I thought I could make him happy. Now I could make him love me.

The doctor gave me the nutrient pills to eat. I had one big last meal, and when I woke up the next day I started my skin. It made me sick, that I needed that last meal. I'll never tell William what I ate. I wished on a star that night; wished that once I started my skin, I would no longer love food as much. I would hate food, and never dream of eating it in such quantities again.

I know my parents won't try to find me. They don't know how to control me any more, and I never thought I'd get to say that. They can't deal with me because I'm different from them now. Just like the world is different so they ignore it. They ignore me almost completely. I no longer make any sense. They haven't been to visit me. They don't even know what I look like any more.

Only William makes sense to me. Only he loves me. On the way home from that party, he asked me if I believed in God. I told him the truth and waited for him to laugh. I do believe in God. I believe he is a man in the sky who will be there when I die.

William didn't laugh. He said, "Well, you must believe that your body is a temple of God then. He created it."

I hadn't believed that before but it made sense.

William said, "You should worship the temple by making it as beautiful and adorned as possible. The way you look now, I don't see that you love God at all." But he wasn't trying to talk me into skinning. He was just helping me make up my mind.

I decided I'd have another ring in my ear, and one in my nose. That would be enough. I was angry with myself for not being braver, but that's the fault of my parents. They are so cowardly, so incapable of change, what could you expect from their only daughter?

The weeks that followed are quite blurry to look back on. One of the pills each day was all I had. I'd suck on the pill, just enjoying the taste of something.

William was so good to me. He combed my hair and washed my arms and legs, and he brought me a glass of water to swallow the pill. He didn't know I sucked the pill and sipped the water slowly, made it last all day. I love water. I love the taste of water. I have a whole jug by my bed now, and I can drink as much as I want. I have flowers as well.

"This is your home now," William said. He's so sweet to me.

He brought me books to read in those weeks, and read to me a little bit. I watched his mouth move upside down; he has one ring in his top lip, one ring below. He has a jewel in his nose, six studs in each ear. His nipples are pierced, and his belly button. His penis is pierced but that's all he has. I love all his rings. They make him look like the people on TV. William made me touch every one of his rings.

"In Roman times, the more holes a man had, the greater the man he was," he said. "And these in my lips, reward for a brave act."

"Which brave acts?" I asked, though I knew one of them. He had not had the ring in his top lip when he met me. He had done it the day after our first sex.

"Many brave acts," he said. He protected me from the truth.

Then I was in hospital. I awakened to William's sweet breath; he leant over me, waiting for me.

"I'm so proud of you," he said. His eyes were strange, excited, his face feverish like I've never seen before.

I was too weak to move but he lifted my head and propped it up on the pillows.

"You've lost a lot of blood." William said. "The skin drug thinned your blood and you bled more than usual."

Around me, women who had skinned walked with crutches, or sat in bed like me. All of them were beautiful, their skin in folds, their flesh gone.

"Why have you brought me here?" I asked William. He wants me to see this beauty and suffer, I thought.

Then I looked at my own body. I was skinny, and I was the most beautiful woman in the room.

William had shown me how much he loved me, because he had gotten me holed while I slept.

There was a ring between each of my toes. Rings in the skin below my ankles. Rings down both arms. Rings, I could tell, in my ears, nose, lips, eyebrows and cheeks. I could feel rings all the way down my spine, and one at the very base.

I was naked, as were the other women in the room. I saw my pubic hair had been shaved, and six rings were there.

"It hurts," I said.

"We couldn't let you have an anaesthetic," William said, laughing at silly me. "That can pucker the skin. Can't let you have puckered skin.

"You have to be careful of infection," he said, and I watched as he gently and lovingly turned each of the rings piercing my body.

He is very regular. He will be here soon to turn them again.

THE SAMENESS OF BIRTHDAYS

On the night of my birthday, I tripped as I climbed out of the cab. No one noticed, not even the cab driver. He was already on the look out for his next fare; I was already invisible.

I'd get into the club no worries; the tear in my black stockings would only help.

I nodded at the bouncer, and he shook his head. I ducked under his arm and I was in.

The place was packed. I could smell their veins, the blood pulsing, inviting, their heat reaching out and taking just a little of the chill from my bones. People made a path for me as I walked to the bar. I remember my master, Damon, having that same affect. I always spare a thought for him on my birthday; my master, the one who made me immortal.

I sat at the bar and ordered a tomato juice. I love the stuff; the colour and texture, anyway. The taste is always that little bit…disappointing.

A young woman stood by me and I glanced quickly at her; after fifty years I am practised at choosing well. I don't mind which sex I take (though I admit young boys are my especial favourite—so grateful) but I do like them acquiescent.

The young woman glared at me, and I glanced down at my hands. In the strange half-light they seemed cobwebbed with lines and I tucked them into my lap. I ordered another drink, added vodka this time. Sometimes I'm asked for ID; I was always a young-looking twenty-one, and I have not aged a day since Damon sucked me into a vampire.

An older man stood next to me. What was he, forty-five? I laughed at the sight of him, red face, shaved head barely hiding a large bald patch, white cotton shirt rolled at the sleeves. Fat belly overhanging jeans too tight. I don't mind fat. Plenty to grab hold of.

He smiled at me. I saw the imprint of a hand on his face. He touched it gently.

"Rejection gets harder to take the older you get, ay?" he said.

"I wouldn't know," I said.

He smiled. "I guess not."

I bought him a drink, though, and another, and decided he would do. He had no wedding ring and said he was a travelling salesman.

I feigned drunkenness, collapsing into him, and he was all concern. "Let me help you home," he said. He couldn't believe his luck.

At my door, I fumbled to pay for the cab. "Will you help me in?" I said, avoiding the uncomfortable moment of indecision.

"Of course," he said. He told the driver to wait but I waved the cab away.

He helped me up the path and unlocked the door with the keys I gave him.

"It can be hard to see at night," he said, and I laughed at his innocence. I had been seeing only at night for many years now, working nightshifts, sleeping safely indoors by day.

He didn't have that something special. He didn't deserve to be a vampire. I would take his blood but not turn him.

I offered him a glass of wine but he preferred a cup of tea. Didn't matter, either beverage would conceal the taste of my intended additive. I've a degree in Pharmacy—what did Damon say? "You'll have the time and ability to achieve anything."

I knew what stuff worked.

He looked a little nervous so I stopped staring at him, turned to open a packet of chocolate biscuits. I've tried every new bikkie over the last fifty years, and it's one of the things I anticipate—what will they come up with one hundred years from now? What will I be sampling, and will I still remember my favourites when they are many years extinct?

"I should get going," he said. He had realised by now tonight was not to be his lucky night. I have had very few lovers since Damon; none can compare. It was that vampire soul of his, devouring and creating me all at once.

"Okay, go," I said.

I heard a heavy thump.

"If you can," I said.

He lay in a lump on the floor, a mountain shifting and heaving.

Timing is very important. You need to cut them while the blood is still coursing, before it thickens and stops. I can't stand to bite them. People are so dirty; the taste of them is foul. I travelled to Africa via a nature documentary and studied the Masai way of drawing blood from cattle into bowls; this is the method I use, but my cattle are not left to live another day.

I would have liked to travel in person, but how to ensure night stayed with me? There are delays and stopovers and I must travel vicariously.

That is a regret.

Damon never taught me the magic of flying, and I have never felt the instinct.

That is another regret.

When the man was emptied and I had drunk my belly swollen, I stored his bottled blood in the fridge and thought about disposing of his body. Damon did teach me that. He said to leave them where they lie. Vampires don't leave fingerprints or any other evidence.

Usually I don't bring them to my house, but I was tired, tired and hungry, and it was time to move on, anyway. I've been in this place for twenty years; time to move on before people wonder why I haven't aged. I would leave tomorrow night. Enough time to pack my bags, finish the blood, sleep, and farewell this pleasant home.

I sat alone and sang happy birthday to myself.

I often celebrate alone. When you physically never get older, you tend to let people forget your birthdays. I hate to lie about my age. I'll often have a quiet drink, alone for a while but attended by the end of the evening. I have confined myself, over the years, to one victim per annum, on my birthday. I travel each year, to places within a night's distance, so it would be a brilliant and unlikely flash of conceptual connection-making by the police to draw the lines and notice how someone dies every year, disappears or whatever, on that day. I don't turn them all. My master told me you need to be selective; there are plenty of vampires already and we don't want to crowd ourselves out. That's what he told me. "You're so special. You've got something the others haven't got. I've got it, too. So has…"

You should have heard the names he told me. Famous people, good and bad. Actors and killers. Most of them I thought were dead. He smiled at me, kissed my ear and his tongue went in and gave me a shiver. I was an innocent twenty year old, a lot of us were, then. But I was really innocent, living at home with Mum and Dad and hardly ever going out. A couple of friends from the office talked me into the celebration.

"Come on, you can't spend your twenty-first sober. It'll be fun. We'll look after you." They kept their promise, brought me drinks. Men kept approaching them, chatting to them and being turned down. I had just one guy come up to me, the one who would be my master. He said his name was Damon. He got me talking then listened to me. It was nice. He told me I was sexy but I that hid it with my clothes, my hair. My skirt was too long, my jacket unrevealing. "He's ugly," the girls muttered to me when he went to the bar. "Dump him." It was fifty years ago but I still remember that moment of confusion.

"Ugly? Really?" To me he was achingly handsome. Because he spoke to me. Listened to me. Touched my face. But when the girls said that, it seemed his face twisted, changed. He WAS ugly. Pimples, bad haircut, cheap clothes.

They laughed at him when he came back. He brought me a vodka and orange, tomato juice for himself.

"You don't really drink tomato juice, do you?" said one of the girls. In answer, he drank the lot down and wiped his mouth. He winked at me. Suddenly he was handsome again.

"Come for a dance," he said. He took my jacket off for me. I only had a camisole underneath but I was feeling brave and wild. The girls squealed at me.

We danced and Damon tried to kiss me.

"I can't," I said. I just wanted to be honest. "I don't want to lead you on."

He laughed and squeezed me.

"You're a sweetheart," he said. We danced a bit more then he took me to sit in a quiet corner. He got me another drink.

That's when he started telling me how special I was, not like the others. It was hard not to believe what he was saying. I was special. He shocked me when he leant over and gently bit my neck.

"It won't hurt anymore that that," he said.

"What won't?" I said. I wanted to be clear. I was not going to sleep with him. I knew that.

"Making you like me. Immortal."

I looked at him but he wasn't laughing.

"I'm three hundred and sixty-one years old," he said. "The year I was born, hey, it wasn't much different to now, you know? The Russian Tsar's brother was killed. Countries invaded smaller countries. There was a new pope—he didn't last long."

I shook my head. Then he began to mutter in my ear, murmuring details, how his underwear felt in 1672, what colour the moon was the night Lincoln died, things that made me stare at him in horror.

He unbuttoned his shirt and showed me a scar on his belly. "That's where they tried to stake me, what, a hundred and fifty years ago? Missed my heart by that much. Immortality is amazing," he said. "You deserve it, too. Just think of what you can achieve!" Then he kissed me, and in that kiss I saw worlds past; a sinking ship; a burning pyre; a feast for hundreds; a wild and passionate dance.

He told me he'd take me home and it seemed the only way. The girls told me to stay but I said I was going.

On the way to my place he told me of his powers. Success in all things comes to immortals, to vampires. I could see his body glowing in the dark and I thought of my quiet, slow life, how I always sat up the front on the bus and never had an answer ready when people spoke to me.

As I climbed out of his car (the porch light was on, my mother's silhouette in the family room) he said, "It'll take three nights. When do you want to start?"

I imagined the cup of milk my mother would have waiting for me. The thought sickened me.

"I'll need to tell Mum I'll be late," I said.

He reached over and opened the door for me.

"Mum, some of us are going for icecream," I said at the door. She peered over my shoulder. "It's Nerida's car," I said, flushing.

"Don't come home too late, church tomorrow," she said. I felt a tear then, because I knew I would not be able to enter a church again.

"Okay, Mum," I said, and I ran back down the path.

"Will I still love them?" I asked.

"You won't care," he said.

He smiled, his teeth glinted white and sharp and I felt a sick thudding thrill deep in my belly.

He drove to the local park and leaned over and bit me. It hurt a little. "That's just part of it," he said. He slid his hands up my skirt.

"You need my seed as well. We need transference."

"But I don't want to."

"It's a small price to pay for immortality. Imagine, you'll be around two hundred years from now. You'll see a world so different to this one you'll think this moment, this time, was a dream. My head's full of dreams. A future you can't even imagine."

"But I don't want to get pregnant."

He laughed.

"Vampires are sterile," he said. He should know, I thought, after all these years. He should know.

He told me so much and he felt so cold, his teeth were sharp, his scent intoxicating, his car sleek. He kissed me and eased my clothes aside and slid into me.

I don't know if I liked it or not.

"We need to do it twice more. Then we can be together forever. I'm so lonely," he said. He laid his head on my breast, and I stroked that dark hair.

He drove me home.

I didn't go to church the next day.

He came to collect me when the sun went down.

"This is Damon, Dad," I said. "From work." Already I felt braver, stronger, more able to state my opinion. Dad was a little stunned.

"Hello, young man," he said. "Where are you two off to?"

"Bowling tonight," Damon said. And that was true, we bowled, then he bit me again and entered me to give his seed and I felt I could live forever.

"You will live forever, we will live forever together," he said.

I asked him to go on a picnic the next day and he said, "Sunshine, darling. It's one thing you'll have to give up. And mirrors; so long as you eat meat you should be able to see their blood glowing through."

I'd told him I couldn't drink blood and he said, "You're so sweet. You may find you love it. Most of us do. "

He told me I didn't always have to drink blood, I could eat raw steak. He said I could turn people without seed, but I would need to drain their blood completely. He told me I needed to keep moving every twenty years or so, and how exciting that was, a new life, a new life every generation.

"You should make the most of tomorrow," he said. "It'll be your last day in the sun."

That didn't worry me too much. I'd never been an outdoorsy girl.

He picked me up again the next night and this time we didn't even go bowling. He seemed a little distracted. We had sex, but he didn't bite me.

"What?" he said. "Oh, right." He bit me.

"Is that it?"

He smiled. "That's it, my love. Sorry I've been distracted. I was worried it wouldn't work. You're the first one I've turned in such a long time. But I can see the glow already. Tomorrow night we'll make our escape and begin our life together."

When I got home I blocked off my window and packed a small suitcase. I didn't know what vampires needed.

For breakfast I had some uncooked bacon. I hoped that counted. I told Mum I couldn't go to work and I spent the day saying goodbye to my things.

He didn't come till after eleven.

Dad wasn't impressed.

"They're after me," Damon said. "And you, too, now. You can't trust anyone, not even your parents. We have to separate. Have you got any money?"

I had a little.

"Good. Use it to get as far away as you can. Fly like a bat." He kissed me tenderly. "I'll find you," he said. "I'm sorry it's worked out this way, but I swear I'll find you."

That was fifty years ago. It's been a long, dark fifty years. I craved the sight of daytime people, the normality of them, so in one of my homes I had a video camera set up above my door on the main street. I spent hours watching them, their bounce and vigour.

Night people don't smile as much.

Damon was right. I did begin to crave fresh blood. The occasional victim, on my birthday. Plenty of raw meat. The last few years I've felt too tired to get out of bed some nights. It's the quality of merchandise. Things aren't what they used to be.

Damon was wrong about vampires being sterile, though. I could fall pregnant easily enough, but my womb rejected them every time.

Little aliens. Little mortals.

I missed the sun on my face.

I laughed sometimes in nightclubs, to think what people would think if they knew how old I really was. I stopped looking in mirrors because mirrors lied. I knew I only looked twenty-one. That was the truth.

They must have staked Damon. He never did find me.

And today I am seventy-one in human years.

And today I realised Damon's betrayal.

Bang bang bang bang

I'm on a rolling bed

Bang bang bang

My chest hurts.

Lights above me one two three a corridor

Bang bang bang

Did someone stake me? I reached up to touch my chest.

Nothing.

"S'all right, dear. Just your heart. Gotta expect it at your age, dear. You'll be all right. You look a tough old thing."

Bloody rude bitch. I closed my eyes; the bed stopped and I heard them speaking.

"I reckon she's pretty good for seventy-one. Makes an effort, you know. Hope I give a shit when I get that old."

"A mirror?" I said. Is that my voice? That croak?

"There y'are, dear," said the nurse.

My eyes were all I recognised. Same blue as ever. The rest, oh, god, so old, so old, my heart it hurts oh god my limbs I guessed the ache of them was not a need for blood, it never had been it was aging, he lied he lied he lied and the pain of it sucked my last and lonely breath of air and turned it to mist.

THE SPEAKER OF HEAVEN

Linda was putting the final stitches into a cardigan for her elderly neighbour when the phone rang. It was often that way. The timing was often so fine. She tore the wool with her teeth, tied the knot, and answered the call. She had a new client.

She packed her basket with a few biscuits, a pen and paper, some cooling lotion and other small things which rustled and clicked. She covered the basket with a deep green cloth and was ready for work.

It was an elderly man this time. His grandson sounded distraught but cool. It made them feel good to call her, made them feel like they were doing something to help the dying.

Linda drove carefully to her client's home, humming soft tunes to help her think of what she would say, what she would do.

The young one was waiting at the front door, watching anxiously but glad, she was sure, of an excuse to be away from the bedroom.

Allowing the contents of her basket to clink reassuringly she climbed out of her car. They liked to think she had tools to help her with her work; tools they couldn't afford or understand. This seemed to comfort those who called her. She seemed prepared to them, ready for any emergency.

"He's in there," the boy said. She took his hand and held it.

"You're very strong," she said. He blushed, proud and ashamed of that pride with his grandfather going.

"In there," he said.

The door was closed.

"Tell me," she asked clearly but quietly, "what does he fear?"

"What? I don't know, he never said."

"What does he hate then? What does he mainly hate?"

"Cold. Hates being cold. The ads on TV he shouts at. Cold tea, but that's the same as cold."

"That's lovely. That's good."

Linda opened the door.

"Would you like to say goodbye?" she asked the boy.

"I already did."

"Good. I'll be out soon—don't worry. You've done a good and loving thing for him."

She slid into the room and closed the door with a click.

The man on the bed knew who she was and smiled.

"Come, talk to me," he said.

She placed her basket on the bed, giving it a shake so he could hear the goodies rattle. She sat beside him where he lay. She sat tall and straight, her back a concrete wall. A moment of falter, a loss of surety, would break the spell.

She took his hand in one of hers, reached over and stroked his brow.

"Close your eyes now," she said, "close your eyes and you'll see darkness. Nothing more. That's how it begins. Blacker than any night, than any cat. The sun has never touched this darkness and no warmth was ever there."

The man whimpered. "It's dark."

"Yes. And it's cold, like liquid ice. Cold. Your blood feels frozen and sluggish. Your steps are slow and your hair will crack in the iciness."

"Cold, is it?" he asked, his eyes screwed tightly.

"Very cold. But you walk on, rather than sit still. And soon you are rewarded. Your eyes are stinging because ahead is a pinpoint of light. You walk more quickly now, and you see that it is golden and just looking makes you feel warmer."

"Fire," he said. "Fire, is it?"

"Fire, it is as you move closer. It is still an image only the size of your hand, then your head, but already you can feel its heat."

As she spoke, she reached into her basket and found her tin of tiger balm. A little on her fingers, then she rubbed it into his forehead, his wrist.

"I can feel it now," he said.

"Walk closer then, and the fire is yours. There are many fires, and you may choose your own. You may stand by the fire, or you may go to a house heated always. You will find those you love there and you will never, ever be cold."

He smiled and shivered and walked to the fire. It was a miracle she never got used to; how many of them could give it up just like that, once they lost the fear. Once she told them where they were going.

Linda drove home to find Terry waiting. He fingered the cardigan she had finished for their neighbour, his eyes blurred with tears.

"Can I give it to her?" he said. He had nothing to give himself. Linda nodded him towards the front door.

From an early age, Linda had watched her mother knitting, and the house always full of sick people. She connected knitting with healing, as her mother taught her to do.

Her mother did not advertise her skills and would only heal her friends.

"You can only heal what you understand," she told Linda. This was a lesson Linda remembered, though she didn't have the friends her mother did. She didn't have the skill, or patience, for keeping them. Although she lived in the same house all her life, Linda had no childhood or school friends. She had her husband, her clients, and she was happy.

Her maternal grandmother was also a healer; a spiritualist. She spoke to dead children and lovers, gave deliverance to the grievers, absolved them of guilt. Linda felt this way was closer in kind to her own than her mother's; she and her grandmother spoke healing words to the spirit. Her mother had dispensed healing for the body.

Linda had no desire to have a child for herself, no desire to pass the gift of healing on. Her view of the world was not as positive as her mother's was. She saw the world for all its horrors and did not want to bring a child to it, because she would only wish for it the pleasures of Heaven. Terry never knew of the tiny ones she had sent to Heaven from her own womb. Three in all; and she had whispered to each of them in the waiting room, her hand on her still-flat tummy, on each occasion.

She wondered what sort of people they would have been. What their Heavens would have been like, had they grown to adulthood.

Her father had a very different upbringing from her mother, and he could never accept the sort of healing the women did. Until Linda saw his Heaven; the first she witnessed.

He was sitting in his chair on the veranda, reading the paper and being quiet about his pain. She was only twelve—she loved his quietness, his normalcy, and found her mother's strangeness embarrassing.

She touched the wedding ring on his finger, touched his finger.

She saw a strange world. Her father was there, young, strong, his step healthy. Around him there was no sickness, no age; she saw no sad people. The vision frightened her. Yet, when she described it to her father, he smiled. He took her hand and squeezed.

"That sounds like Heaven," he whispered.

He died soon after. It took her many years to accept that she did not cause death. She sensed it. Read it. She saw Heaven.

It was a very busy week. She knitted two socks and a pair of mittens, and her throat was hoarse from speaking.

Her body ached. Terry came home from his pottering pursuits and was sympathetic to her pains, not their cause.

"You're nearly forty," he said apologetically. "Bodies change. You've seen enough of it to know."

She took a shower to rinse away the age, and there she saw her own Heaven for the first time.

White mountains, pure and silent. Snow drifting to their peaks; a gentle breeze whistling somehow.

She paused in the soft soaping she always gave her body and let the picture in. Nothing more than that, though; the mountains, the snow, the breeze.

Water ran the bubbles into the drain, and she reached for her towel. The vision terrified and comforted her at the same time. Terrifying, because death was close and she wasn't ready. Comfort came from the mountains, the thought of climbing them alone in the world.

Her sister called, wanting to celebrate a business success. Linda agreed to meet for lunch, thinking that indulgence would cure her tiredness.

The meal was far too expensive, a little pile of vegetables and a little lump of meat, and she could have cooked dinner at home for ten people with what she paid.

And she didn't like being offered the senior's discount.

"I have young eyes, don't I?" she asked her sister. They shared height and nothing more. Her sister, only two years younger, had different responsibilities than Linda had. She ran office and home efficiently—spirituality would wait until she was too old to enjoy life.

"You have a young heart as well, it's just hard to see it through that dress. It makes you look twenty years older."

Linda wore woollen dresses. Her sister had one just like it, and the message was clear. Don't give me any more.

There was a crash on the street in front of the restaurant; she sensed it as it happened, sensed that she was needed.

It was a young woman this time, and obviously beyond a doctor's help. She had been thrown through the windscreen—no seat belt?

Linda pushed through the crowd to kneel beside the girl.

"Don't touch her," someone said.

"I don't need to," she said. But she leant over and touched her lips to the girl's ear. She whispered, "Where you are going there are no cars. There are only wide open spaces. There is no confinement, no straps or rooms or closets or caves. You travel by balloon and if it takes forever, you will never care."

A shudder, then, and the girl was gone.

Linda rose and walked back through the crowd. She would not be paid, but money was not important. She had never worked for money. It had never been necessary. People often paid her for her work, because it evened the score; they were not beholden to her. She performed charitable acts with the money. Mostly she delivered meals-on-wheels to the old and infirm. She gave food to the dying and found them in need. Her husband thought this a little ghoulish, a little desperate. He couldn't understand how addictive seeing Heaven was. How good it felt, how beautiful the vision could be.

Not always, though. She had seen some frightening things, from people outwardly good and sweet. She saw a man in a blood bath, slaughtering women. She saw a woman with slaves caressing and probing her. She spoke honestly of these Heavens; they belonged to her clients, and they needed to hear them.

The crowd parted to let her through, watched as she walked away.

Her car lay ahead. She looked forward to reaching its comfort. She felt unwelcome amongst people who didn't understand.

"My son needs you." A whisper. Linda stopped walking. A woman stood behind her. "He needs your help. What did you say? How did you make that girl smile?"

"I told her of the Heaven she can expect to find. I see the future, but only when people know they are dying."

"My son is dying. He's only a baby, only twenty-two."

"That's very young to be dying. Is there no hope?"

"He will die very soon."

When Terry came home, Linda was sitting in the dark. She did not blink when he flicked on the light.

"I met a woman today whose son is to be killed by the State."

"That girl-killer? That rapist, torturer, that man who laughed when his crimes were described, who added details which made the jury sick? Him?"

"His mother wants me to go to him."

"You can't speak Heaven to a creature like that. Only Hell. You can read his mind aloud to him."

She had to be very forgiving to Terry. She couldn't snap at him, because it hurt him so badly. He could only cope with kindness. Their relationship from the start was based on his reliance. They met when he called her to speak Heaven to his mother. For many years he tried to make her tell him what she had seen. He wanted to know what Heaven his mother was in.

"Not for you to know. She is happy, know only that." She regretted the marriage when he begged her in this way. How could she tell him his mother had dreamed not of his father, long dead, but of food, mountains of rich and lovely food?

They married not only because Terry needed to so badly, but because they had sad things in common. Both had lost their parents. Orphans. Neither brought friends to the relationship. No relatives either, apart from her sister. They had been alone; by the time his mother fell sick and he wanted to soften the departure, they had both decided that solitude was best. Then they had each other. And their inheritances, ensuring their comfortable station. He had an office he sat in, but it was her work which was important. He was jealous of the attention she gave her clients. They became the one thing in her life, and he had to wait until they were gone before he was her focus again. He had no one but her.

Terry would not help Linda make a decision. He would not discuss evil, he said. He rarely felt so strongly but the media was intense in its witch hunt of the boy. She felt more anger towards Terry, in the weeks that followed, than to any of the strangers who wished to control her.

She smiled at these people while ignoring them, and only Terry knew how truly angry she was. She fantasised, not for the first time, of living entirely alone, her only human contact strangers; clients and those who provided food and services.

She saw her heavenly mountains often; each time she thought of the boy. She thought perhaps it was his Heaven she was seeing, but the place was too perfect not to be hers.

She had a home in the mountains, a cave, lined with fur and clean and warm. She saw the home and felt it. She ate simple food which did not require cooking. She walked out into the cold and tended animals; set free trapped birds and fed bears too thick with cub to move well.

"I have spoken my own Heaven," she thought. She had always feared what her Heaven would tell her about herself, what deep desire she had not admitted. Now she knew what was ahead, she could choose to leave early, to fall into Heaven. But she had more work to do. She saw that clearly now she no longer feared Heaven.

She did not tell her husband of this Heaven. No time would be long enough to prepare him for her death; he would do all he could not to believe in it.

She found it hard to believe; she should be dead by now. Why would the vision come when she was meant to live?

It seemed a sudden thing, fame. In her desperate need, the mother spoke to whoever would listen, and Linda became public property. There were times when she was fearful. People knew where she lived and they delivered things to her; bibles, newspaper photos of the victims. Photos from people's private collections. People demanded she refuse a mother's request.

It was strange that people believed without investigation that she could see Heaven. They believed just in case, because they did not want their favourite killer to die happy.

Terry left her alone, and she sat knitting and knitting, click, clicking, leaving the TV off to miss the boy's face, wanting him to be a person, not an image.

She rang his mother. "What does he fear?"

"Nothing. He's afraid of nothing."

"What does he hate?"

The mother did not want to answer, because the words would mean she had accepted his guilt.

"He hates laughter. People laughing at him."

Linda looked at the pictures of the laughing girls who died and could sense a little bit of Heaven in each. The girl who was kept alive for a while, who he had loved and killed; she went to a Heaven where she was large, her skin unhealthy, her body odorous. A world where she never felt threatened or wanted.

Linda thought of the mother's voice, her face, the way she accepted his guilt but still loved him. The mother believed he had goodness. Linda had never judged people for their beliefs and behaviour. She needed to accept their hatreds and fears in order to speak their Heaven. She decided she would ease the mother's heart.

The prison was a place she had seen before; it was the place where they killed people legally.

There were crowds there to scream at her, few supporting her fairness, most calling her evil.

In and out and clang and click and stares and moans and there he was, looking scared for someone without fear.

He would die soon, and she was to help him on his way.

He nodded at her and smiled; a test. She didn't smile back. She showed no glimpse of humour or amusement.

He lay on the bed which was pulled into the centre of the room like a hospital bed. The doctor sat on one side, his equipment ready. She with hers on the other.

His mother sat on a stool at the end of the bed, a judge with good and evil on left and right.

Linda took one arm, the doctor the other.

They began rubbing at the same time, he to anaesthetise for injection, she to feel his skin, feel him.

His eyelids fluttered.

She leant close and whispered, "You will wake in a grey world. You will be grey and around you all is grey. The air is thick, insulated, but your lungs fill nicely. It is very quiet. You hear no laughter, and you meet people who only smile with love."

He smiled.

His mother held her tears. She could see his peace, his comfort, and she would not make him sad or guilty.

The Speaker of Heaven rose and left the room.

There was not much passion in her life, but now she felt a need for warmth, real warmth from the man who loved her.

Terry was stunned when she reached for him. Any duty he felt towards making love to her had faded into affection, when he realised with relief she had no desire for that part of their married life. She was too much his protector for him to feel lust. This night, however, he sank into her passion.

The phone rang. Terry hunched into himself; he hated to answer the questions, take appointments. He couldn't face all that talk about death.

"I'll get it," Linda said. Trying to keep cheer in her voice, not letting her tiredness show. There were so many of them now.

"Hello?"

"Linda? Oh, hello. It's Marie." The boy's mother. "I just wondered if perhaps you were free for dinner Saturday, and your…um…too. Nothing too formal, just family and a few close friends…"

Linda felt numb with shock.

"Marie, I'm afraid I can't socialise with clients." Though, of course, she had married Terry. "It wouldn't be ethical."

"But you're the only one who really understood him. No one else ever tried."

"I saw his Heaven, and the vision comes unbidden. I can't offer belief, or disbelief, in his innocence. I can't make him a good or bad person. I couldn't keep him alive."

"Oh," Marie said. A mouse on the line.

"I'm sorry, Marie. You'll need to turn elsewhere for that sort of support. I'm sorry about your son."

"Oh," she said.

Linda flopped onto the couch next to Terry.

"She thought I was her friend!" she said.

"Aren't you?" Terry said. "You must think he was innocent to do what you did."

"I don't think anything," Linda said. She rubbed at her eyes. She accepted that Terry had judged her and found her wanting. There was a shifting in his eyes, as if he was uncomfortable looking at her, where once he gazed at her for hours. She shivered to think she may have lost his unconditional love. But it was a shiver of anticipation, unbidden; the anticipation of being alone. She felt a sense of relief to be no longer perfect.

"I love you, Terry," she said, testing herself and him.

He nodded. "So you say," he said. "But if you really loved me you wouldn't have gone to that terrible boy."

The phone rang and she went to it. Interview request; denied.

"The public have a right," said the caller.

"To what?"

"To you. They'll wonder why you'll be a hero to a killer but not to them."

"Let them call for an appointment," she said.

She felt tired and soiled, needed a shower.

She saw Heaven: She soothed her dry mouth with snow; it tasted like sugar, or watermelon. She was not to die yet; her reward for her work was to see Heaven. Anticipation.

So she sat, and knitted, and saw, and spoke. She would do these things until she was welcomed to enter the land of white mountains, the land of a furry cave, the land she knew would be hers.

THE SMELL OF MICE

My father breathed with little sucking pops, as if each breath had to be drawn through plastic wrap. There was no other sound in the room except for a gentle tearing as Matthew changed the bandages on my father's legs.

"You're a good doctor," Dad said.

Matthew smiled. "I guess you didn't see me riding up on my bike. If I was a doctor I'd be in a Jag. One day. This is looking better." Matthew always wore starched white shirts. Starch his only perfume.

"Thanks to you," Dad said. Because Matthew's touch was deft and thoughtful, and there was no hatred nor resentment in the changing of the bandages, he was the only person Dad didn't despise.

Dad said, "You think my legs are bad, you should see how the women in our family die. All swollen up, faces, bellies, necks, like their skin gets too fat. You'd laugh if you saw it happen to someone else."

My hand flew to my neck. "Dad!" I said. "But my throat is thick and sore."

"Put it this way, don't go planning a wedding. Make the most of now, girl," Dad said. He winked at Matthew. "Lots of wedding nights, no wedding," he said.

"Little do you know," I thought. I didn't like to think of that patch of semen on my thigh, the rest of it dribbling out of me. Matthew vomiting as if the very act was poisonous to him.

I saw Matthew to the front door. He said, "When was your last period?" I shook my head. I was sixteen; this was too embarrassing.

He sniffed at me and said, "It's your smell. Pregnant women have a certain scent. It's like I can smell the baby inside."

He came back the next day with medicine for me. "To fix you up," he said.

I took the medicine he gave me, and that night my stomach felt like it was being shredded from the inside.

"Mum," I moaned.

"What is it?" Mum shouted from the other room.

"I'm bleeding."

"Yuck," my little sister Finola said. "Gross."

"It's just your Rags, you stupid girl. Get some toilet paper then come help me."

I crawled to the bathroom. The pain made me vomit; I held the mouthful until I could spit it in the toilet, not wanting to mess the floor. I needn't have bothered; blood trailed in clumps behind me.

I sat on the toilet, bending over to squash the pain away.

Blacked out.

Woke up lying on the floor. My lips began to move, strange words and I squatted, let the clots squeeze out. I muttered as I scooped and swiped the blood, scooped and swiped, I muttered the words then the pain was gone and I felt as if I could float.

I ran a warm bath.

These words were clear in my head: "Burn it, burn it," and I rose from the red-now bath. I scooped up the small clots and took them to the hearth.

I threw the tiny bits into the fireplace and wrapped a crocheted rug around myself. Pain tugged at me and blood trickled down my legs as I reached for the matches.

There was no smoke as the embryo burnt.

Not really believing I would see anything but wanting night air on my skin, I walked outside and stood in the middle of the street.

I gasped. It was there, just as the witch said it would be; a thin plume of purple smoke a long way distant. I walked slowly inside and dressed in clothes I found on the floor.

"I see smoke," I told my father. He panicked as he always did and limped outside.

"Where?"

"There."

"There's nothing there," he said, "Ya bloody little time waster. What if I'd called in the fire department? Hey?"

"What's going on?" It was Finola. She held our father's hand.

"Bloody Tamsin's seeing things."

"Smoke," I said. "Over there."

Neither of them noticed the blood on my legs.

"I can't see anything," Finola said, but she would say that. She was six and wanted my father's favour.

I began to walk towards the smoke. I felt light as air. A feather on the wind.

"Where are you going? Your mother wants help with the dinner."

"I'll be back in time."

"Now, Tamsin."

"I'm hungry," Finola said.

I gave in, went inside to halve the potatoes, cook the chops, shell the peas.

The smoke was still there after dinner. Very faint, very distant, but there. Just as the witch had told me it would be, six years ago, on the day I disappeared for a week:

Inside the house, baby Finola suckled, suckled, draining my mother of energy and patience.

"Don't forget nappies," my mother said. "Tell Reba to put it on the account." And the baby cried, and I ran.

"Don't talk to strangers," my mother shouted.

I ran to the shops, ten years old, allowed out on my own. "There and back, Tamsin, I'm timing you."

"I'm timing you," I said as I ran. "And you spent fifty million hours being nice to the baby and one minute being nice to me."

I stepped on every crack I passed. I reached the supermarket and found the things on the shopping list. As I stretched for the frozen peas, the ones at the back because the ones at the front were old, I heard a low, tortured yowl. I peered over the side of the freezer cabinet.

There, between the bread stand and the cabinet, were Reba's cat and a small grey mouse. I heard a high-pitched squeal as the mouse dislocated its bones trying to get away.

"He's got a mouse!" I yelled. "He's got one!"

Reba came to see. There was a brittle crunching and the mouse was still. Reba hugged herself. "There must be a witch flying over. When your cat brings you a mouse, there's a witch about."

I bought cheap nappies to give the baby nappy rash.

Reba, breathing hard, put the things in a bag. She leaned forward and I could smell nail polish. I had seen her in the light, out the front sucking a cigarette like the baby sucked the tit.

"Keep an eye out for that witch." I looked at the wart on Reba's nose, her taloned fingers.

"Okay," I said.

"Here's a lollipop," Reba said. I knew the lollipop was ancient, would shatter in my mouth and taste of dust, but I took it.

The shopping bag was heavy. It banged against my legs. After a few steps I stopped. Thump thump I heard and I moved, not wanting to be near the laundromat with its huge thumping dryers and I always imagined cats in there, dogs, thumping against and denting the walls of the dryers.

I hobbled with the heavy shopping bag, staring up at the sky, watching for a witch, looking for a broomstick.

"Hey!"

I fell hard, landing on my knuckles.

"Stupid girl. You didn't see me. You weren't looking."

Teary from the pain, I stood up.

The old woman smelt of mice. She had few teeth, many bags. Her words whistled but I understood her.

"I'm not supposed to talk to strangers."

"You don't have to talk. Just listen. You're the one to listen, my dear. I've been watching you. You're the one."

I was frightened. The old woman was closer to me now.

"Say yes," the old woman said, "and you'll be rich beyond your wildest dreams."

"Are you rich?" I said. I was being smart. This woman couldn't be rich.

"I was, once. I got tired of it. Say yes."

"Yes," I said.

The old lady brought out a roll of lollies.

"You eat and listen."

I took the lollies and they were the best; they were soft and delicious and I didn't have to share. I couldn't smell mice while I chewed, I smelt fruit, sugar cane, chocolate cake still in the bowl. The old woman whispered to me, words which made no sense and some which did.

"You are only young. It's a good place to start. I was already old when I was told. Now I'm tired. I've had enough. But I can't die until I've told someone and I'm telling you. You will tell someone one day. When you're tired. But that will be many years from now. Many, many years. If you work hard you could live forever. That doesn't happen in your family. Ask your father what happened to all his sisters. And his mother."

I listened carefully without speaking.

The old woman spoke, muttered, nodded her head. Her voice went on and on and it seemed to me that the sun rose and set and rose again.

In truth the time that passed was even longer than that; the old lady stopped talking, said, "Good girl," and shifted away. I asked my mother later if there were any dead old ladies and she said, "Don't be morbid."

My shopping was still at my feet and I picked it up, thinking my mother would be angry at waiting for it. It smelt, though, something rotten, and I looked in the bag to see meat gone bad. Milk solid in the bottle. Then I heard a scream.

"It's her! It's the missing girl!" and I was bundled up and taken home, and I never got back my missing week, I never told anyone what the old woman said, and I waited, waited until I grew into my new power.

When Matthew came again to do my father's legs, I made them both a cup of tea and gave Matthew an oatmeal biscuit.

He grimaced. "You know, some people live off imported French biscuits, so fine they melt on your tongue," he said. He bent close to me. "So how are you feeling?"

I shook my head. "I feel terrible. Still sore and sick."

"But fixed?"

"I guess so." I didn't tell him about the smoke I had seen.

"Did you hear about the man who had maggots in the sore on the roof of his mouth?" he said, and he told me more, terrible stories I liked to hear.

As the days passed, my mother began to stare at me, my father to turn away. Mum said, "I thought you were dying. I thought that's what was making your belly stick out. I thought it was happening. What did you do to stop it?"

We both glanced over at Finola, watching TV turned up too loud.

"Whatever you did, you'll have to do it for your sister in ten years. Otherwise she's gone."

I looked at Finola and felt a coldness. This was how my father must feel. This iciness of the soul. I thought, "I don't have to do anything. There is nothing I have to do."

I wondered why my mother didn't treat me as a precious thing, knowing the disease I carried would kill me young, but realised she resented giving birth to children who would not live.

"Why have children?" I said to her once I knew about the disease.

"We love children. We love you as babies. And your father didn't tell me until it was too late."

The ten years passed quickly. My father lasted for three of those years; I didn't travel home for his funeral. Matthew and I had moved far away, another city, where we fell into the habit of performing illegal abortions in our kitchen, to fund his University Degree. No one was ever hurt. We perfected our methods; we were very good. We made a good living. Once Doctor Matthew had qualified, we opened his Therapy Rooms. And behind the Therapy Rooms, the Clinic.

The life-giving Clinic.

Then my sister began to sicken. Thicken.

"It's the angioedema," Mum wailed on the phone. "It's terrible."

She sent me photos of my sister, swollen. "Help her, you must help her."

I knew I could help her. I just needed to pass on the knowledge, help her fly. Help her to see the smoke.

I caught the bus to work, flicking through the photos Mum had sent me as we travelled. When I arrived, the client was already waiting.

"You're looking well, Amanda. Doctor Matthew will be pleased," I said. "How many weeks is it?"

"Twenty-nine. And I feel like shit."

I laughed. "I'm sure a good talk will help you."

"I really don't know, I'm so stressed. I've got all these people giving me a hard time about my diet as if I was some evil bitch for not giving up dairy and wheat."

"Everything in moderation." I smiled. "You do need to watch the stress levels, though. The sort of muscle-tightening we're talking about can seriously damage the baby."

"You're kidding."

"I'm not. My sister's husband died before her baby was born and the stress caused so much damage to the baby it couldn't breathe. Came out brain-damaged. He still can't move, poor little thing. He's nine, now."

Amanda stared, horrified, at me.

"But I've been really stressed. My husband lost his job, and I'm not working—we've got no money! I had to sack the cleaning lady yesterday. I mean, I'll get another one next month but the place is a pigsty till then."

I shook my head. "I'm sure everything's all right."

I answered a call.

"I'm sure," I said.

"I can't feel the baby moving," Amanda said.

"Look," I said, "We can do some really unobtrusive tests. The politically correct wouldn't agree with them because they find out whether your child is perfect or not. He's a good doctor, Doctor Matthew. He's a prenatal expert as well as a therapist. I can ask him, if you like."

Amanda said nothing.

"Just to be sure," I said.

"Just so I know," Amanda said.

"That's right." I smiled.

"You're staring at my belly. Like you know something."

"I don't know anything," I said, my mouth dry with anticipation.

I awoke early on Clinic Day. I loved these days beyond any other. Mum called while I was in the shower, "Help her, you must help her." I let the answering machine record her distress.

I dressed carefully, washed carefully, using the no-scent soap he preferred.

The bus always seemed slower on Clinic days. I told the pregnant woman in the seat behind me that flushed cheeks in pregnancy were a sign of a Down's Syndrome child. I gave the woman Doctor Matthew's card and said, "Just so you know." Then I walked through the Therapy Room reception and into the Clinic.

"Only me," I said.

"Hello, Tamsin. My fairy god-princess." Doctor Matthew kissed my hand. He was dressed beautifully, as ever. Italian clothes and shoes, made by hand for him in Rome as he stayed nearby, doing whatever it was he did to the locals there. He loved to be wealthy.

He stood staring at his prized photo of the Custer Wolf in death. The most hated animal in North America had been manipulated into submission; head bowed, legs spread.

"He ripped open the bellies of pregnant cows to get at the foetuses," Doctor Matthew said. "Just for the foetuses. People hated him for that, though he was just providing for himself, you know? They hunted him to the death." His hedgehog cushion sat on his desk, a round small cushion prickly with long, shiny needles.

"We've got four lined up today," he said. He flicked through the pile. "Down's, missing limb, enlarged head, no genitals." He threw down the papers. "Don't these people ever get a second opinion?"

"Not the ones who make it this far," I said. "The ones we're here for."

"If anyone knew what we were doing, they'd loathe us like they did the Custer Wolf. Now let's prep."

We worked through the familiar routine and I loved it, the instruments, the cleanliness, the anticipation.

Doctor Matthew said, "After this one, do you know what I'm going to do?"

I shook my head, concentrating on getting the equipment just right.

"I've found a surgeon willing to deal with the body dysmorphics. The guys who hate their arms or legs. For the right price, he'll service their needs." Doctor Matthew laughed. "Can you believe it? I'm testing the very limit of what people will do for money. Haven't found it yet." His nostrils flared. "First one's here," he said, sniffing the air like a dog.

I greeted the client at the door. "Nothing to eat this morning? Good," I said. Doctor Matthew sat on the corner of his desk and smiled.

The client said, "We're planning a proper burial. We'll name him, too. We need to do this." I flinched in surprise.

Doctor Matthew said, "Yes, many people feel that way. Now, let's check these results, hmmm? Before we plan anything."

He flicked through the pages in front of him. I knew he was angry at me for not identifying an unsuitable client earlier.

"Oh, my goodness, you're going to like this news. Your baby is fine. Perfect! You won't be needing our services after all."

"Oh, my God," the woman said. She held her belly and cried. "Oh, my God, I feel so guilty. I nearly killed my baby."

"You'll be a perfect mother," Doctor Matthew said, and I led the woman out.

"Tamsin? Can I see you, please?" Doctor Matthew said. I closed the door and sat down.

"She wanted the body, Tamsin. We don't accept those clients, Tamsin. You know that as well as I do, Tamsin." The doctor gritted his teeth each time he said my name.

I was shocked. I remembered recruiting this one at the Mum's and Bub's shop.

"She seemed so detached when I did her interview. I'm sorry I missed that one." Yet he had missed it too.

"Don't let it happen again," Doctor Matthew said.

"No," I said. I felt the loss sharply.

Doctor Matthew neatened his desk. He said, "We'll need to think about moving on, I think."

Then Amanda arrived without her husband. She came quietly into the Clinic, neat, polished shoes, ironed linen shirt, subtle makeup.

"Have you got someone to drive you home afterwards, Amanda?"

"No. My husband wouldn't come."

"Oh, well, never mind, we'll book you a taxi, don't worry about it."

There were tears and tissues. She stared at the Custer Wolf.

"Poor wolf," Amanda said.

"Yes, I know, it breaks your heart. He was the oldest living wolf. A hero in his time," Doctor Matthew said. "Let's pop your robe on now. No good waiting for this. It's a tough decision you've made but the right one, and I wouldn't be doing this if I didn't think so," Doctor Matthew said kindly. He leaned toward her. "You have as much right to this as a man has to get rid of a stomach ulcer." He smiled. "Off we go now."

Once Amanda was under, Doctor Matthew said, "How many weeks?"

"Thirty-one."

He winced slightly.

"She paid a fortune, Doctor. It'll be alright."

Doctor Matthew injected her with saline solution then we waited and induced labour. We pulled out the foetus. It was whole. Perfect. Doctor Matthew took a long needle and pierced the temple.

He liked to be sure.

"Why don't they get a second opinion?" Doctor Matthew said. Putting the blame onto them, passing it on. Doctor Matthew used his scalpel to remove the bits he needed. I never asked him how much he sold them for. He made sure I wanted for nothing.

I muttered, my eyes on the foetus, my fingers on the foetus, and I'm sure he never asked me what I said because the idea of knowing struck him dumb with terror. I lifted the body and held one end of the bandage in my teeth. I wrapped the foetus tightly. My cheeks glowed, burned, I knew Doctor Matthew watched me. I placed the body into a prepared box. Doctor Matthew thrust the needle into the hedgehog cushion.

"Jesus fucking Christ," he said, and threw a box of tissues into the corner of the room. "Fucking mice. God, they stink. Can't you smell it?"

He rubbed his nose. I smiled. "I guess so," I said.

We wheeled Amanda into the recovery room. Helped her home. Then began on the next. Clients never saw each other.

I finished bandaging the last foetus and said, "I need to eat. Coming? Come on, I'm starving," and I was, but I liked to share the feast, and Doctor Matthew was my favourite dinner companion, matching my gusto, admiring my appetite.

We walked to a nearby Lebanese restaurant where the concept of feasting was understood. I ordered before I sat down. Devoured bread, dip, lady's fingers, kebabs, the rice and salad and chicken which came, the wine, my hair was loose and frizzy, electrified, and I spilled food without noticing. The waiters were nervous of me and brought me extra food without being asked, sweet food, and coffee, and they watched me eat as they always did. Doctor Matthew bought wine, hundreds of dollars the bottle, and laughed when he knocked his glass over. He bought liqueurs, tossing them back as if they were water. He tipped so highly the waiters probably considered quitting.

Doctor Matthew licked his lips to clear them of the last drops of Cointreau. His silence didn't bother me; I knew what he was thinking. I repelled him, and yet...

"I must be getting home," he said. I nodded.

"So what else is on the agenda?" I said. He reddened. I knew he was excited rather than embarrassed, and that under the table he was touching himself.

"I've found someone willing to sell his wife's ashes," he said gleefully. "Can you imagine what the rest of the family is going to do?"

"I can't imagine," I said. Bored now. I wanted this part to be over. Sometimes I looked at Doctor Matthew and thought, "You're doing this for the joy of material gain and the pleasure of manipulation. I'm doing this for my life."

I arrived home, my belly full. I felt tired now, but excited. I knew that what I was about to do would invigorate me.

I put my things away and tidied up a little. I tidied the children's room, which was never messy because there were no children. And the husband's study, pens and paper there, envelopes, things ready for the business men did. There was no husband either, but I had things ready for them all, just in case. A man with two born children; that would be perfect. I didn't trust myself with pregnancy. The witch had told me, "If you can make your own, my dear, all the better. All power to you." But after that first loss, I didn't want to go through it again.

Sometimes, after a ritual, my new energy was so intense I would stay out for days, the glow of me drawing people in. It was nice to come back to a tidy home. I dusted my things and emptied the fridge of potential smells. I took the rubbish out. I emptied the washing basket into the machine, stripped off my nurse's uniform, threw that in. Stripped off my underwear, my bra, threw those in and set the machine going.

I drank lots of water. The first few times I practised the ritual I'd returned sick, dehydrated. Now I drank plenty of water beforehand.

I put on a long black dress. That would do me well when I hit the clubs later.

I did my hair up in a bunch. I brushed my teeth. I put shoes into a backpack, and my wallet, and more water. My keys.

The washing machine load finished and I hung out the clothes. The sky was grey and it would probably rain but I didn't want the clothes rotting in my machine.

The fireplace was clean, swept that morning before work.

I took the three little bodies, unbandaged them and burnt them in the fireplace. There was no smoke. The bodies felt light, like nothing. I would not have thought they were real if I hadn't seen them emerging from their mothers. For a moment before I threw the bodies in I felt a little sick. I thought, "I could freeze these bodies and carry them interstate to save her dear young life," but the witch had said I'm giving my life for you and I was not willing to give my life for Finola. My father would not have died for me. I am my father's daughter.

I didn't wash the babies. They were covered with a pinkish dust, stuff from their mothers, blood and the waxy stuff babies are born with. I didn't wash the babies because I was concerned that would give them humanity. They were part of the ritual. Their burning meant I could see what I needed to see; a plume of smoke would show itself in the distance for each soulless, smokeless body.

Mice squeaked in the walls of the house.

"You have no soul until you leave the womb," the old woman had told me. "Unborn babies have no soul. They give off no smoke when burnt." The old woman's words filled my stomach and throat.

The bodies I burnt were never smoky. The bandages smoked, though, when I did those. An ember blew off and I ducked my head away. I burnt the bodies and my vision cleared. It was like the burning clarified the colours I could see. Black. White. Purple.

It was a beautiful, clear, warm night. I went into the street.

There were three plumes of purple smoke, far away, far apart. I felt great energy as I walked. I felt like a dream, all dressed in black, my dress a little transparent in the moonlight. I walked a straight line, feet bare to feel the earth, over glass and stones, through puddles.

When I came to a house I rose and glided over the roof, then sank back to the ground again. It was a good time for cats; mice running frantic, uncaring. Dimly I was aware of the crunch of bone, mice snapped up in their distraction by greedy cats wanting to please their owners.

The purple plumes of smoke showed to me alone in the moonlight.

No one answered when I knocked at the first home. I entered, pushing open the back door. The elderly woman had died making a cup of tea. The smoke of her life-force was still rising and I leaned over and sucked it in, filling my belly with the apple-scented stink of it. I left and walked quickly, quickly, and I found a dead teenager by the side of a playground. His life-force smoke was thick and rich and made my head spin. Then I walked to find the other house, always following the smoke. Here there were children, an hysterical wife, police. I wondered if it was worth it. The risk of exposure. Doctor Matthew had scheduled six more terminations for next week and those sacrifices would show more life-force smoke to me. More life, more years. I turned from the family and let the smoke be.

I staggered home three days later. There was a message on my machine but I couldn't tell from whom.

All I could hear was sobbing.

THE GRINDING HOUSE

Albadara: a bone which Arabs say defies destruction, and which, at the res-urrection, will be the germ of the new body. The Jewish name for it is Luz, and the "Ossacrum" refers to probably the same superstition.

Brewer's Dictionary of Phrase and Fable.

It was a strange migration. The birds were walking, not flying. Hundreds of them walking, pecking, pecking at dead birds along the way, walking on.

"Shouldn't we call a vet or something? Someone to take the dead ones away?" Sasha asked. They stood in front of the concrete block of flats they called home.

"What's the big deal? They're only birds, Sash," said Rab. "Birds die all the time. They're stupid."

"But there's so many of them," Sasha said. Parrots, rosellas, crows, magpies, sparrows and cockatoos. Dozens of them. "Shouldn't someone at least take the bodies away?"

They heard a rushing, a whispering, then a thump.

A seagull landed with a squelch ten metres away from them.

"Splat!" Bevan said, lighting a cigarette and squinting.

He hated the sun.

Nick squatted down by the split bird. "You're a long way from home, mate," he said. He poked it with a stick.

"Come on, you're late," Bevan said. He fidgeted, shuffled his feet. He wanted them gone so he could have the place to himself. Get his work done. The toilet was filthy.

Sasha squatted beside Nick, holding her huge knitted bag on her knees. "What happened to it?"

Rab said, "Sash, it's a dead bird. It died for fuck's sake. Can we move on?" He ate a peppermint.

Nick said, "Have a look at it. It looks sort of smooth inside. It's weird."

"I don't want to look at it, Nick. All right? Come on. I want a seat on the van today," Rab said.

Bevan wouldn't look, either. "Can you go? Please? Come on, the van'll be there in five minutes. Sell well today. I feel like steak tonight," he said.

"I hope we get somewhere flat," Sasha said.

"Yeah, no hills to walk and people are always fatter in flat suburbs," Nick said.

They reached the collection point just as the van pulled up. A big, white, windowless van that made Sasha nervous. The moonies drove vans like this, full of wild-eyed devotees carrying flowers. Telecommunications companies sent their poor young sales teams out in these vans, too, dropping them, disoriented, in the suburbs.

Sasha, Rab and Nick climbed in and registered. Another team was already there. They sat huddled and silent amongst boxes of 'Slenderize'. Something about the van made them all huddle. A blonde girl widened her eyes when she saw Nick.

"Hey, folks," Nick said. "Where're they dropping you today? We're hoping for the caravan park. People are always fat and lazy there, and they just throw money at you."

Nick threw his fist as if releasing coins. The other team flinched. "Nothing," Nick said. "If you could be sure they were washing their hands it'd be the perfect place."

The van pulled up outside a cinema.

"Team One," the driver said. The silent group shuffled out. The blonde girl smiled at Nick.

"Lucky you," he said. "Clean toilets. And don't forget, there's always spilled popcorn after the movie's over. Sneak in before the cleaners and you'll score a cup full. Wave it under people's noses. Just the smell of that stuff makes you fat."

"Bye, Nick," said the blonde girl. She had tears in her eyes.

Nick winked at her. "Spend some of that cash on me, darling, and I'll make you very happy," he said. She smiled.

Team One walked past a policeman who was dragging a homeless man by the scruff of the neck, and they stepped around to avoid the vomit.

"You've got no chance with her," Rab said.

"Mum says cops used to help people. Sounds like bullshit, huh?" Nick said.

The van dropped them in the city.

"Excellent. No door-to-door today," Nick said. He took off his shirt, leaving a purple singlet that clung to his chest. Sasha tied her shirt up under her breasts. Rab rolled his sleeves to show his biceps.

"God, we're gorgeous," Nick said.

"This is a shit job," Rab said.

Nick squeezed his shoulder. "It's not a job, it's a calling."

The brothers had met Sasha three years earlier, when together they collected for charity. For a while she motivated them to be the top team. Bevan used to sit and watch them, feeding off their energy. Sasha always wondered why he'd hang around people ten years younger than him. It was better with him at home.

No one gave, now, though. They bought; they never gave.

Rab was the star salesperson. He could make his dark-blue eyes leak tears and people bought out of sympathy. Sasha did okay but she was so eager and angry she put customers off a little. She insisted the team give ten percent of their earnings to a charity, which annoyed the others if they wanted to eat.

"It's a tithe, that's all," she said. "It's fair."

The company they worked for gave them a generous forty percent of sales. They'd sold books before, and shoes, and services of various kinds. Forty percent was generous.

Nick would leap around like a clown, drawing the crowds in for the other two to approach. His sales figures were always down but the crew worked together. They knew he sold low because he was helping them sell high, so they looked after him.

Sasha tilted her head toward a man telling her he already had 'Slenderize' and didn't need any more. That she was no better than a prostitute.

"Fair enough," she said.

"You look like a little bird with your head angled like that. You should turn your head away so you can't hear the arsehole," Rab said.

"I'd still hear him with my head turned," Sasha said.

Nick shook his head. A little later he whispered behind her back, "I love you." She didn't respond.

"Don't tease her," Rab said, though he smiled, his tight-lipped smile so different from Nick's broad one. He thought his teeth were no good. Too many lollies.

"Tease me how?" she said.

"Nothing," they both said.

Rab looked up and down the mall. "There's one. Just getting money out, got a girl with him. He'll want to impress her."

"How can you see that far? I hate your eyesight," Sasha said.

"Here he comes. Look at him. Bloody gold jewellery. You do him, Nick. You're good with rich people."

"You gotta get over hating rich people, Rab," Nick said. "Or else go work for one, making their beds or something." He flinched from a sudden cramp. "Fucking hunger pains," he said.

Rab laughed.

Nick leapt around so fast he looked like a rubber man. "Excuse me, excuse me, sir?"

The man said, "I'm busy."

"Young lady? Are you busy, too?" Nick raised his eyebrows at her. She looked him up and down and said, "Very."

"Too busy to lose some weight? I know you're looking gorgeous, perfection is in the eye of the beholder, but we've got a machine here to tell us if you need to lose just a little. And perhaps lose a little stress, too. We've got it all in 'Slenderize', the complete weight-loss-mental-health programme. It's even got an anti-cancer agent in there."

The couple stopped to listen.

"It's a free test," Sasha said.

The man rolled up his sleeve. "Why not?"

Sasha held his hand and felt his pulse. It wasn't necessary but men liked the physical contact.

She pressed his forefinger to the small screen Nick held.

It flashed.

"According to this, three weeks will take you to optimal weight for your height and age. And the lithium in the product, which occurs naturally in spring water, by the way, will help you stay happy during the programme. We're all on the maintenance programme."

The three of them smiled gloriously.

"Do me, now," the woman said. They tested her.

"Eight days to optimal weight. I would have said three, but you gotta believe the machine," Nick said.

The woman said, "So, are you two twins?"

Rab and Nick winked at each other. "Believe it or not, no. I'm older by just seventeen months. Never a year and a half, mind you. Seventeen months," Nick said.

The couple bought the recommended dosage and walked away, heads together, laughing.

"Thank fuck for that," Rab muttered.

They sold eight more programmes then got a little bored.

Rab said, "I need a new music player. Let's go buy one."

"We're not spending our money on more equipment for you, Rab," Sasha said. "Nick, give us a song."

Nick started singing, right into people's faces. He got pushed away a fair bit but that didn't bother him. Making people angry excited him in a strange way.

Rab disappeared to buy coffee, but his plan was to have a quick snooze in one of the café's big armchairs. He managed ten minutes before the manager poked him awake and kicked him out.

"This is not a charity place," she told him. The manager was so angry she forgot to make him pay for the coffee.

Rab brought back spring water for them both. "With naturally occurring lithium," Rab said.

"So long as it's naturally occurring," Nick said. He swallowed a pill with his water. "Gotta use your product," he said.

"Excellent," Sasha said. "I'm that thirsty. Thanks, Rab."

They were tired. The performance needed to sell 'Slenderize' wearied them. The bright lights of the mall made their eyes ache. They sat down at the base of a massive flowerpot and talked about going home.

A cop came along and told them to stand up, move along.

"We're just having a rest," Nick said.

The cop got out his notebook.

"Name?" he said.

Nick froze for too long, so the cop angrily gestured for his hand and pressed his finger to the notebook screen.

"Nick Albadara." The cop looked at Nick. "According to this your bank account is empty. You should be starving."

Nick grinned. "I am pretty hungry."

The others laughed.

The cop half closed his eyes. "You'll need to earn some money soon, mate, or you'll drop below the poverty line. You're that close to dropping down a class level. It's hard to get up from there, believe me. Don't try to get money for nothing because you're already marked down for begging." The cop tore at a nail. It seemed to crack away like thin china.

His kindness made Sasha's eyes water. "It's all right, we've made heaps today. We just haven't registered it yet."

They heard crying; low, childish, exhausted crying. They turned and saw a woman, younger than them, really young, and in her arms was the crying kid.

"Help him, help him," the woman said. She spoke quietly. Exhausted.

The cop took off his jacket, and Sasha put her knitted bag on top of it. When the woman put the kid down, he lay still, crying in that terrible way.

"What's the matter with him?" Rab asked.

"I can't hear what you're saying," the woman said.

"Speak up, Rab. You're such a soft talker," Sasha said.

"I said what's wrong with him?"

"His bones hurt. His stomach. His head, his feet. He hurts all over. It hurts to breathe. The clinic says it's growing pains but he's not growing. He can't move anything now. First his feet then his hands, now he can't move."

"There are no tears," Sasha whispered.

The woman bent down to the boy. She kissed his cheek. "I'm sorry, darling, I have to show them." She lifted open the boy's eyelids.

Sasha gasped and turned away. Nick couldn't look either.

The cop said, "Jesus." He picked the kid up. "We've got to get him to hospital."

The woman wept noiseless tears of terrible empathy for the boy. She stood strangely.

"They won't take him until he's dead. Then they want him. The doctor won't see him, I waited three hours, and he wouldn't see him."

The boy struggled, and his breath rattled.

The cop said, "I'll pay. I'll pay for him." He squeezed the boy hard and they heard a cracking. The boy could no longer scream.

"Careful," the woman said. "Oh, God, careful." She reached for the boy and sank to the ground with him. He flicked his eyelids open and they saw bone there, his eyeballs covered with thin bone.

There was a crowd gathered now, muttering to each other, rustling their shopping bags as they jostled for a look. Nick, Sasha and Rab, all of them crying, tried to shield the mother and her son from view. The boy no longer cried. He sounded like he was breathing through a tube, then a straw, then…nothing.

The mother wept. Sasha watched and finally realised what was odd; she'd hunched her shoulders up and never dropped them.

The cop got on his radio and called for help.

"All right. I don't know what's going on, but they want us to wait here," the cop said to them.

"I'm not hanging around here," Sasha said.

"You'll have to wait, they've said," the cop said.

"What's your name, mate?" Rab said.

"You don't heed to know," the cop answered, taking his hat off and scratching his head. "Henri. You're supposed to pronounce it French but I never do. People always get it wrong and I don't worry about it. They think you're a dickhead if you do."

"He's freaking about something," Nick whispered to Rab.

"What'd they say to you?" Sasha said. "Because you know you're in it, too."

"I was instructed to contain the affront. I said there wasn't an affront, we just tried to help. But they hit my number." Henri held up his notebook. It flashed red.

"What is it?" Sasha said to the mother. "Is it something contagious? What is it?"

The woman sobbed without energy, as if she had nothing left inside. "He started getting sore and stiff. He said his bones ached. I said, okay, you need milk and cheese. Build up your bones, and he loved that. It made him happy for a while. A little while. But he got so hungry…then his eyes…and he couldn't hear me. His friend is the same. Why the children? What is it?"

Nick stretched his neck. Spread out his fingers. "It's making my bones ache just to think about it."

The cop looked helpless.

"Can't we get her somewhere comfortable? And the child?" Rab said. He stood with his hands on his hips. "I think we should all go and sit down. We'll go to that outdoor café, over there—we'll have a coffee, we'll wait for them. It's the best thing."

The cop said, "Look, I don't see why you can't just wait. They'll be here in a second."

It was five minutes before the uniformed medical team arrived, "Medical Team" in large letters on their backs, "P.D" underneath.

"Police Department?" Nick asked. Henri shook his head. The medical team carried equipment, but they had no interest in the physical well-being of the group. When they picked up the little boy there was the faint crackle of bone and the mother wailed, "Don't break him! Don't break him."

The medics carefully laid the dead boy on a stretcher and covered him. One of them took the mother firmly by the elbow.

"Leukaemia," he told her. "Mercifully fast."

To Henri they said, "Names and addresses. Nothing to worry about here. Leukaemia. A new form. You can't catch it. Names and addresses, and we don't want this family's privacy invaded. We want them left alone now."

Henri turned to Sasha and said, "It's a new form of leukaemia." He shook his head. "Not like anything I've ever seen." He registered their names and address on his notebook.

A crowd gathered, and Nick and Rab took advantage of it. "For the boy," they said. "The mother."

People gave very little and soon Nick and Rab gave up.

Nick fell very quiet.

"It's terrible," Sasha said. "We're all upset."

Nick looked at her. "Yeah, but I'm thinking about Dad. He's been walking stiffly. And he's quit work."

"It couldn't be this. Not the same thing. I'm sure he's fine, mate," Rab said.

They looked at the mother. She was quiet now. As they watched she took a deep shuddering breath then flinched, as if her lungs hurt. As the medical officers led her away Sasha tried to hug her but she was too limp.

"Let's get out of here," Rab said.

The cop checked his notebook. "I guess you can go. We'll be in touch if we need to speak with you."

Sasha kissed him. "Thank you," she whispered.

They walked quickly away.

They waited for the van to take them home again. The driver was angry they'd sold so little, didn't care why they'd stopped selling, and he refused to drive them home.

"Most people have already got the stuff, mate," Rab said. "You can't sell what people have already got."

The public bus took forever. Sasha sat in the back, crying, sick with what she'd seen.

Bevan was waiting for them when they got home. "Where've you been? The shops are shut now. I had to cook bloody vegetarian. No salt. I'll add my own later." He waited for a response. None of them spoke. "What's happened?" he said. "Did you lose the money?"

"You wouldn't understand," Sasha said. She stumbled to the room she shared with Rab.

"I might," Bevan said.

"We just saw a kid die," Nick said.

"What? An accident or something?"

"Nah. Leukaemia, they reckoned. I never heard of leukaemia like that."

"Plus it took ages to get home. We had to get the bus and the Rangers won the footy today and there were bodies everywhere," Rab said.

"It's worse when they lose," Bevan said. "I fuckin' hate it when they lose."

"How patriotic," Rab said. "Loyal barracking for the local team from someone who can't even catch a ball." Any child's death made him angry, mostly with the parents for allowing it to happen, as if somehow parents could keep their children safe from accident and disease. Their sister had lost a baby to cot death, and he blamed her. She didn't watch enough.

Nick was sick to his stomach and could barely eat or drink. He wanted physical contact with the others and kept patting them, sitting too close, wanting to be near.

They sat together on milk crates, resting their plates on an upturned box. Old newspapers made the crates a little softer.

Nick, suddenly starving, drank a litre of milk before he began his meal. He always smelt sweet, as if the lactose rose to the surface of his skin and sat there like perfume.

They could hear the TV in one of the flats, the football game replayed. "Kill 'em, Kill 'em," they heard. Football wasn't much of a game anymore.

Sasha held her plate on her knee and ate rice, kelp and steamed vegetables.

"At least have some soy sauce on it, Sash," Rab said. "If you're going to eat seaweed, cover the taste for fuck's sake."

"They put anchovies into soy sauce sometimes. You have to be vigilant." She held her spread fingers to her eyes, mimicking a vigilante mask. The joke didn't lighten their mood.

For dessert, she sat with a bowl of peaches. She never smelt as sweet as Nick did.

They drank beer. Bevan smoked. Sasha finally said, "That poor kid. And his mother. Oh, my God."

Everyone was quiet again. A bird fell out of the trees; such a common thing they barely noticed.

Then Nick jumped up.

"I'm going to look inside that fucker," he said. He lay newspapers down on the grass, put on gloves and found a sharp knife. There were three dead birds in their backyard. Nick picked up one and laid it down on the newspaper. It was smooth under his fingers. He felt no ribs, none of the skinny little bones that make birds so hard to eat. He cut through the skin and came straight to bone.

A smooth plane of bone.

"This is weird," he said. He went inside and put a big pot of water on to boil.

"You makin' soup for tomorrow night?" Bevan said. "Tell me if you are, and I'll have a break from cooking for a change."

"You're the cook, Bevan. I'm just going to boil this bird."

"You're not gonna put the bird in my pot. Fuckin' weirdo." Bevan coughed.

"It's just meat. Like a chicken. Nothing to worry about."

"What if it's diseased?"

"You can't catch bird diseases. You're human."

"What about that chicken flu thing? That killed about a million people."

"It killed about two thousand, and they all had something to do with the chickens' blood. All right? I just want to see what's going on here."

The water boiled. Nick dropped the bird in, splashing hot water and burning his fingertips. While he waited, he laid newspaper out on the kitchen bench.

The smell of wet feathers. He let the bird boil for an hour then lifted it out with tongs. The flesh fell off, and he pulled the rest away. He gagged at the soup he'd made; feathers, eyes, flesh.

He washed the bird's skeleton in the laundry sink then placed it on the newspaper. He stared at it then carried it outside to show the others.

The bird was one bone.

The wings were as smooth as china, with no give, no bend. The ribs had fused to the backbone.

It was like a small football with some of the air let out. Dents, shallow craters. But mostly smooth. A football with smooth wings.

"No wonder it couldn't fly," Sasha said. "Look at it!"

"We should take it to Dad, Rab."

"I'm sure he's got birds there, Nick."

"We're going there tomorrow, anyway, aren't we? Mum's cooking dinner. And I want to see how Dad is. We need the money, man. They're always good for a loan."

Sasha started crying and couldn't stop. Bevan carried her inside and tucked her into bed, then turned on the TV, wanting to distract himself from the thought of her sad little body. The news showed him an apartment block up the road from them, eight small flats housing eight large families. There was a permanent begging place out the front; a table for food donations; a slotted, locked box for money; a bookshelf for books for the children.

The place burnt down. All exits barricaded. All killed.

A terrible accident. "Questions need to be answered," the police minister said, but he smiled as he said it.

"Anything interesting?" Rab asked.

"Nothin'," Bevan said.

On Saturday morning they waited for Nick to get up and finally dragged him out of bed. Bevan drove, with Nick yawning in the back. The bird skeleton was wrapped in paper and packed in the boot.

"You don't all have to come, you know," Nick said. He read the paper as he spoke.

"Your Mum'll cook us a meal. It's worth it for that," Bevan said. "Better than the fried crap we'd get at my parent's place." They all had a momentary flash of Bevan's parents, huge, both of them, sitting on the couch eating fish fingers.

"Well, thanks, guys. For coming," Nick said.

The road was paved with rubbish; adults, children, cats and dogs picking through it.

"Watch out for that kid, Bevan," Rab said.

"What?"

"The kid," Rab said, louder. The child stared at them then moved out of the way.

When they arrived, they saw a family was camped across the road, socks hanging from a rope strung between two trees. Mrs Albadara answered the door.

"Ah, your father's not so well today. Not so well. He'll be okay. Me, I've just got a little headache."

Mr Albadara emerged then, smiling. He was as beautiful, really, as the boys, Sasha thought. The dark hair, black eyes, dark skin. Perfect teeth. Perfect smile.

"Hello, Mr Albadara," Sasha said. She hated feeling so respectful but she couldn't help it around Mr Albadara.

Nick said, "Dad? Something to show you. Something weird. You won't be able to figure it out. It'll stump you for sure."

"You'll show me in the study," Mr Albadara said. He liked his challenges to be private. Nick followed him to the book-lined room and placed the bird on the large, cluttered desk. Stiffly, Mr Albadara leaned over and unwrapped the bird. "I always said you should have been a vet. You're so good with animals. Ha ha."

"I didn't kill it, Dad! It just landed in our backyard."

His father poked at the bird with a pen. "Hmmm. It brings to mind the eternal bone, which won't burn. You can't crush it. You can't grind it or suck the marrow out, which will disappoint you. I know you can't see a bone without wanting to suck it."

Nick laughed. "What bone?"

"You don't know? Albadara? It is the name of the eternal bone. The bone from which the body will be resurrected."

"That's what our name means?"

"I'm afraid so."

"You know we saw a kid die yesterday. His eyes were covered with bone. And inside the dead bird it's the same thing. And you, Dad. You seem so stiff. This boy was stiff."

"Yes. I'm a little worried, too. Sudden onset is always of concern. I will see the doctor very soon." Mr Albadara stood up, stretching high to reach an ornate treasure box. He winced a little. "My ribs," he said. "Ah, in here. I had forgotten." Mr Albadara scrabbled around the things in there; a golden piece of cloth; a string with knots tied in it; a miniature eyeglass, a small rock.

"Here," he said, handing Nick a dusty, blue, perfect glass globe the size of a clenched fist. Inside sat a pearl gray triangle.

"What is it?"

"That's an ancient bone. Very old. It's an indestructible bone."

"It can't be. How old?"

"That I don't know. But it proves to me eternal life. I used to show this to you and Rab when you were children. I'd almost forgotten it existed."

"But you don't believe in religion."

"I believe in that." He gazed at the globe. "Jeremiah would be fascinated by this. I must show him."

"Who's Jeremiah?"

"Oh, just a friend. A most unusual man. You'll meet him. Another time, when we're all at the farm. You think this house is full of junk, you should see his home. Old books, antiques, anything with information from the past. He doesn't think enough information is being passed from generation to generation."

"I didn't know you had any friends, Dad."

His father smiled and nodded. "You tease me," he said.

The others were in the kitchen. Mrs Albadara was making tabouleh and spicy rice, stuffed vine leaves and spinach fingers.

Bevan watched intently.

"You're so fast," he said. "Sasha, even you'd like this stuff. Hey?"

There was no answer. Sasha and Rab had stolen away.

"Let's go spying. Show me your old room. Something to take our minds off this bone thing," Sasha said, tugging at Rab's hand.

"Let's find a place to lie down," Rab said, grabbing her, kissing her. Peppermint passion.

It was a big, old house, full to squeezing with books, specimens, models. Sasha loved it. She could spend hours in that house, if she didn't have to talk to the parents; they made her feel stupid. She loved just looking and wanting half the things she saw. There was a wax skull. A candlestick made of ebony. Books, unsorted, in piles. Dusty glass statues; a horse, a girl, a wishing well. Ornate pens. Cards of all kinds. Empty pewter frames.

In the upstairs study, the library, which was his childhood bedroom, Rab said, "Come sit with me." He pulled her onto the couch and stroked her face. Thrust his fingers into her hair and pulled her towards him.

She kissed him back, crawling onto him, wanting to absorb him. She moved about, finding a position until he said, "Keep still."

She slapped him gently. "Don't tell me to keep still. I hate keeping still." She rolled onto the floor and crawled around, looking for things.

"There's treasure everywhere here," she said. She pulled out a silver bookmark from under a chair.

"Keep it," Rab said. "They'll never miss it."

Bevan said, "I can watch the cookin', Mrs Albadara, if you've got things you need to do."

"You're such a nice man," she said. "You need a nice girl." She smiled. "Let me think of someone for you."

Anyone with a hole, he thought. He stirred the pot, checked the oven. There wasn't a lot to do. He opened her spice jars to sniff them, understand them.

Just to see what was inside, he lifted the lids on the containers lined up on the pantry shelf.

In a tin marked 'bread' he found a mess of things; tiny bells, a ring, three fake tattoos, four silver balls and a voucher for free coffee, many years expired. And money. Notes and coins, dirty and crumpled.

Bevan looked over his shoulder. She hadn't returned.

He took a quick count; two hundred dollars in notes, twenty-five dollars in coins. He took one hundred dollars.

"Petrol money," he said. "Toll money." Money of his own, not money the others had earned. He put the tin back and checked the dinner, hoping Mrs Albadara would come back soon to tell him what to do next. He tried to imagine his own mother teaching anyone to cook.

Never.

Mrs Albadara caught Sasha coming out of the bathroom. She said, "So, Sasha, come sit with me. I feel I know so much about you. The boys never shut up. Sasha this, Sasha that. I've met you all these times but we've never talked, dear, and I've got photos, would you like to see photos?"

Mrs Albadara squeezed Sasha's hand as if they shared some great secret. She pulled out baby photos of Nick and Sasha realised she thought she was Nick's girlfriend.

"Mum! What're you doing? Sasha doesn't want to see those!" Nick said, catching them together.

"I don't know. Any chance to see you naked," Sasha said.

Mrs Albadara slammed the album shut.

"Maybe another time," she said. "I smell burning. What is that Bevan doing to my kitchen?" She limped away.

When they were alone, Nick said, "You shouldn't talk like that in front of my mother, S."

"Fuck your mother."

"It's not her. It's me. You give me ideas. Dirty little ideas I should be spanked for."

Sasha laughed. "Just good friends, Nick. Just good friends." But she smiled at him, confusing him.

"Dinner!" shouted Bevan.

They sat down at the large table laden with food. Sasha felt a little guilty, thinking of the family across the street. But this was food she could eat, and she gave into it.

"If only your sister could be here, too," Mr Albadara said. The others exchanged glances.

"She doesn't come here anymore," Rab said.

They all helped to clean up.

Mrs Albadara wrapped the leavings in newspaper then gave the parcel to Rab. "Bin's out the front."

The end of the parcel was damp and leaked over his shirt.

"Jesus, Mum. I've got rubbish juice all over me."

She sighed. "Sometimes I wish we still had plastic bags."

Rab rolled his eyes. "The Good Old Days."

His mother snorted. "They were good. People cared about each other. Wealthy governments gave money to poor countries. You could go to the doctor even if you didn't have the money to pay. The government would pay."

"Why would they do that?"

"And they'd help you if you couldn't find a job. Not throw you in jail."

"Doesn't make sense, Mum," Rab said.

His mother turned on him. "You don't care! It made sense. But the more it became about money, then it didn't make sense."

Bevan said, "I would've hated the tax payin' business. I wouldn't want any of my money payin' for some loser to get his cold fixed up or whatever."

"People used to do it, then they got the idea they shouldn't."

"We're all right, anyway, Mum," Rab said.

"And that's all that matters, isn't it?" she said. "Take a clean shirt of your father's. In the drawer." Rab found a wide-striped one that made him look years older.

"Can't we give the leftovers to the family across the street?" Sasha said.

"They'll take it if they want it," Mr Albadara said.

"So you've never taken a plate to them?" Mrs Albadara said.

"I cannot lie to you. Once I did. Maybe twice."

"Perhaps you'd like me to take it over to them, served on a silver platter?" Rab said. Sasha wrinkled her nose at him. Nick ignored it all, reading the newspaper.

They were back selling 'Slenderize' on Monday.

"God, I hate Mondays," Sasha said. "People are nasty on Mondays."

"People are nasty every day, Sash," Rab said.

"But everyone walks so much faster on Mondays. It's like they feel guilty for their weekends and want to make up for it."

They watched an elderly man limp by.

"Like him. God knows what he got up to," Sasha said. As he passed them they saw his coat was slashed to shreds and the back of his head was covered with blood.

They all turned away.

Nick jumped in front of three young girls.

"Girls? Girls? Good, are you?" They laughed. One covered her mouth with her hand and Nick saw grime in the knuckles and nails.

"No bath at home? Don't your parents wash you?" The girl hid her hand behind her back.

"We don't live with our parents."

"But where do you sleep?"

"Who can sleep?" the girl said.

"You be careful, girls. See?" Nick pointed. In the distance a teenager kicked a woman who was bent over clutching her stomach.

"See? There are bad people about. You be careful," Nick said.

The three girls walked away. "We need to keep moving. They told us to keep moving," the girls said to Nick. His attention was lost, though; he'd found a dead rat and was wrapping it in newspaper.

Rab grabbed his arm. "Come on, time's wasting," he said. "Let's go find a doctor's shop. That's easy money."

They found a queue that went around the block, the poor waiting for a doctor who'd see them. They sold forty-two weight-loss programmes to the people shuffling, standing patiently.

That night they had steak. As Sasha was washing up a woman came to the door, collecting for charity. Rab answered; Nick was immersed in the newspaper and didn't hear the knock. The woman recoiled from the smell in the house; Nick had boiled the rat then tried to burn its bones and the stink was all-pervading. Trying not to breathe through her nose, she said, "We are returning to the terrible days of asylums. This is what they found on a recent raid." She handed Rab a photo; an emaciated, twisted child lying under a putrid sink on filthy tiles, pants around his ankles, holding hands with another naked child.

"They were both moaning when they were found," she said.

"How come that kid's got a beard?" Rab asked.

She looked at the photo, then at Rab. "That's faeces," she said.

"I can give you ten cents," Rab said. "That's about all I can manage."

The woman said. "There are women being raped in these places. They need medical treatment and they won't get it for less than ten dollars. Some of these women are torn from anus to vagina. They'll never have children."

"Shame," said Rab, and closed the door on her.

"Hey, Sasha, I'd like to tear you from arse to cunt," Bevan muttered to himself. He heard Sasha, sometimes, in the room next door, in the house they all shared. She loved it. She worked Rab till he dropped and still wanted more. Bevan'd give it to her if she let him. Fuck yeah. He'd give it to her. Bevan watched her skinny arse as she washed the dishes and fantasised grabbing it, her turning around and laughing. He fantasized she was his wife. Young, but not too young. Not too innocent.

"Stupid woman. What does she think is going to happen?" Rab said.

"Do you always have to be so negative?" Sasha said. "Just because you only think of yourself and what money you can make doesn't mean everyone else does."

"Look around you, Sash. No one gives a shit about anyone."

"You certainly don't."

"Hey, enough with the bitchiness, all right? I've had it with you." Rab turned and left the house.

There was a cat on the footpath outside. Motionless. Only the tip of its tail moved. Rab gently shoved it aside with his foot and it felt smooth. Hard.

Nick put his arm around Sasha and kissed her head. "Don't worry about him, S. He's more stressed by this whole thing than he'll admit. Come on, I'll take you out for a drink. Mum gave me some money for 'us time'."

Sasha said, "How did she get the idea I was your girlfriend, not Rab's?"

Nick kissed her hand. "No idea." They dressed up a little, laughing. Sasha put lipstick on.

"Where're youse goin'?" Bevan asked.

"Just out for a while. You can come if you want," Sasha said. Bevan looked at her. "Nah, promised to go see me olds. Have fun."

Sasha and Nick ran out of the house. Free. A van marked "P.D." was parked nearby. The medical team emerged, carrying a body bag.

"Another one? What the hell is it?" Sasha said.

There was a hum like electricity in the air, and she realised moaning was coming from houses all around them.

Bevan stayed away for two days. His parents took more time than expected. Things to sort out. Rab also stayed away, tired of feeling in the wrong all the time.

Bevan arrived back first and noticed nothing different.

Sasha said, "How are your parents?"

"Arrested. Dad can't move, and Mum can't look after herself. And the two of them eat more than they earn. I left 'em some 'Slenderize' last time but I don't think they took it."

"Oh, no," Sasha said.

"They're so fuckin' fat they had to get wheeled out." He poured down a beer. Grinned. "I'm livin' off beer from now on." He was glad the onus of caring for his parents was gone from him.

"And their eating habits differ from yours how?" Nick said.

He sat close to Sasha.

Rab returned the next day to find his belongings alone in the bedroom. Sasha's things in Nick's room. He said nothing because the phone rang. Their mother.

Nick wouldn't get out of bed. "My stomach hurts. I can't eat. Bring me some milk, a milkshake, chocolate, come on, S," Nick said. He pushed Sasha.

"You seemed okay last night," she said.

Nick tried to smile but his face was stiff. "Are you sure about this?" he said.

"No. But it's what happened so there you go. I'm happy. Rab'll be fine. You can share me." Sasha felt her heart beating faster most of the time. Like it was matching the beat of unheard music.

"Best of both worlds, huh?" Nick groaned. "I really feel bad. My ribs feel like they're sticking into my lungs."

"We should take you to a doctor. They might be able to help."

"I guess."

Sasha got up and made him a milkshake. Rab was in the lounge room, packing music into an overnight bag.

"What's going on?" Sasha said.

"Funny question, coming from you, Sash," Rab said. He smiled and kissed her on the cheek. "Dad's not well. Bevan's going to drive me out to the farm to see him."

"I want to come. Nick's sick, too. We could nurse them together."

"We could."

Sasha took the milkshake into Nick. "We're going to visit your Mum and Dad. They've gone to the farm. Wanna come?"

"I guess. I want my Mum."

"I can be your Mum."

"I doubt that, S," he said. He pulled her on to the bed and kissed her. His mouth felt hard and tasted of milk.

Sasha took Nick to the doctor. She sold her favourite necklace to pay for it.

Nick came stumbling out. "Lithium," he said. "It's just the side affects of the lithium. Nausea, drowsiness, tremors."

"So stop taking the lithium."

"They want everyone to keep taking it," Nick said.

Nick sat in the car while the others packed bags and filled the boot. They took their last supplies of 'Slenderize'. Bevan drove; he always drove. Sasha joined Nick in the back.

"Changin' of the guard, I see," Bevan said. He looked in the rear-view mirror, seeing Sasha stroking Nick's head. "Must be my turn next." He coughed.

Sasha ground her teeth. "I hate clichés, you know, but…last man on earth and it wouldn't happen."

Bevan was silent. Rab could see his gaze flicking from side to side and worried about his concentration.

Nick said, "What about your olds, Bevan?"

"What about them?"

"Is it this bone thing they've got? I heard something on the radio about it and there's stuff about it in the papers," Nick said.

"Wouldn't know. Can't get in to visit them. All I know is, they're gettin' fed so they'll be happy. Why, what is it?" He coughed.

"This bone thing. Sore bones. Symptoms from some hormonal thing, I don't know."

"The doctor said it was the lithium," Sasha said.

"It's gotta be more than that," Nick said. He fell asleep with his arm tucked up under his chin. It took two hours to get to the other side of town. Traffic was heavy and there were accidents, more accidents than usual. People were walking along the freeway and it looked weird, like the walking birds.

A strange migration.

They reached open ground and drove through the lush greenness of it. There were milking sheds.

Nick sat up. His arm was tucked under his chin.

"What are you doin'? You look creepy," Bevan said.

"I can't put my arm down," Nick said. "I can't move it."

Fused.

"We should get a job here on the way back," Nick said. "It looks really nice here." Rab had to turn down the music to hear him.

Bevan drove without talking, smoking furiously.

As they passed through their third toll booth, Rab said, "How's the petrol going?" Bevan flicked a look down. "We'll have to stop soon." He lit a cigarette with one hand. The smoke reached over to the back seat.

"Bevan!" Sasha said. Bevan wound down his window and hung his right arm out. He drove left-handed. His arm was covered with a long-sleeved top; he rarely bared his skin to the sun.

Bevan pulled into a petrol station and Rab said, "Where did the money come from?"

"I borrowed it from your Mum's bread bin," Bevan said.

"Stole it!" Sasha said. "You stole it!"

Rab was quiet.

"It's petrol money," Bevan said. "Wanted to pay for it myself for a change."

"Mum loves you. She would've given it to you, if you'd asked."

Bevan grinned. "I didn't want to be under obligation to your Mum." He squinted at the gauge. "That should do. That'll get us there." He stuck his head in the window to reach for his wallet.

As they neared the Albadara's farm, Bevan said, "So I'll just drop you off, will I?"

"You gotta come in for a while," Sasha said. "Weren't the fields different last time we were here? When was that?"

"We came two Christmases ago. Remember? We hated it," Rab said.

"Are you sure we haven't been since then? I can't believe we haven't been out of the city in all that time."

"We've been busy."

There were fields of flowers. Dozens of different kinds. Lush purples and reds.

"Let's stop and get some flowers for your Mum. They're so colourful," Sasha said.

"I need a piss anyway," Bevan said. He got out and urinated one step away from the car. The smell of ammonia made Nick's eyelids snap open but he closed them quickly. The light hurt him.

Sasha ran into the fields and picked some flowers. Their stems were white and seemed brittle; they snapped easily.

"What sort of flowers do you think they are?" she said.

"No idea," Rab said. "I don't know stuff like that. Nick is the romantic type. Ask him."

Nick was answering no questions. He'd seen a dead rabbit beside the road. "Get that for me, Rab?" he said.

Rab shook his head in disgust. "You're a fucking lunatic, you know that," he said.

Sasha breathed in the scent of the flowers.

"It's rich. It reminds me of something. Smell them." She thrust them under Rab's nose. He pulled away.

"I know it's not a good smell, but aren't they beautiful?" she said.

"I can smell them already, thanks. Too strong. Let's get away from here." His urgency startled her into movement.

Minutes later they reached the Albadara's farm. There were a dozen cars parked out front.

Mr Albadara came out to greet them, walking stiffly, slowly. He watched as they took Nick out of the car.

"Him too? He can't move his arm?" Mr Albadara asked.

Sasha tried to hand him the flowers. He waved his hand at her. "I don't want them, silly girl. Throw them away. And wash your hands. Did you breathe the pollen?"

"Aren't they beautiful?" Sasha said. She smiled, willing him to smile back and make it all right.

"They smell of flesh," Mr Albadara said. "Don't you realise that? The sweet smell of flesh just before it begins to rot. They're burying the poor over there. Lining them up, piling them in. These flowers grow overnight and they stink. Go dig one up and you'll see. Try to pull it up by its roots and you'll feel a tug. Those mutated flowers grow straight out of the bodies of the dead. Pollination spreads the flowers everywhere else. They grow like weeds, this mutant breed."

Sasha threw the flowers away and blew her nose. The stench was there, now she knew what it was. There was a sick feeling in her stomach, as if she'd eaten meat and enjoyed it without knowing it was meat. She'd sniffed so hard at those flowers, wanting to identify the smell.

Mr Albadara said, "There is more than one graveyard. So many people die, of so many things, with so little money. They plant the flowers to cover the fact. They don't hide it but the flowers are there to make people forget the bodies are there, forget people are dying of hunger and deprivation."

"But there were no graveyards or signs or anything. What're they doing? They can't bury people like that."

"They're dead, they're poor, they have no one. Anything's possible when no one cares," Mr Albadara said.

Sasha thought of the dozens of fields they had seen. Hundreds of these flowers, with bone-brittle stems. She thought of Rab's disgust in the flowers. "Did you know this?"

"I thought everyone did. What else are they going to do with the bodies?"

"I can't believe you didn't tell me."

"I can't believe you didn't know, Sash."

Mr Albadara said, "The roots travel down to where the nutrients are."

"We saw a kid die. Actually watched him die," Sasha said.

"Ah," Mr Albadara said. "Yes. Nick told me."

"He was all stiff, like you and Nick. He couldn't see, though. His eyes were all closed over. They told us it was leukaemia."

Mr Albadara snorted. "Doubtful. Very doubtful. I bet they snapped him up. Raced him off."

Nick nodded and hugged his Dad with one arm.

"The proof will be found in the bones of the children," Mr Albadara said. "Come in."

Sasha held back, watching the others help Nick through the door. It was too strange. Mr Albadara was too strange. She was scared of it all.

"Come on, Sash," Rab said kindly. He put his arm around her. The strength of him made her feel weak.

"I'm all right," she said.

"You've come on a good day," Mr Albadara said as they walked through the house to the backyard. "We're having a little party."

Bevan stepped forward. The backyard was full of women thirty years his senior. Some men but not so many. All the guests were stripped to bare skin and underwear. Rab had noticed this in the city, too, in the public parks. People spending as much time in the sun as possible. They craved it. Bevan usually covered up, with his red hair and white skin. People didn't trust him, so white. The darker the skin the healthier.

The guests had taken off their hats and thrown away the sunscreen. They were getting naked.

Bevan smiled. "Ripe for the pickin'," he said, and walked with his ape's walk to the table of drinks; arms out from his body, fingers spread, legs a little bowed.

"He's such a sleaze," Sasha said.

"At least he's leaving you alone," Rab said.

Bevan did okay. The older ladies liked him, and he liked any woman who liked him, old or young. He could flirt with them, the old ones, and they believed it, because he was gap-toothed, scar-skinned, short-bodied. Their self-esteem was so low, most of them, they could believe an ugly man with BO would flirt with them. They wouldn't have believed it from Rab or Nick.

Bevan slicked his hair down but it sprang straight back into a mess as he walked up to a woman with fat ankles and dry, brittle hair. "Gidday, love," he said.

Nick groaned. They helped him to sit and Sasha found him a glass of milk and a straw.

"God, all these boring people," Sasha said.

They sat together, clustered on chairs, perching on table edges. Nick, intent and curious, sat beside his father near the pool. "What do you think it is, Dad? This bone thing? I boiled a rat the other day. It was like the bird. Creepy. Tried to burn it."

"I'll tell you what's creepy," Bevan said, standing with his hands on his hips between them. "No beer! Where's the beer?"

"There's plenty of whisky," said Mr Albadara.

"I want beer!" Bevan's face reddened like it usually did after a dozen.

"Beer won't help you," Mrs Albadara said, coming over to calm her guest. "Here, have some milk. Energy milk," she said, pouring whisky straight into the carton.

Nick walked stiffly to the table.

"I smell cheese," he said. He picked up a handful of cheese cubes with the unfused hand and filled his mouth with them. He chewed. The pain went away just a little. He took a carton of milk and sculled it, dribbling milk down his chin.

Everyone was doing the same.

The sight of them all with milk moustaches and beards made Sasha laugh.

"Want one?" said a white haired woman. Her face spasmed and twitched as if she was amused. "You look like you could do with one."

"Sasha, this is my Great-aunt Terry," Rab said. "Not bad for her age, is she?"

"I don't eat any animal products," Sasha said. She felt like she needed to apologise for her food choice.

"None?" said Great-aunt Terry.

"I'll take it, Terry," Rab said. He sculled the milk.

"You know what they're saying," Great-aunt Terry said, "It's not the side affects of the lithium after all. Tiredness, and body ache and that. They're saying it's hormonal. And you can only treat it with calcium and Vitamin D. Studies have shown the more sun the better. Don't you just love it?"

Bevan drank straight whisky. He hated milk. He coughed as the liquor hit his throat.

"There's nuts, on the table, and more cheese," Mr Albadara said.

"Cheese is an animal product," Sasha said. She hated the way she sounded but what could she do? She took a kelp pill. Sometimes it was all she had to eat. She whispered to Rab, "You do realise your Great-aunt Terry is insane, don't you?"

Nick was still eating the cheese and drinking milk. Sasha thought he stank of it.

Rab watched her.

"Happy with your choice?" he said.

"I haven't made a choice."

"Really?"

"Why? You bothered?"

Rab laughed. "Is it all completely meaningless to you?"

"The sex part is. The morning part isn't. And the talking part."

They were quiet. They watched Mr Albadara, livelier than he'd been in a long time. He wandered around squeezing and stroking people, saying, "How are you feeling INSIDE?"

"Your Dad's scaring me. What's up with him?" Sasha said.

"I don't know, Sash. I guess he's just worried about people." They watched him walking stiffly amongst his guests. His arm movements were stiff and jerky. His smile seemed bigger than usual.

"Did your Dad get false teeth?" Sasha asked.

"Leave him alone, would you? You've done nothing but criticize since we got here," Rab said, staring at her.

Sasha turned her back. "I'm going for a swim," she said. She dropped her clothes at the side of the pool. Her bright yellow bikini brought gasps of envy from the guests.

Rab and Nick watched her for a while, then Nick said, "I want to talk to Dad. Help me in."

Rab took his arm and they found their father standing in the corner of the sunroom. Just standing. Rab helped Nick to a sofa and sat on a stool.

"Dad," Nick said. "How are you feeling?"

"Fine, fine," their father said. "Same as you, I suppose. Not so good. You?"

"I'm a little scared, to be honest. You should have seen this kid die, Dad. It was horrible. The medics took him away so fast. They wanted him for his organs. For other kids."

"They'd have to crack him open like a lobster. He's all one bone, now. Spurs, they're calling it. Yes. I've been hearing a little about this new disease. The bone grows at an alarming rate, they say."

"That's what it feels like. It feels like I'm all bone and my blood can hardly get through my veins," Nick said.

His father nodded and said, "They should name the disease after us. Don't you think?"

Rab frowned. "Why?"

"Because our name means the eternal bone. You boys have forgotten everything I've ever told you. It is an ancient name meaning the eternal bone."

"So this has happened before?" Rab asked. "It must have happened before to have a name."

"That's a point. A good point. I wonder if this did happen millennia ago. If the bones fused, the bones strengthened. And the mythology sprung from that. I'll get back to you. I've got some literature because of our name. Let me read and then I'll call you. Go now and leave me to study." He stumbled as he turned. Rab leapt up and grabbed his arm, helped him to sit beside Nick.

"Dad?" Nick said. "Are you all right?"

Mr Albadara shook his head. "No. No. I don't want this to be over. I don't."

"What, Dad? The party?"

"My life, Nick. My life. I'm not ready to go."

"Who says you're going? You'll be all right."

"I won't, you know. It's too late. For me. Maybe they'll figure it out in time for others. Lord, I hope so. But Nick. Nick, you too. I'm sorry to frighten you. I'm so sorry," his father said.

"You always tell us the truth."

"I try to," his father said. "I'm not too good at lying."

Rab looked at them, their limbs held stiffly. "I'm feeling it too," he said.

"Not like this," Nick whispered.

There was the sound of girlish squeals below.

"Ah," Mr Albadara said. He smiled, satisfied. "Come on." He shuffled downstairs and struggled to open the back door.

"Jeremiah! My friend! You old misfit," he said. "I always know when you arrive because the women make a noise!"

"Here at last. At last!" the man said. He was dressed all in white. Close-cropped white hair and a broad brimmed white hat. The heavy scent of aftershave. He smiled, snarling his damaged, ivory-yellow teeth at them. His face was smooth and tight, too much fat squeezed into too little skin. He held up a bottle of white wine like an Olympic torch.

"Glasses, my friend? Glasses!" he said.

"Come, let's sit inside. Away from the rest. Rab. Nick. Sasha. You too, Bevan. Let's visit with my friend," Mr Albadara said. Mrs Albadara sighed and collected huge glasses for them all. Mr Albadara couldn't hold his properly, and he splashed wine all over his pants and shoes.

"You're getting wine on the carpet," Mrs Albadara said. She was exhausted from being hostess to so many visitors so much of the time.

"That's why we're drinking white," Mr Albadara said. "No stains." He and Jeremiah found this very funny.

"I'm sorry. Sorry. I'm here to make the arrangements. I'm so sorry for your loss," Jeremiah said. He stood up to clasp Rab's hand but Rab just stared at him. He went for Nick then gave up, putting his hands in his pockets.

"What arrangements?" Rab said. "What loss?"

"He's already made mine. So he's here to do Nick's. Normally you'd have to go to see him," Mr Albadara said. "But the moment I called him and said it was an emergency, here he is."

"I don't normally make house calls," the man said. His mouth twitched as if he was trying to be serious but couldn't help seeing the funny side. "My place is up at the top of the hill. I call it 'The Grinding House'. I'm hoping the name will catch on. 'The Grinding House'."

"Are you a doctor? We don't need a doctor. We've already seen a doctor," Sasha said.

"He's the funeral director," Mr Albadara said softly. "We need to decide what we'll do with Nick. They're asking that most people be cremated. It allays the fear of infection. People who can't afford it are going out to the fields. I know what I want to do, and your mother, but we want to include you in the decision. We want to be part of the research, so our deaths are not in vain."

"You want that. I do not," Mrs Albadara said. "This is wrong."

"It can't be wrong if it is for the greater good. The Greater Good. What is wrong is burying bodies which could help save humanity," Jeremiah said. His voice was soft, clear, determined.

"Ah, hello? Still alive here?" Nick said. He tried to smile and said, "I'm tired."

"And me. Come, I'll lie with you, my darling," his mother said. Rab helped Nick to rise.

Mrs Albadara curled up in bed with Nick, and cried softly. Rab went back to Sasha, sitting nervously with his father and Jeremiah.

"Rab, we need to talk. This is happening and I don't want the decisions left to you," said his father. "Listen, I want to be honest. I want to describe it to you so you will have some understanding. The stomach pain is first. That ache, and a loss of hunger. Or great hunger, ravenous, accompanied by terrible nausea. You can feel the smoothness inside your belly. The fat hangs there like a pouch."

Sasha tucked her legs up and squeezed her eyes shut. She tilted her head away.

"This is what happens. First the feet feel stiff and the heels sore. You can't bend your toes. Then your ankles feel stiff. It is worse overnight. You wake up in pain. As you walk you feel the bones crackle. Like walking on eggshells. Your fingers, too. You can't move your fingers. When you sleep you try to lie with your fingers comfortably held. You try not to point your toes. Because one morning you wake up and your fingers have fused. You can't bend them. If your toes are pointed they will stay that way."

Instinctively they all curled their toes.

"You know then that you don't have long," Mr Albadara said. "Your knees and elbows stiffen. If you fall asleep with them wrapped around yourself, you will have to break them to move them.

"Your neck stiffens. Your groin feels painful. When you walk it is like your pelvis is mortar and your spine a pestle, grinding, grinding.

"Your breathing becomes difficult. You no longer feel your ribs, just a smooth breastplate, like armour.

"You urinate sitting down, a thin, painful, stream. You can't defecate. Small pebbles eke out.

"Then your ears. You can't hear. There is bone across your eardrums. This happens very quickly. It can happen in a day with the worst growth happening at night."

Rab got up and moved next to Sasha.

"When the bone grows over your eyes you need to make yourself as comfortable as possible. You need to lie down. Before your throat closes over you need to take a drink. Remember though that you can't urinate. Your bladder will be full, and there is no way to release it. The poisons of your waste will be absorbed back into your body, but this is not what will kill you.

"You will know the sensation of bone growth by now. You will be able to feel the bones growing and fusing.

"Your sinus cavities close.

"You lie there. There is a sinking feeling, like you are about to succumb to anaesthesia. You feel like your eyes are open but you can't see. Maybe just a sense of light before the bone grows too thick across your eyes."

His father cupped his eyes with his palms.

"It is very painful. You remember growing pains now."

He dropped his hands to his lap, clenched his fists.

"Your skeleton smoothes into one plane and the top of your throat seals as the base of your skull closes in. If you don't panic you have maybe an hour of breathing before this closes altogether, the last bones merge and you can't even struggle for breath." Mr Albadara sank back in his chair, tears wetting his cheeks.

"Rest, now, my friend," Jeremiah said. "Rest." Mr Albadara closed his eyes. Jeremiah moved closer to Rab and Sasha and whispered, "I've seen a skeleton. They're not telling people. It looked like an alien. An alien! Like the aliens people say they see. It looked like he had one bone. He was smooth. Smooth. No joints or gaps. Some bumps—ankles, knees, hips, elbows. Some bumps on the head. All else was smooth."

Rab got up and stood by his father. "Dad?"

"It's almost inevitable. The fusion," Mr Albadara said, blinking rapidly. "We're born with four hundred and fifty bones, which fuse to two hundred and six by the time you're an adult. The top of your shoulder is still not fused at sixteen. It's the last to merge. The skeleton is so very separate from the man. Almost anonymous. You know who a man is just by looking at him, but a skeleton you need to study and guess." He closed his eyes. "I'll rest, now. Nick is resting, and your mother. Rab, I want you to go with Jeremiah, just so you understand."

Jeremiah stood, his fingertips pressed together in a triangular shape.

"Come on, then," Jeremiah said. "No time like the present. I'll take you with me, then bring you back a little later. Come on!"

"We might as well see how bad it is," Rab said. "Come with me, Sasha?"

They travelled in the hearse. The blackness of it made Rab and Sasha whisper. Jeremiah drove to the top of the hill. A professional sign, painted black letters on a pale blue background, said 'The Grinding House'.

"Does he think it's funny? I don't get it," Sasha whispered.

"He's just a fucking lunatic, Sash. There's nothing to get," Rab whispered.

Sasha shook her head, then scrabbled in her bag. She picked out a bottle of 'Slenderize'. "I thought it sounded familiar. The place where they make 'Slenderize'. It's called 'The Grinding House'. You don't suppose . . . " They stared at each other in horror, then snorted with laughter. "Surely not."

'The Grinding House' was an A-frame building. A triangle on a hill.

Rab and Sasha followed the funeral director inside. They didn't hold hands, although Sasha wished they could. She knew she had to be the strong one this time, and tried to pay attention to Jeremiah. She angled her head toward him like she always did when she was listening carefully.

"How's your hearing?" Jeremiah said. "Is it slipping away? I notice things. I've always been like that." He reached over and picked a piece of lint from Sasha's sleeve. Flicked his own shoulder.

"It's only that I see you tilting your head to listen. It's one of those funny things. I don't know if it's a type of aping behaviour or if it helps them listen. I know it's one of the first signs that their equilibrium is going. Body, soul, spirit." He smiled as if they should know what he was talking about.

Rab said, "She's always done that. She doesn't want anyone to know she's a bit deaf."

Jeremiah ignored this as if he were deaf himself. He led them through a passageway lined with books. "You could start at that end and work your way to this and you'd be educated when you finished. All the necessary knowledge. All knowledge. Schools teach you nothing. Nothing. No parent should send their child to school. It should come from the older generation. Passed on. The Grandparent, the Parent, the Child," he said. "Did you hear about the children sent to a school of known, very wealthy paedophiles? They are taught the beauty of big/little love. This is true."

Sasha said, "We actually knew someone whose little brother went there. They took him out the other week."

Jeremiah nodded. "You see? No parent should trust the system. No parent! So what do you think of my sign? Enticing?"

"This isn't a hotel," Rab muttered. Sasha waved the bottle of pills at Jeremiah. "The place that makes these is called 'The Grinding House', too."

Jeremiah frowned. "Hmm. I was hoping nobody would notice. I stole the name, I'm afraid. I liked it. Seemed a waste on a chemical company. Pure waste."

"So you don't make 'Slenderize' here using dead bodies?"

Jeremiah laughed until tears came. "No. No, I don't. I think they're based off-shore. That's where their naturally-occurring elements are to be found."

Sasha yawned. Rab said, "About Dad ... "

"Ah, yes. Yes. And Nick, too, if I'm not mistaken. Both of them before long. They'll be sadly missed. We always say that but for him . . . he is a good man. Sadly missed. He is very proud of you boys. And your friends. You're good for him, you young people."

"He isn't that old," Sasha said.

"No, no, he isn't. Terrible loss."

Jeremiah led them to a little chapel.

"If you'll wait here, I'll check his notes. He is very clear about what he wants and he wants me to make it clear to you. Sit and let the atmosphere take you. People say it's very calming here. Very calming."

"But most of your customers are dead," Rab said.

Again, the funeral director seemed to be deaf. He nodded at them and walked out through the chapel door.

"What an awful man," Sasha said.

"If you had to choose, sex with him or sex with Bevan, who would you choose?"

Sasha stared at him and didn't answer. She walked around the room, reading the names of the many dead. The room seemed to be sound-proofed; there was a kind of muffled roar which made Sasha think of trapped air.

There were ceiling-high doors cut into the walls.

"Where do these go, I wonder?" she said.

"Don't open them," Rab said. "God knows what's there. Bodies or something. I really don't want to know." He crunched a peppermint.

"They're just cupboards. Can I look? I hate that man. I want to know his secrets."

She tugged at the big silver handles but the doors were locked.

"What has he got in there?"

Rab shook his head. He sank into a pew and put his head into his hands.

"It's still all about you, even with Dad dying and Nick nearly gone."

Sasha stared at him. She sat beside him, held him.

"I don't want to think about it. I'm gabbling. I'm sorry."

She squeezed him, pulled him close. He cried then. It took his breath away.

"I can't breathe properly. I feel like my lungs are going." He cried.

"Good," Jeremiah said. They had not heard him come in. "I was concerned that man wasn't to be mourned."

Rab said, "Just because you don't see the tears doesn't mean they aren't there. You don't need to witness things for them to be real. And he's not dead yet. I'd appreciate you not acting like he is."

Jeremiah passed a small folder to Rab.

"He's very clear, here. Very clear about his remains. His bone-ash to be used for research purposes. Though it's the children they say hold the answers. The bones of the children."

"Mum doesn't want that," Rab said.

"It's the only way we're going to fight this terrible disease," Jeremiah said, rattling his keys in his pockets. "The Pathology Department know my eye for detail. That's why I was asked to help. The Department knew I could manage the work. I am the record keeper. The chronicler. I have everything ready for the Pathology Department each week, and I'm given a receipt. I've been asked to store it all here." He opened the cupboard. Lined up, row after row on cheap plywood shelves, were baby food jars filled with grey ash.

"Four thousand, eight hundred and ninety-three," Jeremiah said. "All catalogued." All with stickers saying "Property of P.D.."

"You're very organised," Sasha said. Jeremiah took her hand and she felt him squeezing hard, assessing the bones in her fingers.

"It used to be there was always one bit that wouldn't burn. Not always the same bit. But always one small chunk. Now, these latest bodies, sometimes it's the whole thing. The whole thing." He mimicked grinding. "Usually we grind any left-over bits down and add them to the ashes. It's an art, you know. The fire needs to be incredibly hot to burn the bone."

"Nick tried to burn a rat's skeleton after he read in the paper about it," Sasha said. "They were right. It wouldn't burn."

"It stank, though," Rab said.

Jeremiah showed them a small pile of triangular gray bones. "These need to go into the grinder. Animal, vegetable, mineral," he said. "Three."

"You've burnt a lot of people," Rab said.

Jeremiah chuckled. "Oh, I didn't burn all of those! No. Those have come to me from around the country. I am the record keeper." He took Rab's hand, squeezed it. "Men are more solid in the bones. They absorb the calcium better than women do. That's why women are more likely to suffer osteoporosis and broken hips. That sort of thing. Broken wrists. Broken arms. A broken finger. Broken toes."

"Are you going to name all two hundred and ten bones?" Sasha said.

"Two hundred and six," he said.

———

Mrs Albadara was waiting anxiously when they returned. "I wish he hadn't made you go to that man. Why go to that Jeremiah? I don't like that man. He makes my friends nervous."

"That doesn't stop them fighting over him," Mr Albadara said. "It's disgusting how they behave. He's not interested. Can't they see that?"

"He only likes them when they're dead."

Mr Albadara snorted at his wife then turned to Rab. "Now let's see how Nick is," he said. "Take me there." Rab helped his father to the room where Nick rested.

Nick cried when they entered. "Dad. Dad. Dad."

"Your grief makes me feel my life hasn't been wasted," Mr Albadara said.

"What is it, Dad? What is this thing?" Nick asked.

"It's the end of life as we know it," his father said. He placed one hand on Rab's shoulder, one on Nick's head.

Rab laughed. "You're such a drama queen, Dad."

"Are your bones aching yet? Can you feel it? Come to me when you're like Nick," their father said.

"I'll never be like Nick. Sorry to disappoint you."

Nick stared. "Spurs isn't that bad, Dad. They're saying only a small percentage of the population will be affected. We're not talking the end of the human race. Not even close. Just the end of you and me."

"You don't think that's the end of the world?" his father asked. He tried to smile but his cheeks and jaw were stiff. He could only talk quietly.

"It's very comforting having you here," he said.

"That's good, Dad. But I feel like I need to get out a bit. Just to get some air. I can't breathe. Take me somewhere, Rab," Nick said. He called out, "Mum? I'm going out."

"You're not going anywhere," his mother said, coming with a cool cloth for his forehead.

"We'll just take him out for a drive, Mum. Just for a little while. Okay?" Rab said. His mother tutted.

Bevan loaded Nick in the back. "God, he's heavy. All bone and no flesh," Bevan said. He got into the driver's seat.

"Anybody want anything before we go?" He cleared his throat.

Nick cried in pain and with frustration. "Milk. Get me some milk." Nick couldn't stop drinking the stuff. It was like breathing. If he stopped for a minute he felt like he was choking. He lay reclined to drink. Sasha poured the milk though a funnel into his mouth. It sickened her; the sound of Nick gulping repulsed her.

"Start driving," Nick said. His voice whistled, like he was talking through a straw. "I want you to drive."

Bevan started the car. "Where to?"

"Just drive," hissed Rab. Nick sighed as the car started. Already the rumble had eased a little of the pain.

"You might as well take him to Jeremiah. The ghoul. Save us a trip later," Rab said. Nick whistled, then laughed like nutshells crushed underfoot.

"Shut up," Sasha said. "Just drive," she told Bevan.

She felt Nick's neck stiffen.

"I can feel tears. It feels like they're dissolving my eyeballs. I can't even see light anymore, S. My eyes have fused over. I can see a whole new world. Strangely attractive."

His sinuses had filled in so he talked in a strange, nasal voice. Rab looked at Nick until his neck ached. He rubbed at it, grimacing.

"Is your neck sore, Rab?" Sasha said. "Is it stiff?"

"Cry while you can," Nick said.

Rab flexed his fingers. There was less give than there had been.

Bevan slowed for some cows blocking the road.

"See you for the Sunday roast, you stupid cunts."

Nick made a noise like laughter. Sasha and Rab laughed, too.

"Don't stop," Nick whispered. "Keep moving." Bevan backed up, going slow at first then faster. He turned the car in a spin and took them back the other way.

Sasha reached out to put her hand on Bevan's shoulder, to thank him for understanding.

They got back to the farm well after dark. The party was still going; people in the lounge room laughing with their white teeth showing. White-haired Great-aunt Terry looked at Nick then said to Rab, "Shouldn't we call the medical team for Nick? They've asked everybody to let them know."

Sasha sat beside her and held her hand. "Can we leave it for tonight? They can't do anything for him."

"We'll have to call them tomorrow. Okay? They like to be informed. P.D, you know," Great-aunt Terry said knowingly. "At least let us get him a doctor. I just read about this new thing they're talking about, where your bones don't dissolve like they're supposed to. You can get help for it, I heard. He needs help."

"I'm okay," Nick muttered. He was propped up in a chair. His mother fed him and wiped his chin. As they ate dinner, noodles with kelp for Sasha, fish and chips covered with salt for Rab and Bevan, bread soaked in milk for Nick, Sasha whispered to Rab, "The idea of those medical team people coming makes me physically ill. Are they still telling people it's leukaemia?"

Rab said, "I guess it's beyond that. I don't know. Maybe we should leave tomorrow, early, before anyone can call the medics."

"But where? Where are you thinking of going?" Sasha said. "I don't want to go back to the city."

Rab said, "We'll think of somewhere. Okay? Away from people. It'll be okay."

When the meal was over they all slept.

Nick did not wake up.

Sasha found him dead in the bed beside her. She held him for an hour until the others woke up.

"What are we going to do with him? We can't take him to that terrible Jeremiah," she said.

"Dad wants him there. It's what he told us to do. Love you, Nick," Rab said.

Sasha didn't dare say it.

"Can't we just bury Nick ourselves? No one'll know," Sasha said.

They heard Bevan singing in the shower.

"Surely that'll be okay. It'll be better," Sasha said. They talked in whispers, wanting to keep Nick to themselves for a bit longer. Bevan came out of the shower, rubbing his hair with a towel.

"Dad's already paid. He paid for all of us. He thinks it's important. Come on, Sash. You're talking crap. This is what has to happen."

"I guess, then. I don't want to go there, though. That Jeremiah makes me sick," Sasha said. She stroked Nick's hand.

"Rab and I'll do it, Sasha, with their Mum and Dad. You stay here and rest," Bevan said. He'd dreamt of being with a woman the night before. That always cheered him up.

"The thing that's killing me is how I'm going to tell Mum," Rab said. "She's downstairs thinking he's still alive."

"She's prepared, at least, knew it was coming. She'll be able to say he's not suffering anymore. But what about your Dad?"

Sasha held Rab's hand as he told his parents. The grief was terrible. Tired.

Mrs Albadara could barely walk from the desolation. Bevan had to carry Mr Albadara who looked different, and Sasha realised his teeth had fallen out overnight; his gums hard, protruding with jaw.

Sasha watched them drive away, and, when she was alone, cried. She sorted through Nick's things while they were gone, her way of saying goodbye, and found his box of skeletons. The bird, the cat, a rabbit, the half-charred rat. Examples. His work.

Sasha stared at the box then picked it up and took it to a field. She held it for a while then began throwing the bones away.

Rab came up behind her.

"What are you doing?"

"They stink. These bones stink. I can't stand the smell of them. How was the funeral?"

Rab lifted his hands. "Yeah, great Sash. Happy day. They burnt him up, and Jeremiah couldn't even wait till we were gone. We heard it. The grinder. I swear I could smell bone."

"What did it smell like?"

"You wouldn't like it."

Rab's mother stood in the kitchen, screaming.

"How could this be right? This was not a burial. This was a desecration. My son, my son."

Rab's father was too stiff to hold her. She screamed at him, "How could you allow this to happen?"

"It's information that could save us all."

"My children are not information. They are sacred from my flesh. Will you consign me to the same fate? Rab? Our grandchild?"

Rab and Sasha stood in the doorway. Bevan was outside, washing his car.

Rab looked at Sasha. She nodded, her face white.

"This is our sacrifice for the human race. We are the intelligent ones. The educated ones. It is our responsibility," Mr Albadara said.

"I despise you. I hate you. I hate you!" Mrs Albadara screamed, then she collapsed at her husband's feet and wept, holding his legs.

Later, Sasha and Rab went to her bedside where she rested with a cup of tea, pictures of Nick and Rab as babies.

"How did you know?" Sasha whispered. Mrs Albadara smiled. "I wasn't sure. Where's your father, Rab?"

"He's with Jeremiah. At 'The Grinding House'."

"Good. Now listen to me." She rose up, and her sudden strength was almost frightening. "You must get away. I cannot have you all left to Jeremiah. I don't want you to end up in a jar on the shelf. You must go before it's too late."

"It's already too late, Mum. It's over," Rab said.

"Go anyway. Just drive."

"But where?" Rab said. He was so tired he could hardly talk.

"I know a place," his mother said. "It's an almond grove, a beautiful place. I passed it once, with your father. There's a little cabin there. It seemed uninhabited but you'll have to see. Go there, all of you. Maybe take another woman. Pick someone Bevan likes. To keep him company. I worry about him a little. And tins of food. Water. Books. You'll think of things.

"Go to the almond grove. The place where the almond trees grow is very warm and there are no frosts. When it rains the water is slowly absorbed into the hard, dry ground. Did you know an almond tree looks like a peach tree? That a peach tree smells of bitter almonds? It is beautiful there.

"Now Nick is gone, I think you should go to the almond grove. Leave us. It is better for you there."

Rab said, "We'll go tomorrow. Spend tonight together. But maybe we should just go home to the city."

"Maybe we should try to find this almond grove. I don't think home's the way it used to be," Sasha said. "I think it's a good idea. We should go tomorrow. I'll tell Bevan."

"Do we take anyone else with us?" Bevan said. The only women he'd seen here were in their fifties. Too old even for him.

"Let's just go," Sasha said. "First thing in the morning."

None of them slept well, and before dawn Sasha and Bevan had packed the car. Sasha led Rab to the front seat. Then they drove, past fields of bone flowers marching like soldiers. They listened to the radio, music and ads, no news. An ad for 'Slenderize' told them, "Now with added iodine."

"What the fuck's that for?" Rab said.

"Something for our own good?" Bevan said.

"There's iodine in kelp," Sasha said. She looked at Bevan. "And in that salt you pour on everything."

Bevan laughed. "So I'm a good guy?"

They had been driving for two hours when Rab clutched his stomach.

"I'm hungry. I'm so hungry."

Sasha ripped the ringpull on a can of spaghetti. "This'll fill you up till we get somewhere."

Bevan drove with his thumbs sticking out. Sasha sat with her feet tucked under.

"You're not stiff at all, are you, Sasha? You're not feelin' it even a little. That shits me," Bevan said.

Sasha shook her head. "I wonder how the others are going. The other vegans I mean. It's gotta be the animal products. Not all of them like kelp but none of them touch meat."

Bevan snorted. "Yeah, whatever. I'm not givin' up meat just cos you say so."

"I'm not asking you to. I don't care what you eat."

She closed her eyes.

The traffic was steady. Reasonably smooth. Police cars amongst civilians ensured the rules were followed. One man was arrested for driving with his arm out of the window. He was pulled over, his car taken away.

They passed through another toll booth, handing money to the uniformed cop there. "I wonder where Henri is. That nice cop. He's probably been killed by one of them by now," Sasha said.

"Let's hope he's all right," Rab said.

People stopped often at the roadside food stalls. There were hundreds of them, all along the road. People shovelling food in, ravenous. Some served food to the cars and that made it even easier. Everyone was so hungry.

"I'm still hungry. I'm still hungry," Rab said. They had to stop and get him food before the nausea set in.

Bevan pulled up at a roadside stand. Dust was thick in the air and they could see it settle on the food. Rab grabbed meat on a stick, six of them, smothering them with peanut sauce. The food slid into his mouth so fast the cook laughed and thrust more at him.

"Eat! Eat!" the cook said loudly as she turned away.

"I'll just have some rice, please," Sasha said. The woman didn't respond. Sasha spoke louder, shouted. Rab limped around the table and waved at the woman.

"I can barely hear," she said loudly. "My ears are closed over." Her voice was nasal. "Nice to be out in the country, hmmm? It sounds awful in the city now. The chaos. You don't get that kind of chaos here."

Bevan said loudly to the roadside seller, "You should meet us where we're going. It's an almond grove. It's supposed to be beautiful."

She nodded. "Okay. I'll visit." She smiled and they could see her teeth were just hanging on.

"Her jaw's pushing through," Rab whispered. He wriggled his own loose teeth with his tongue. As he walked back to the car he suddenly wasn't sure where the ground was, where the sky. He stumbled.

"Dizzy?" Sasha said. He rubbed at his ears until the dizziness faded.

"It's okay," he said, though he couldn't even hear his own footfalls.

There were four people parked at the next picnic rest spot. A young boy, an older girl, woman and man. A family. The son was curled up into a ball. The parents took it in turns to rock him.

"How are your kids going?" the father said. His shirt was like Rab's, fatherly.

"I'm not a father," Rab said.

The parents exchanged sorrowful glances.

"I wish we could look after you, too. But we're going to my parent's place. They have a built-in pool." The mother smiled. Her neck spasmed grotesquely. The boy groaned.

"Come find us at the almond grove if you can," Sasha said. She hugged the girl. "It'd be nice to have a friend."

"Yeah, we need more friends," Bevan said. The mother stared at him.

"It's a chance to rebuild," Rab said. "That's why we're going." He tripped over nothing, fell to the ground.

"We'll see," the mother said. Sasha tried to hug the girl again but the father pulled his daughter in close. "I'm sorry to be rude, but we're trying not to have physical contact with strangers."

"You don't get Spurs through touch," Rab said.

"They don't know how you get it." It wasn't the only time they came across this. People avoided touch.

The mother's phone rang. She answered it nervously. "Yes? Yes. No. He's still all right. Hang on, I'll check." She put down the phone and spoke to her son. "Darling? Can you hear me?" The little boy blinked at her, nodded. She picked up the phone. "Yes, he can still hear. Can we bring him to you? Can't you do something? Please?"

She put down the phone, weeping. The father said, "That the medical team? Are they coming to help?" She shook her head.

"God, that poor kid," Sasha said when they were out of earshot. "He's going to suffer like that little boy in the mall."

"They oughta shoot him," Bevan said. "Take him out of his misery."

"That's not funny."

Bevan drank a can of beer, slugged it straight down his throat.

"I wish you wouldn't do that," Sasha said. "It comes out of your pores and you stink." In answer he coughed.

At their next stop, a man sat surrounded by the debris of a feast. "You can feel it growing, hmmm? If you lie still you can feel the growth of it. Hmmm? The intensity of the calcium. The appetite of bones." He poured milk in. They could barely see him swallowing. It was like his bones absorbed it before it even left his mouth. He twitched and fidgeted, his legs shaky.

"Don't you love the sun?" the man said, though his skin was red and blistered. "Don't you just worship it? Feeding the bones. Helping them fuse." He lifted up a blanket with a flourish. The smell of old wool wafted over them. Beneath, he'd laid out row after row of rusty old cans of food.

"Buy some food," he said. "Good food." He had a price list, written on dirty cardboard.

"You are kiddin', aren't you?" Bevan said. "An old can of beans for five bucks?"

"I could charge ten. In fact, for you, it's ten. Per can."

"People aren't going to buy it."

"People already are, hmmm. The smart ones. Haven't you figured it out yet? It's the food. The milk, the meat. Even the vegetables, but not as much. You've got to eat pre-Spurs canned food until it passes. What else are you going to do? Look, it's the food. We want it too much, the need is too desperate for it to be healthy."

"We can't stop eating, mate."

"No. But you can eat this old canned food." Some of the tins were bloated, misshapen.

"Arsehole," Bevan shouted. "Takin' advantage of people."

"That's where the wealth is."

"Come on, Bevan. There's plenty of food around." Sasha grabbed his arm.

"I wouldn't eat it," the seller said. "I wouldn't."

"We're not buying your food, creep," Rab said.

"Hey?" the man said. "You speak too soft, mate."

"I said Fuck Off!" Rab shouted.

He limped away, leaving Sasha behind.

"It's because of how we treat the poor. That's what I reckon. The poor people live off food full of this super calcium. It kills them, they're burnt or buried in pauper's graves. We get this lush earth, these flowers, and it spreads. No one likes the flowers, do they? Couldn't sell those for free. You want to buy yourself some cans, lady. You really do. Fifteen dollars a can. Hmmmm?"

"Arsehole," she said, and walked to the car. Rab and Bevan watched her.

"Do you want to lie down in the back seat?" Sasha asked Rab.

"I'm not that bad yet," Rab said, though he slumped in the front, hating the constriction of the seatbelt but unable to sit up without it. His eye was caught by movement.

"What's that over there? That thing running?" Rab said.

"That's a tree, mate. You're seein' things," Bevan said.

"It's a bit blurry. That's all."

"You know, we should have done like your Mum said. Got supplies," Bevan said.

Rab said, "We're not going to arrange women for you, Bevan." Bevan didn't answer.

Later, Rab said to Sasha, "I can't trust any of my senses, Sash. I'm hearing things, now. I thought you said, 'I've never loved you. I hate you.'"

"I didn't say that," said Sasha. "God, Rab. I love you. I love you."

"You just loved Nick more."

"No, no, I didn't. I can't even express what that was. I honestly didn't think it would bother you. It was a mistake. I was a joke to him. But he felt bad about you. He really did. He thought you were taking it too well."

As they drove along, Rab said, "Stop the car. I think there's an earthquake."

Bevan said, "There's no earthquake," but he pulled over and waited until Rab stopped shaking.

"There's a roar in my ears. What's that?"

"Your ears are closing over," Sasha said loudly.

"I don't want Bevan's to be the last voice I hear."

Sasha sat and whispered in his ear until he fell asleep.

"We're gettin' close, I think," Bevan said. Two days had passed. He drove like a zombie, dangerously tired.

Rab held Sasha's hand. He couldn't release his fingers. He hadn't grabbed her too tight or her fingers would be bloodless. His eyelids were closed. He opened them to slits and she could see bone there, grown over.

Bevan stopped at the side of the road and they carried Rab to the grass. Sasha slid her fingers out of his grasp. "I'll get you a peppermint. Wait there," she said. She walked to the car and Rab spoke urgently to Bevan through the small hole of his throat.

"This is for her, now. You're dead, too, and she's going to be all right. You've got to get her to the almond grove. Make her safe." He spoke loudly because he could barely hear himself.

For Rab, the feeling of immobility was terrifying. He could barely see, barely hear, and each breath was not enough. He seemed to project himself into the ground, he could feel the earth covering him.

Rab could feel his skeleton, his one-bone, leaching its calcium-rich marrow into the earth. The earth growing rich and loamy, good planting dirt. The grass growing lush and green vegetables so beautiful you desperately craved them, and all grown on the mutant calcium of his bones.

"Don't bury me. Burn me. And the others. Don't put us in the earth here. Burn us." He screamed the words but as he screamed the base of his skull closed over and the last thing he felt was Sasha's wet face against his cheek.

A rattle in Rab's throat made him fight for breath. He struggled and writhed in Sasha's arms as he tried to suck air in. She heard the cracking of his bones as he threw his arms up.

"How is he?" Bevan said.

"He's bad. He's so bad. Let's get him back in the car, and we'll go over some bumps or something." She slid a peppermint between Rab's lips.

Bevan drove off the road and the car shook and rattled.

When he stopped, Rab was dead.

Sasha looked at Bevan. She held Rab close.

"Petrol's pretty low, Sash. I'm thinkin' we should save it for emergencies. Not take him to Jeremiah."

"He wanted to be burnt properly."

Bevan coughed. "We'll do a better job than that creep. Really. It'll be all right. I don't want to be burnt by him either. When we get to the almond grove, I want to dig two holes. We'll put Rab in one. You can put me in the other."

"Maybe we should burn him."

"We'd never get the fire hot enough. We'd just burn his flesh off. I'd rather him go into the ground lookin' like that than seein' him as a one-bone."

"Yes. Yes. All right." She turned away. They opened their windows and Bevan drove until he found an open supply store. "We need things. Water, tin plates. All the things we'll need for campin'. Mrs Albadara gave me heaps of money."

"I guess you're under obligation after all," Sasha said. "Why didn't she give it to Rab?"

"She thought he'd waste it. Spend it on somethin' worthless. She trusted me."

They filled their car and Bevan started the engine. "Ready?" he said. "Let's go." It was further than they expected; six hours passed before Bevan said, "That's it. That's got to be it." It was beautiful. They both sighed.

He opened the door for her and she climbed out. As she walked toward the grove, he pulled Rab's body out, dry retching. "The stink'll never go," he muttered. He ran to catch up with Sasha.

As they entered the almond grove they fell to their knees and shovelled in almonds. Starving.

They walked through the grove, their feet crackling. "It's the nuts," she said. They heard crunching. A terrible sound. "It's just the almonds underfoot," Sasha said.

"Yeah," Bevan said, but he could feel the bones in his feet crackling.

They found a small cabin with two rooms and a fireplace. Thick sawn pieces of tree trunks for chairs and a packing case for a table.

"This is as sophisticated as our place," Sasha said. There were four chairs and she sat in one and cried, thinking all four chairs should be filled.

"Missin' the boys?" Bevan said. He tried the tap. Dark water came out. He walked outside to check the tank.

"The cover's blown off so God knows what's in the water. It smells pretty foul. I say we drain the tank, fix the cover and start again. We've got two cases of drinkin' water to go on with, and there's a runnin' stream I can hear. For washin'. Let's go check it out." Sasha shook her head.

"Sasha, you can't sit here thinkin' about the boys. All right? It's us, now. We need to decide on the water, find out what food there is about. Come on."

Bevan was right; it was a running stream and the water looked fresh.

"This is fine," Bevan said. "We'll be fine. Pick up any sticks you see. Dry ones for the fire."

"I'm not an idiot, Bevan. I can see what there is to do,"

"I know, Sash. But you've never been campin' before, have you? I know a little more than you, here."

Bevan's feet crackled. "Who would've thought I'd outlast those other bastards so you and me could get together."

"That's not going to happen, Bevan."

"But you were askin' for it. You told me."

"When?"

"In the car. When you massaged my shoulder."

"It wasn't a massage. I touched you on the shoulder for being so nice to Nick. I thought you understood. I wasn't leading you on, Bevan. Honestly. I haven't done anything to lead you on."

"You did, you bloody did, you were tellin' me." He walked towards her and Sasha felt suddenly afraid.

"Bevan, things don't happen so fast. Okay? You need to be patient. Now let's move on and pretend this never happened. All right?" she said. Her shoulders felt stiff.

"Did you hear about these lovers?" Bevan said. His voice was muffled as he hunched over. "Fused together, I heard. They were almost one-bone and she said, let's die together, so he was fucking her, I heard. And her gash fused over. Closed up. Snipped his dick off like a sausage."

"That's horrible. Why would you tell me a story like that? You don't even care about Rab or Nick. You couldn't care less."

"I'm happy being the last man alive, Sash."

He imagined his seed joining that of Rab and Nick. A child born with three fathers yet only one to call Dad. He held himself in, imagining it in such detail he had to turn away from her to hide. He didn't want to rape her. He wanted her willingness. That was part of it. He would wait, be kind, and she would learn to love him.

"Don't call me Sash," she shouted. "Never, ever dare to call me Sash." She turned and ran to the cabin.

"Fuckin' idiot," Bevan said to himself, clenching his fists. "Think before you speak, you fuckwit."

He left Sasha alone for a while. When he entered the cabin she smiled at him as if nothing had happened. Forgiveness.

A certain routine fell into place in the almond grove. Bevan fed Sasha, collected water for her, listened to all she said. He was so sweetly attentive Sasha wondered if she should wake him out of the fantasy. But he was so good to her she couldn't stop herself from taking advantage. He was all joky and jovial, trying to entertain her, make her laugh. It didn't work. He tried too hard.

He found an abandoned vegetable patch, and he cleaned it up before leading her there.

"It's gonna to be okay. Look. We can grow vegies. There's stuff sproutin' already."

"That's good. We can get it going in case more people arrive. Like Mrs Albadara."

Bevan was silent.

"We could go and see if she wants to come," she said.

"There's no petrol, Sasha. All we can do is go places close to home."

They put signs out on the freeway, hoping to make it easier for people to find them.

It was two weeks before a visitor arrived. Bevan was tending the tomato plants, already in fruit when he discovered the garden. Sasha washed their few dishes, loving the feel of the cool, fresh water running between her fingers. Birds sang overhead, and she had a moment of clarity; that this was okay. Then she heard a noise.

"Bevan! Can you hear that? A car!"

He stood up, wiped dirt across his sweaty brow. "They'll drive past."

Sasha stood up. "They're not. They're not. They're coming!" She dropped the plates and ran to their hut.

"I'll get the basket, fill it with nuts. They'll be hungry and thirsty. Bring the mugs, fill them with water," she yelled to Bevan.

He watched her go then shook his head. "It was nice with just us," he said to himself. He rinsed his hands and filled two mugs with stream water.

"Hurry, Bevan," Sasha shouted. She ran to the sound of the car, near where Bevan's was parked.

"It's stopped!" she said.

Bevan caught up to her. They heard one door slamming.

"Just one. Or the others too sick to get out," Sasha said.

They could see the car, now.

"Or Jeremiah," Bevan said."

"Oh, fuck, not that ghoul. He's come for Rab. I swear. Hide."

"We can't hide from him forever," Bevan said. "It'll be okay. We'll just tell him how it is with us and he'll have to fit in."

Together, they walked out of the grove to greet Jeremiah.

"Hello, Bevan. Still with us?" Jeremiah said as he reached them. "And Sasha." He bent and kissed her hand. She smelt decay and ground teeth.

He looked around. "Rab? Where is Rab?" Sasha and Bevan exchanged glances.

"You must be hungry, Jeremiah. Have some nuts. Water. And Bevan, any tomatoes ripe? Could we have some?"

Bevan nodded.

"Still feeding the masses, Bevan? You're the cook, aren't you? You are. Mrs Albadara spoke highly of your skills. Spoke highly."

Bevan felt sudden intense grief, like his brain filled with blood. He touched his nose, thinking he had a nose bleed.

"Here, a hanky," Jeremiah said. The linen was clean and crisp. "I cut up shrouds for them. The best of materials."

They sat to eat. Jeremiah placed another handkerchief on his log chair.

"Have you got any other suits? White might not work so well out here," Sasha said.

Jeremiah smiled. "You are not the arbiter of all good taste, young lady. Not by a long shot."

He reached into his bag and brought out a globe. "I had a presentation to make to Rab, on behalf of his father, but he is no longer here. I cannot imagine Mr Albadara wanted either of you to have this, so I will keep it myself until we locate Rab."

"What is it?" Sasha asked.

"Beginning, middle, end. Heaven, Earth, Hell. Three," Jeremiah said.

"What's three? What are you on about?" Sasha said.

Jeremiah watched her lifting food to her lips. She chewed a little stiffly.

"The eternal bone is shaped like a triangle. All things important are triads. This is an inheritance of many generations of the Albadara family. Many, many." He glanced sideways at Sasha's belly.

"You're looking well," he said. "Baby coming, is it, or have you taken to fattening foods? Baby?"

Tears ran down her face. She was bereft of all strength. Nothing left to stand up with.

"It's a baby," she said.

"If I could be assured that infant was next-in-line, I would pass this into your caring."

"It's one of theirs. Rab's or Nick's." Sasha felt her cheeks burning with shame.

Jeremiah tutted. "We'll have a sense when the child is born. Until then I'll keep the globe. Mr Albadara would have been very sad to know Rab is gone, too. On his death bed he told me, 'Go do what you need to do. Find them.' His wife had confessed where she sent you. Such an honest woman, at the end. She, too, wanted me to deal with Rab." He paused and smiled. The smell of decay hit Sasha and she had a sudden image of a toothworm swallowing the inside of his teeth and leaving waste to fill the hole.

"So where is he?" Jeremiah steepled his fingertips together in a triangle. "Where have you put him?"

"Would you like some nut milk?" Sasha said. She stumbled in her haste to get away. Jeremiah held her elbow to steady her. He pinched so hard she felt her bones bruising.

Sasha collected nuts, gathering them in her lifted skirt.

"You're like a little squirrel," Jeremiah said.

She screamed. "Don't sneak up!"

"You could use my grinder to make the nut milk," he said. "I brought a portable one. Not so portable, really. That would be much easier, little squirrel."

A soft pull and clunk made Sasha jump.

"So nervous," Jeremiah whispered. "It's only Bevan killing our dinner."

Bevan lumbered through the grove to them, holding aloft a rabbit in one hand, his home-made slingshot in the other.

"Got one!" he said. It made Sasha's shoulders heave, and with the heaving she felt stiff, and she knew Spurs was beginning in her.

"I'll store these nuts in the hollow tree, near the water tank," she said, lifting her skirt full of nuts. Bevan stared at her legs, his mouth open.

Jeremiah said, "Little squirrel."

Bevan felt in his pockets, fidgeted. He walked to his car and searched it meticulously. He ripped up the carpet.

"Fuck fuck fuck," he said.

"What's the matter, Bevan? Trouble?"

"I can't find any smokes. Not one."

"Ah, well, Bevan, in this little world of ours we all have to make certain sacrifices. I have left my business behind. Sasha has lost her brother lovers. And you have no cigarettes."

"Just get me some in town, will you?"

"It's possible. I intend to travel to the Pathology Department to deliver my jars." Bevan sat down, tired. "Thanks," he said.

Jeremiah said, "When I come back we'll talk about Rab and his parents' final wish for him."

While he was gone Bevan and Sasha made plans to leave but in the end absolute lethargy and fear of the unknown kept them in place.

"I don't want to leave here just to get away from him," Sasha said.

"I'm just spewin' I'm not the last man left alive," Bevan said. "It'll be okay. He'll get bored and leave us, soon enough."

"Shouldn't we think about moving Rab? I don't want him found."

"Do you really want to dig him up?"

Sasha stared at Bevan in horror. "What are we going to do?"

Jeremiah returned five days later. "They refused to take delivery. Can you believe it? They told me to keep hold of them." He had been shopping, and emerged with bags of food. "I got some honey. You'd like honey, wouldn't you, Sasha?" he said. "You could rub it on your tummy if you won't eat it."

"No, I don't like honey. Is it even safe? The bees caused the cross-pollination of the bone flowers. How safe do you think the honey is?" Sasha asked.

"We don't know, do we, Sasha?" Jeremiah said. He sighed as if with deep exhaustion and began to walk the perimeter of the almond grove, seeking disturbed earth. "I'll find him, you know," he told Sasha as he passed her for the third time. "There's no point in hiding. Don't you understand this is important for the future of the world?"

"What future?" Sasha said. She held her belly. "I can't bear to think about the world my baby will be born into."

"I think the world is going to be a place you're happy with. Completely vegan," Jeremiah said.

"For the wrong reasons."

"Does it matter?"

A car drove past and Sasha looked up. Hoping.

"I keep thinking someone's going to stop. Someone else must come," she said.

"How would they know about it?" Jeremiah said, picking his teeth.

"We told people. We said this was the safe place. We told them to come."

"Maybe you gave them the wrong directions. Hmmmm?"

"We put signs on the road. Didn't you see them?"

Jeremiah shook his head. "Gone, I'm afraid," he said. "You know that Mr Albadara came to think that Spurs has happened before? He was quite certain by the end. There is nothing new under the sun."

Jeremiah sat with his portable grinder between his feet. It was a massive thing. Once in position it was hard to move. It was like it had taken root and would need to be dug up.

"They say that civilization can be traced back to the time we learnt how to control our environment," Jeremiah said. "And the grinding of the grain was part of that. Once they had their grinding stones, they were not so keen to move about. They stayed, planted crops, kept herds. Some people say that was the beginning of the end of the world. That all progression came from there, and that it all led to this." Beside him was a sack of bones. He turned the handle, grinding, grinding, dropping in a bone and singing as he ground away.

"Are you plannin' on stayin'?" Bevan said over the terrible noise.

"For a while," Jeremiah said, smiling. "For a while." His ivory teeth were like sharp bones sticking out of his jaw.

"What about your job?"

"The Grinding House is where you make it," he said. "And what you make it. This is our Grinding House, now."

He turned the handle. Sasha's teeth screamed at the sound, throbbed in rhythm. Bevan muttered, "Fee Fi Fo Fum." Jeremiah said to him, "It really should have been the Albadara boys here. That would have made for better symmetry. Rab, Nick, Sasha. Three. You never did quite fit, did you?"

Jeremiah asked Sasha to collect almonds as he worked. These he tossed in his mouth. The ash he bottled and labelled and added to his pile.

When the pile was complete, Jeremiah summoned Bevan.

"You don't have to do as he says," Sasha said.

"I know, but he seems to know what has to be done. More than we do. And now I've done one thing it's hard to say no to the next. Being a leader isn't for me."

"I thought you were a brilliant leader," Sasha said.

Bevan smiled. "I can't do it, Sasha. I can't take over again. Maybe when he's gone."

Sasha watched as Jeremiah demonstrated what he wanted Bevan to do. Bevan started to dig.

"He wants a bunker to bury the jars in. Somethin' deep and safe," Bevan told Sasha.

Jeremiah said, "I've got plenty more jars. There will be plenty more. We need another pit. More, Bevan. We need to preserve these ashes. Did you know we have cellular information from grain burnt in ten thousand BC? Preserved by the burning. This is what we're doing. Preserving information for the next inhabitants."

Using newspaper, he wrapped the jars carefully, reading the headlines and snorting. "'Slenderize Final Link to Spurs'," he said, shaking his head. "Skinny little fools." He rested the glass globe amongst the jars.

He placed the triangular concrete block he'd bought in town over the bunker.

Sasha sat alone in the cabin listening to the grinding, the digging. She wondered when the others would start arriving, the hopeful ones who had heard of the almond grove.

She would welcome them, of course. This was a place of charity, of helping the poor and needy. She would tell them the rules; that all must be shared. That no animal products must be ingested.

She felt a great thirst, though. A terrible, terrible thirst. And a hunger she had never felt before. Belly aching hunger.

She didn't want to starve the baby in her womb. What she was eating was not enough. Her baby was telling her that. Her stomach ached with need.

There were cows in a field nearby, and a farm not too far away where she exchanged almonds for eggs.

Her first sip of milk made her gag, but she felt it in her bones, calming them.

The eggs she scrambled, ate with bread.

Then she slept, feeling like a good mother.

Sasha could hardly move. She relied on Jeremiah to feed her, clean her. Bevan had gone off in the car for food and never returned. Sasha imagined he had died; she knew he would not desert her. Her baby moved very little. Sasha slept a lot. She awoke one day to find Jeremiah staring at her.

"You know you won't be able to have that baby normally. Vaginally." She blushed at the word. "And you haven't got long. You need to decide what to do."

In the end the decision was made for her. She was so stiff she couldn't move, her arms fused by her side. She couldn't run, couldn't leave, and there was no one to carry her. She wept as Jeremiah came for her. "I'll look after it, don't worry," he said. "It'll get a good education." He had equipment collected on his last trip and he gave her pills to render her unconscious. "Say goodbye," he said. His foul breath filled her throat and vomit rose.

"Goodbye," she whispered.

Jeremiah sliced open her belly. Inside her womb the baby's bones had fused and merged until all that was left was an almost perfect oval inside a curled up body.

"The bones of the children," Jeremiah said, and he went to ready the fire and clean the grinder. He had work to do.

SURVIVAL OF THE LAST

The boy I kept captive in the glass tower said, "So, old man, will I be watching the New Year's Party? Or is it dangerous to my health?"

I didn't answer. I never do, for fear of saying the wrong thing. Bane is the only Last One in this country so a lot rests on his head. There are two others in the North, three where the ice was, and three on the other side. Ours will be last of all, though, I'm sure. We take such good care of him.

"Come on, old man. What's the deal? I'm willing to be quiet if you'll ask the glass to stay clear for tomorrow night. I want to watch."

He was so innocent. He knew nothing of the trickeries and plots you need to get your own way.

Just the thought of those games makes me tired.

We are all so very, very tired.

He rested his palms against the glass walls and peered down.

"They're gathering already. Can I have the windows focus?"

I said the words and the windows magnified the people below. Everyone needs the help of the windows; our eyes are weak. We can't hear well either, but that's all right, because we don't talk much.

"Ah, he speaks," the boy said. He hated that I spoke only to the machinery.

I stood watching with him, wondering why anyone bothered. We had our big party, just four years ago, to ring in the fifth millennium. We all know it will be our last. I look at Bane, though, and I know he doesn't appreciate what he has. Those extra few years. He will waste the time, fritter it. I would not fritter a moment, if I were a Last One.

My grandfather could remember a time when we weren't dying. He was wrong, of course; the human race has been dying for centuries. In his day they denied it, continuing to grow, produce, use, procreate.

Though even then procreation was a miracle. In ancient times there were sometimes two, even three children born to one family. My grand-father was one of just thousands born in an entire generation; I was one of dozens.

Bane is precious to us.

I took him his bowl of bread and coffee a little early this morning. As I called the door he started chattering, as he has the six years I've guarded him. I liked it better when I was caretaker of the empty tower, before he arrived. I liked it then.

I didn't answer him.

"Old man," he said, "why preserve your spit? You'll outlive all of us."

If only, cruel boy, I thought.

Bane liked to have conversations with himself, taking my role, giving me terrible things to say.

"Old man, what do you like most about your life? The chance to see you naked, little sir. That is worth a glass of real milk. And what do you remember of real milk? My grandmother's tit, of course, my mother being as dry as the air in Hottest."

Another trick to make me reveal my ears. Bane knows all old people hate Hottest. We cannot bear the glare, the heat. Hot is all right, and lasts for five months, so you have time to acclimatise.

Hotter lasts for one month and serves only to prepare us for Hottest.

Bane is not bothered by heat. His high glass home is cooled by the sun, and he has never stepped foot outside. The sun burns so hot but we still worship it because it runs everything for us.

My oldest friend, Nadir, came early for his shift. I found him standing at the base of the tower. Hand shading his eyes, looking up at the boy who looks down.

"Don't stare at him, Nadir."

"He's the one in the glass house, Mort. Staring at us. Look at him, so young. Pitying us our age."

"Perhaps you'll live forever. Be the last left alive."

"No chance of that if we do our job properly, keep him happy."

We didn't discuss how Bane cried himself sick, until his cheeks were red and blotchy and his eyes puffed into slits.

My next shift began with Bane hammering at the door. "I'm lonely, lonely, lonely, lonely. Bring me a friend." If he knew what was ahead he would pray for death. Will it, dream it, desire it.

He can't stand to be alone.

I love to be alone. I am never lonely. Why should a boy such as he be given the privilege of absolute solitude? Why not give it to one who would revel in it?

After his coffee and bread he cried in the exercise machine as the equipment did its work. He always cried.

"What were you doing this morning?" he asked me. "You looked quite strange."

I was running. That was what he saw. I didn't answer him. He laughed.

"Running. Late for work. Late for the jail," he said. He had recently discovered the concept and realised most people were free.

Bane said, "Have you decided about tonight? May I stay up and watch?"

He was very good all day, didn't mock me, make noise, demand anything. He cooked; he is a very innovative cook caller. He called a loaf of bread with a flavour only he had thought of. Something old which tasted real and made you want to eat again.

The boy is never satisfied. I gave my nod, permission for him to watch, but he wanted company. "Bring me a friend. Now, or I'll bite my wrists out. I will." He placed his teeth gently on his wrist. Even a mark will mean trouble for me.

He was tired of behaving.

He was greedy for company. I was not eager for him to have friends, because they told him things he didn't need to hear. Who he was, why he was there, what was expected of him. They told him ways he could end his life and how he could end the lives of others if he loved them. I could have told him such things, but I kept my mouth shut.

I called a woman to him.

This was youngest one we ever brought him, just ten years older than Bane. She was quite pale, some strange genetic throw-back which should have been eradicated years ago.

She was very experienced and oily as well, exuding it, thick and yellow, from her pores. He liked this one because she was different from him. He was short, brown, one of us. Although I don't like to watch I am ordered to—I don't like to because I know he knows and it is uncomfortable. Sometimes he'll display his genitals, agitate them for my viewing.

He ignored her afterwards, called up a food drink and stood with his back to her, looking down at the people outside.

"Are you really going to be the Last?" she asked him.

"Last what?"

"Last One left alive. Are you really going to live forever and look after the world?"

My heart pounded at the thought of being that man.

The boy stared at her, then reached out his hand and squeezed her small, yellow breast.

"Won't you be lonely? All alone?" she said.

He whispered in her ear, and she laughed.

I wondered what he was planning; he had so much energy it made me sleepy just watching him.

They began to have sex again, all oily and yellow, and this time I didn't watch. I would pay dearly for that mistake.

I sat in the annexe I have facing out to the mountains. I like looking out there and imagining, remembering, the growth of the mountains.

It was already high with rubbish but during the angry time bodies were piled there by the machines, and covered with a substance so they would turn to bone. They are called the Angry Mountains and from a distance they're beautiful.

The rocks, the mountains, the sand, these things will live when all else dies.

Only the last person left alive will witness such wonders.

I must have dozed off. We sleep a lot. We like to sleep. Our world revolves around sleeping.

The boy was asleep under his covers and the woman sat hunched by the door. Sometimes he hurt them but it was none of my business. One day he would rule the world; he must be allowed certain liberties.

I let her out. I was thirsty. The dry air, always dry, parches you. I called up some faux eau and swallowed it as she left.

As he left.

He knew trickery after all.

The weather was perfect for his first adventure. We were halfway through Hot and who knew if we would live to the next Hottest? It was a lively New Year's Eve. For some. I sat in the glass tower and prayed for his safe return. I could not imagine why he would come back and I knew that I had ruined many lives with my carelessness. How was I to know who was who? All young ones look the same.

The world would be a beautiful place without people in it, I sometimes think. Brown, dry, that sharp smell I only notice sometimes. Quiet. Safe.

He returned. He told me what happened in a dull, flat voice. "There were so many people. At least one hundred. But they were so quiet. No one talked. No one cared who I was. So strange. And they barely lift their feet off the ground. I couldn't tell from up here. They slide their feet as if they're too tired to lift them."

He wasn't well and was burned badly by the sun. He came back home to be cared for. He thought he could easily escape again.

"A short life is a good life. That's what a woman down there said when I asked her why she was damaging himself. She was throwing herself onto broken glass, dancing with blood flying off in droplets. People didn't make a sound. They just watched the blood as it landed." He spun around as if demonstrating the poor woman's dance.

He was very sick for two days and I knew he had been given some vital. I was so angry with him I let him sleep in his own vomit, didn't help him bathe, let him call his own food. We don't like eating much anyway, or drinking.

He didn't know how much trouble he'd get me in.

"You know that if he dies you will be expected to take his place?" the Captain said.

I was humiliated in front of all the people in the capital for letting Bane out that one night. In ancient times they would have pissed on me, but piss is too precious now. Instead they marked me with paint. They enjoyed it. I could barely breath with them all over me and my lungs, pressing down. While I don't need much air, my lungs ached.

I don't feel pain so much; neither does anyone else. Fights can last for hours, until they drop with exhaustion, covered with cuts and blood. We don't like war but we do like fights.

Pictures of people many generations ago show them with flat chests. Their lungs must have been tiny. Our lungs are huge. We are more efficient than they were—the appendix is gone, our bladders are small. We don't piss much anymore.

I was beaten for allowing him to strangle the oily woman. What was I to do? I am no match for his tricks.

Not long after, I arrived early for my shift and heard Nadir talking to Bane.

"The human spirit is old and tired. We have reached perfection. The animals too no longer adapt. They lie down and die." Bane listened because he loved the sound of another's voice. What is it about the boy which brings out the worst in people?

I wonder if perhaps he is not worthy. People leave gifts he doesn't appreciate. Doesn't he know how wonderful it would be to rule the world?

That night, Nadir killed himself. We took him to the mountains and sent his body to the top. People were crying, praying, but what they were praying was this, "Please let me be next. Give me the strength to follow our lucky brother."

We watched Nadir's body, just meat now, drop onto the mountain peak, and we turned away. Bane watched from his tower.

Was Nadir lucky? The others seemed so sure. But where did he go? Was he dead forever? Surely being alive forever was better than being dead forever.

But we do dangerous jobs machines could do, have dangerous hobbies we could experience in other ways. We let our hobbies and jobs kill us.

My grandfather remembered a time when machines did dangerous work and dull.

I remember a time when the world was angry, not tired.

Now we are tired. So very tired.

Two weeks after Nadir's death, I found Bane bruised and embarrassed. He tried to kill himself by bashing the bed leg against his wrist.

"I was bored," he said. He had grown up since New Year's Eve. Watching people was no longer enough. He wanted to be amongst them.

I knew such contact would destroy him.

People from long ago were much taller than us, too, and barely lived past seventy. Our oldest citizen is one hundred and sixty, though not much of an example. "Kill me," she whines. "Kill me, kill me," as if life is the most terrible thing she's seen. We can't kill her, though. Fey's precious to us in our story telling. Her mother was there when the vision came which ended the time of denial.

Fey says the man was very handsome and his eyes were wet and bright. He seemed full of life.

He walked into the capital unnoticed, found a place to sleep, ate meals. People smiled a lot then. They said, "It's good to be alive," but I know they were unhappy because they brought so few others to life. Even then children weren't conceived or they were born dead. So few born.

He met our Great Poet (I still read her works if I want to summon tears) and they fell in love. She believed herself to be barren and wrote poems about the death of the womb which will break your heart. He was no ordinary man, though, and she fell pregnant.

Ah, the rejoicing.

But as the baby's head appeared, it vanished. The man faded, and he said, "Happiness is an illusion. None of it is real. You must accept and prepare for death so you may drift into death sleepily. Otherwise you will be dragged into it with your throats cut and your lungs ripped out."

Fey's mother was present at this event, when the man disappeared. The poet wrote her most famous work about it.

"That's why we're so tired," the older people said.

"We will not lay down to die," the younger people said. And the time of anger began.

I still bear the scars.

The time of anger ended when the ancient prophecy of the last person alive was revealed to us in our dreams. Across the world, we dreamt, and we began to tally the number of children we had.

In the dream we saw the world brown and dry, an empty place. Then we heard footsteps and a person appeared, cloaked. We couldn't see face or figure. "I am the last person alive. I will look after the world until it is safe and green again, then you will come back. I will wander alone forever if that is what it takes." Then the figure sank to the ground and wept so loudly we woke up.

We have the dream often. One morning, I arrived for my shift and knew that Bane had finally dreamt along with us.

He wept. I patted his eyes. I shook my head. "Don't waste water."

"I don't want to be the last. Please let me die. I don't want to be."

He was such an innocent, to have to suffer the sins of the world.

Bane said, "Why me? Surely there are people who want to live forever?"

I smiled. How well he read my heart.

I gave him the drugs he could use to send himself to sleep. He squatted, his naked body thin, healthy.

"It's up to you," I said. He smiled at the sound of my voice.

"Thank you for speaking to me, Mort," he said. "You have brought a large carrier with you. Are you going on a journey?"

"That will depend on you, Bane. There are others, you know, trapped, expected to caretake the world. If you decide to stay I will care for you. Otherwise I will go to help them depart this world also."

Bane took the pills and lay down on the bed, as I knew he would. I stared at his nude form and talked him to sleep.

"Why should such innocents pay for our evil?" I said. "Let someone else be the last." My voice comforted him as he died.

I began my journey to find the other last ones and offer them a way out. I could not have them taking my rightful place in life. That suffering was mine.

I can walk the entire globe if I follow the roads. Seas are long since dried up in many places so I can get from end to end. World traveller.

I can hear the waves splash around me and the salt drying on the sand.

Sometimes, when I'm walking, I'm thirsty, the sun burns through my covers to my brain, I feel there are people walking beside me, following me.

They are angry.

"Don't give up. What did we all die for?" and there are the ghosts of millions floating along behind me.

Is the last man alive meant to feel so tired?

SALAMANDER

I know this chair well. How many times have I caressed its fine lines, its tender carvings? I imagine the tree alive, can smell its leaves and the soil it rested in.

He caught me once.

"So that's it," he said. "Cold, hard wood." He came home the next night with a bag full of offensive toys, thinking to touch me with their cold rubber, their metal, their wood. I refused their invasion. I slept alone that night, in a bed I inherited from a woman my husband never met. He would not sleep in the bed because she had died in it, but I said, "She was a good woman and her sweetness is in this bed. That is why I love it."

He did not know that the eiderdown came with her from Europe. He didn't know how many ducks shed down for it, how many died. He did not know the craftswoman who wove its cover, nor the soldier who allowed my friend to keep it because she lay down on it with him.

I see the eiderdown burning now, and I clench my fingers around the arms of the chair.

He called me a salamander, a lizard with a body so cold it quenches flames, so he placed me at the centre of the fire. It shows no signs of diminishing. I feel warm, very hot. Perhaps my body is only cold to his touch. I have not been touched by any other, so I can't tell if it is me.

Certainly his touch does not excite me. He has been with other women; he claims to be experienced. He said, "Other women liked this. Others made sounds like this," and he demonstrated.

I said, "Why don't you make the noise then, if you're so good at it?"

I taunted him to leave me but he said I couldn't cope on my own. That wasn't true, of course. I could look after my home, couldn't I? Cook, clean and shop. He could do none of that. All he did was go out to work. I can always go out to work—I can go out to cook and clean. There is no doubt I can look after myself.

It seems he knows that too. I can live without him, so long as I have my house, my familiars. He wants me absolutely, that's why I'm here in the centre of my home, my hands tied to the arms of the chair, my body tied to its spine. He tied me and began to caress me.

"Maybe we should have done it this way sooner," he said.

I gave him an icy stare.

I guess I could have screamed and begged him not to pour petrol over my things. I could have asked him not to bring everything into the lounge room, not to pile them up for me to see.

"I own you and all of these things," he said. "I can do what I like with my belongings." But he carried out a box with his first edition books, his bible, his case of special wine.

I have a very cold heart, he's told me. A heart so cold it will quench fires.

But I love the heat. I love physical heat, the strength of it, the surety. I have a fascination with fire. I think of the flames and how they eat things up; they swallow and gulp like humans. I believe fire is alive. I believe fire is a lover.

I have nightmares about the Great Fire of London which took so much. St Paul's Cathedral and many other churches—those candlesticks, wrought from metals thousands of years old. Psalm books and bibles, the sweat and love, kids bending the pages, waiting to escape. All gone.

Thousands of houses gone; what things with them? What books, what knickknacks and treasures? It burned for days, from The King's Bakery, Pudding Lane, to Pie Corner. Was there such a thing as stand up comedy then? Can you imagine the jokes?

Such things would have burned. In the baker's; the old ovens, bread for the King, tables dark with years of butter and sweat, a recipe, handed down and never memorised, a special note, perhaps, from Master Farryver to his lover, burned in the flames. And the houses—what small items? Sets of bellows, books, clothing. Precious pieces. I cannot bear to think of such loss.

He's forced my best shoes onto my feet so they'll burn too. I can see his dirty finger marks all over them. My shoes never have a scratch or a mark, even the ones I wear around the house. I never go barefoot. I can feel a wisp of hair in my face—unfamiliar. My hair is rarely a mess, though he tries to ruffle it sometimes.

"I don't find that exciting," I say, giving hint that there is something which would excite me.

"Not a hair out of place," he described me once, when we were young. A compliment, then. Now he spits as he says it, as if my neat hair is the cruellest affront.

He had never hurt me; he would never behave that emotionally. But he hit me once this morning and in the afternoon, he knocked me out, like the first one was just for practice.

I awoke to his reptilian touch. I was tied in the middle of this room, my things surrounding me.

I began to weep when they began to burn. I am not quite so cold. I love this house so, love to polish its floor boards, its big sunny rooms. I love touching up the wood, making it live. I only wanted to fill this house with beautiful things then I'd stay and be happy. I love the furniture here, and the books.

I think perhaps my husband is right. I do like things more than people. Things are always beautiful once they are made that way. People and relationships can turn nasty in a flash.

This fire is engulfing time—each item it destroys is at the end of the line of centuries of creation and production.

The candle which was the statue of David, a gift many years ago. What precise and complex chain of events had it taken to reach me?

The original had to be sculpted first so the copy could be made. Hundreds of years where the statue could have been destroyed, hidden, become unrecognisable.

Then for my friend to see the candle and think of me.

Now the thing melts grotesquely, its girth widening and flattening.

It took me a year to pay off the television. He refused to help. He wanted me to exercise my mind, not deaden it. I sold old books, worked in a dress shop, saved and paid and then I had my television. Now it burns, it burns. I didn't sell any of my husband's books. Who would be so cruel? Mine only. His are still here, by the thousands (though I see none in this room. None burn). When I'm not working at the dress shop I read through my husband's books. He hasn't read most of them. He buys them for their spine and pretends to his guests that he devours them. He hates that I have an Arts Degree; can't stand that I know more about something.

I read them all. Many are second hand, and I find old bus tickets, theatre and movie tickets, shopping lists (4 tins c. food, 1 box Wheat Balls, 1 roll toilet paper. I could not understand why someone would abbreviate 'cat' in cat food. I wondered if the cat was a secret, even the writing of its name enough to give the secret away). These little things I kept as companionship. I imagined discussing the books with the owners, merits and failures. I imagined having breakfast, laughing over toast.

People always say they would grab their photos first, in a fire. They are the greatest loss in a flood; the cruellest blow when they are torn in anger. I had photos of my great grandmother, who looked like me, and of my first love.

I had awakened by the time he piled these before me.

"What are you doing with those?" I asked. He had never shown interest before.

"Don't you worry," he said, "It'll all be over soon."

The flames are making me very warm. He'll let me burn and die, here, to prove a point. He'll burn my things, the dress I was wearing when I met him, a piece of jewellery my mother gave me (and there, what caused that jewellery to be made, the metal to be mined, forged and wrought, my mother to have the money to buy it, to see it, even, because it was in a shop far from her home and out of her experience?) I watched this melt in the heat, and my skin began to close in on me.

Perhaps it's true. Perhaps my heart is so cold I will not burn.

Through the flames, through the window, I see him watching me. It must be very hot out there too; I can see the sweat on his face, his red face, but he wouldn't miss this.

My cooking pots are melting. Those are very special pots; now their handles are deformed, they will not settle in my palm like a comfort.

He stares at me, a look of horror on his face. He can't understand how I am still alive. He watches as the ropes which bind me are burnt to black cobwebs, and drop to free me.

I raise my arms and the flames begin to sink into the debris of my belongings.

He has hurt me well, my husband.

He enters the room, step by step, staring at me, ignoring the smoulder.

I raise my arms and lower my head in surrender to his strength. He smiles and opens his arms, forgiving me the sin of survival.

He enfolds me; I enfold him, my arms closing on his flesh.

I squeeze a little tighter, and his mouth opens in surprise as he gently burns and turns to ash.

WORKING FOR THE GOD
OF THE LOVE OF MONEY

———

"A cut or a bruise appears on your body," he says. "You don't remember where it came from. You go over your movements to identify the moment of injury and you worry about memory loss when the answer doesn't come, then you forget it. The matter fades as the bruise fades, as the cut heals.

"If you were to mark into your diary the times this occurred, you would not be kept busy over the course of a year. Around Christmas, most people would have a mark, other times would depend on the individual's areas of vulnerability. The anniversary of a death, perhaps, or an affair. A birthday or a good day at work, or a bad day leading to recklessness. Anything which may cause you to give a coin to a child with black hair, enormous purple eyes, teeth so white they reflect the sun as he grimaces. He is short (or tall, if you are short) and thin. He looks hungry, and you think the memory of his face will never leave you. But you forget him in an instant, you forget him as soon as you hand him the coin he has requested.

"You keep your fingers around your wallet or purse so he can't see the notes there, can't see your driver's licence to come round to your address and ask for more. Can't see the picture of your lover or child so he can't think of them as his own. This is why you so rarely give coins. You don't trust the collectors. This is why the purple-eyed boy wants your coin so much.

"You hand over the coin and you forget the boy. Within a week or two you will have an unexplained cut or bruise."

The purple-eyed boy's name was Tom. He had been with the god for many years. He liked the work. It involved travel, and was an outdoor job. He rose as soon as the sun did, because he slept well. He slept in a broad bed, slept like a starfish, in a dark room. The god did not allow him to have a light in his bedroom.

"Night is for sleeping," said the god, "and sleep is important."

———

But the god's room was filled with light—it slid under his door like a living fungus, and Tom heard him snuffling and grunting in there all night.

He was an incurious child, turned that way by fear. The god liked to talk about the others who held the position before him.

"Better off not keeping any money for yourself," said the god. "I had a boy called Richard once, a boy like you. He worried about the money so much he choked on a coin, it swelled up and filled his throat so he couldn't breathe for all the money in the world."

Tom did not remember any other life than this. He did not think about the lives of other people. He always returned to the god after his day's work.

"Freedom is over-rated," the god told him. "I had a boy who looked like you once. Gerald wanted to talk about freedom but no one tells you anything when you're locked up in jail. Just the other inmates and all they tell you is how pretty you are, pretty pretty, how they love you and how lonely they are. Do you know about loneliness, Tom?" Tom nodded.

Tom knew the god did terrible things. He went out and did terrible things then came home to rest.

Each time, Tom would have to work hard on the streets to collect the coins, then into the kitchen to melt them into a liquid the god could work with. He wasn't to rest during the melting time. Each coin had to be plopped into the cauldron and stirred, plop and stir, plop and stir, and there were thousands of coins. If he paused in his stirring for a moment, the god would roar from wherever he was, and Tom's ears would burn.

Then Tom could rest for a day or two. Eat and sit in the garden, breathe and sit. The god stayed down in the basement, building his armour.

The god looked very handsome when he left home in his suit made of coins. He had gloves and socks, pants and a full jacket. He had a hat with a flap to cover his face. The whole thing glistened and shivered.

He would come back from a trip with rips and scratches, and give the suit to Tom to throw away. Tom would begin his job on the street again, collecting coins from the people.

It took a lot of coins to make a suit but the god could wait. He had patience.

———

"Where did that cut come from? You might remember the boy if I describe him to you. The eyes are purple, like the moment before dawn when you haven't slept, when you lay there all night and begged for sleep. The hair is black as the devil's soul. The teeth are white; they smile at you with love so you can't help but hand over a coin."

The god was very old, and very cruel. He only killed people who were loved, wanting those left behind to suffer. He killed people whose greed brought them across his path, even if the greedy moment had occurred a long time ago, and the meeting was only a distant consequence. To complete his tasks, he took risks—though truly the risks were not great, because he was in no danger, not with his suit on, not with people suffering cuts and bruises for him.

The closest he came to danger was when one of Tom's predecessors had become lazy and stolen coins from a church charity box. These coins had passed through fewer hands and provided a weak link. The god had dived into the water with a little girl and stayed under, his golden fingers digging into her flesh, his eyes seeing well through the mesh of his mask. Feeling her pathetic struggle, he watched her face, her eyes.

Then he began to choke. The weakened suit gave him just enough time to anchor the body into the muddy bed of the river and rise carefully to the surface.

After he made his new suit, he disposed of his lazy assistant. He told Tom the stories of his predecessors because he wanted Tom to learn from their mistakes. Tom would stay young as long as he stayed loyal.

"He smells like lavender in an ancient closet or of your mother or of whatever makes you feel guilty."

Tom was a fearful boy, and he did as the god told him. He listened when the god spoke and did not ask for food when he was hungry or sleep when he was tired.

The god began to trust him, to want to impress him. So Tom heard how the god spent his hours, then he began to accompany him on his outings.

Tom did not have the stomach for his employer's job. He did not like other people but he did not hate them either, and the sound of tears made him sad.

The god began to give him presents and more food, and sometimes Tom didn't have to work, he just wandered around the house, looking at his presents. He began to feel the god loved him, and one day, after an enormous meal of quail, seafood, chocolate, cake, cheese, over and over, the god smiled at him. They were slightly hysterical with food. The god described a moment of great pleasure and Tom laughed at the description of a man trying to resuscitate his wife, when she had a cut throat, she wasn't choking at all, and his air just blew straight out her neck!

They laughed, blowing and puffing for a while. Then Tom said, "Poor husband, though," and laughed again. The god did not laugh. He stared at Tom then left the table.

Tom thought of ways to leave the god, to kill him, or leave him dying, or tie him up and run away. He was made of flesh like everyone else, just strangely put together. He would die if you stabbed him, or smothered him. You could poison him and he would collapse and Tom would be the saviour of many.

The god invited Tom in to watch the making of the suit, and Tom thought he had been blessed.

The stuff was poured into a large vat, where it shimmered and steamed. Tom felt his skin burning as he watched, and later, when he looked in the mirror, he saw that his nose and cheeks were softly blistered.

"Now, you see, Tom? Can you smell it? Smell the greedy sweat from those people's palms?"

He handed Tom a coin.

"The special ingredient," he said. It was an ancient coin, dented by the centuries—a Roman coin.

"Don't find many of those on the street, hey, boy?" said the god.

Tom preferred him to be silent. This joking, this camaraderie, was terrifying.

The god told Tom to drop the coin into the vat and short flames burst out, reaching for Tom. He jumped back.

"It's very hot," Tom whispered. "Very hot."

The god threw off his robe.

He was naked beneath. His skin was vast and white, his stomach distended as if from some huge feast (though he had not eaten, Tom was certain of that). His penis was engorged. Tom laughed at its hugeness. It couldn't be real. It was stuck on.

The god turned to face him.

"Can't have that," he said. The erection shrank into his body.

He climbed two steps to the rim of the vat.

He tested the liquid with one toe, playing the fool for Tom's benefit.

"Just right," he said, and he sank into the bubbling metal.

For one moment, Tom thought he had been released. He thought the god had killed himself, to free Tom because he loved him like a son and didn't want him to live like this anymore, and Tom could have cried for that love, because no one had loved him like that. He stepped closer to the vat and stared over the rim, hoping for a glimpse of the body.

The metal was drawing together and shaping.

It shaped a face, legs, a stomach. It shaped arms. And the god rose from his bath.

Tom whimpered now, because he knew he would die. He knew the god would not let him see this and live.

The god shook like a dog and drops of hot metal flew from him. One landed on Tom's cheek, and he smelt burning flesh before he raised his sleeve to brush it away.

"Off to work," said the god, his voice molten, not strident or mean, but seductive, beautiful. "Why don't you come along?'

Tom hated to go out with the god. He watched things he could not stop without risking his own life.

They went walking through the city streets where Tom had done his best work. The god watched him collecting for a while. He amused himself while Tom worked. He passed his hand into the stomach of a woman who intended to sell her baby once it was born and gave a squeeze. The mother barely felt a thing. She would not know until her baby was born dead.

Tom collected the coins and watched his god.

They found a blind man, standing by the kerb on a busy road filled with cars but empty of people. He was puffing in an effort not to weep and he could not see the purple eyes or the golden suit, he only heard the soft, seductive voice.

"Are you OK?" asked the god.

"I'm a bit lost," said the blind man, "I'm a bit stupid. I told my family I would be fine on my own, but I'm lost now. I can't cross the road."

"There's plenty of cars coming. Now, a break—no. Wait, after this car then—go."

Tom watched as the god led the blind man directly into the path of a bus. Both disappeared under the wheels. The god rolled out the other side, scratched and leaping with excitement.

Tom was not brave, but he was not happy to die, either. As he stirred the pot for the next suit, he thought and remembered and planned.

He heard every tale the god had to tell, and remembered much the god had told and forgotten.

He had a little money of his own—paper money the god had no interest in.

He bought new coins, coins encased in plastic and never touched by human hands.

On the day he meant to leave the god, Tom tried to keep the excitement out of his step as he descended to the kitchen. The god never rose before afternoon. His business went late into the night so he slept in. Tom lit the large stove and set the cauldron on it. When it was ready he began to drop the coins and watched each one melt, watched the liquid spread, each coin becoming part of the golden fluid.

He waited till the pot was half full. He dropped more coins and more, then he heard the heavy footfall of the god pushing his body out of bed.

Tom's whole body shook as he took the plastic folders from his pocket and, still stirring, tore them open with his teeth. Being careful to keep the rhythm perfect, he plopped the brand new, untouched coins into the pot and stirred.

The plastic he shoved back into his pocket.

The god moved silently, and Tom smelt him first. A smell of metal and a smell of heat.

"When will the material be ready?" the god asked, though he saw for himself. Tom thought the mixture smelt different, and hoped the god wouldn't notice.

"One more hour," said Tom. The god bent over the pot and sniffed deeply.

He nodded and went to sun himself.

It was hot in the room.

The god made a new suit and went out. He didn't talk to Tom. Already, Tom barely existed.

The god did not return.

Tom's limbs began to ache, his hair greyed, fell out, his fingernails grew long and ragged. He couldn't see well and couldn't hear. He breathed loudly through his nose.

He received back the fifty years stolen from him, and he knew the god must be dead.

He took nothing from the house. Wanted nothing. He went to a hostel where, until he died, he swept floors and cleaned up vomit, in exchange for food and the freedom to come and go.

"You probably haven't had an unexplained cut or bruise for a while now, have you?" Tom asks everyone he sees. He cannot stop thinking how he never saw the god die—perhaps there is a new purple-eyed child. He asks everyone he sees, "How did you get that cut? Do you remember where you got that bruise? Have you seen a black-haired child with purple eyes, large teeth?" If Tom ever receives the answer he fears, he has no plan but terror.

PUBLICATION HISTORY

"Fresh Young Widow" *The Grinding House*, 2005

"The Glass Woman" *Aurealis,* 1997

"The Blue Stream" *Aurealis,* 1994

"The Hanging People" *Bloodsongs,* 1995

"Bone-Dog," *AGOG! Terrific Tales,* 2003.

"Smoko" *The Grinding House,* 2005

"A-Positive" *Bloodsongs,* 1997

"The Missing Children" *There is No Mystery,* Ginninderra Press, 1999

"In the Drawback" is original to this collection.

"Al's Iso Bar" *The Alsiso Project,* Elastic Press, 2003

"The Left Behind" *Orb,* 2000

"Tiger Kill" *Earwig Flesh Factory Magazine,* 2000

"The Wrong Seat" *Calling Up the Devil and Associated Misdemeanours,*
    Artemis Press, 1994

"Skin Holes" *Strange Fruit,* Penguin, 1995

"The Sameness of Birthdays" *Betrayal,* Ginninderra Press, 2000

"The Speaker of Heaven" *Orb,* 2001

"The Smell of Mice" *The Grinding House,* 2005

"The Grinding House" *The Grinding House,* 2005

"Survival of the Last" *Aurealis,* 2001

"Salamander" *Don't Cross the Water and Other Warnings,*
    Artemis Press, 1994

"Working for the God of the Love of Money"
    Dark Regions Magazine, 2001

ABOUT THE AUTHOR

Kaaron Warren lives in Canberra, Australia with her family. She has been writing horror, science fiction and fantasy stories since she was five and won an Aurealis award in 1998 for her story, "A-Positive." "The Grinding House," from this collection, won the Ditmar Award for best novella, and "Fresh Young Widow" won the Ditmar for best short story. She has been published in Australia, the United Kingdom and USA. Her story "A-Positive," which appears in this collection, has been optioned by BearCage Productions. Kaaron writes novel length manuscripts as well as short stories. This is her first collection..